Shanghaied

by

Margie L. Miller

Lost Gatekeepers, Book 1

Shanghaied

Cover Art by *Debbie Taylor*

The Wild Rose Press, Inc.
PO Box 708
Adams Basin, NY 14410-0708
Visit us at www.thewildrosepress.com

Publishing History
First Fantasy Rose Edition, 2016
Print ISBN 978-1-5092-1115-9
Digital ISBN 978-1-5092-1116-6

Lost Gatekeepers, Book 1
Published in the United States of America

"Run," he yelled as he rolled to the side, wrenching his hand from hers.

Stupid man, did he not get the concept they couldn't gate out of this mess without physical contact? She still felt the low hum of power running through her body, and if he just—

"Run," he hollered again as the eight foot bulbous grayish-clear insect turned what might be a head in her direction and swung the staff toward her with speed defying its gelatinous form.

She spun, hoping the movement wouldn't make her vomit, as Elliott vaulted himself toward her attacker, pummeling into it and grabbing it around its middle. The massive stick swept less than an inch past her face as she fell backward. Landing with a jolting *thud*, all of the air knocked from her lungs and she gasped, stunned for a second before crab walking away from the wrestling insect and her husband.

Fighting dizziness, she desperately searched for a rock or a stick to aid in the fight; vaguely registering they had landed in the middle of some battle between humans and these creatures.

Fabulous.

If it's not a cliff, it's a stinking war.

Surrounded by mayhem, the humans shouted to each other, calling battle cries and working in pairs to cut down the giant bugs screeching at ear splitting decibels. Each pair of warriors grasped long silver sticks with sharp bulbs at the end, and their main focus lay in ramming it into the gut of the massive mutant tick-like things, causing blue lightning to shoot out the end and melting the insides of their victims.

"Dammit woman, run!"

Chapter 1

Jenni had to admit, the man chopping wood in her new front yard made an impressive sight, highlighted by the pink morning sun rising above the tree line on the horizon. With shirt discarded on a nearby log, the muscles across the woodcutter's back and arms displayed beautiful choreography as he hefted the ax in his gloved hands then up, over the shoulder, and down again. Repeat. The sharp staccato of his chopping echoed in the trees surrounding the cabin, rhythmic and soothing.

Rubbing sleep from her eyes, she meandered to a deck chair and settled in, propping bare feet on an overturned bucket. Tucking a strand of dark hair behind an ear, she watched in rapt attention, unable to hold back a sigh of contentment. Folding her arms over her stomach, she smiled. Despite the slight morning chill, a band of perspiration formed over the man's brow. His slightly damp blondish-brown hair swung into his green eyes, but he tossed his head slightly, flicking the strands out of the way, and kept working.

Finished with his current log, he leaned over to select another from the wood pile and Jenni watched his jeans mold over his thighs and rear-end. She sighed again. Her admiration more audible this time; his head swiveled toward her, his face reflecting shock at seeing her sitting on the porch in a cotton-candy-pink t-shirt and black sweatpants.

"What on earth are you doing up at *this* hour?"

Nice. She couldn't blame him, though, given her history. Instead of being affronted, she smiled wider. "Catching the five o'clock show. It's been as entertaining as promised."

His eyebrows scrunched together in confusion as he straightened to face her. "What are you talking about?" He flung his ax at the block, sticking it firmly, and then rested his gloved hands on his hips, all his weight resting on one leg.

"Last evening, when I stopped at Bill's Burgers on the way into town, a group of women in the next booth discussed the 'hot paramedic who moved in a couple months ago.' Apparently, one of them knows today is Hot Paramedic's day off. Which also apparently means as sure as the sun will rise in the morning, at five a.m. Hot Paramedic will chop wood in his yard, shirtless."

His eyes grew ever wider as her story unfolded, and she laughed.

"Why didn't you tell me this last night when I called?" he asked with a strangled voice, his gaze darting around to the distant cabins nestled on the hills surrounding them.

"Because I know what a prude you are, and I wanted to see for myself. And now that I have, I totally understand their discussion about binoculars."

"Binoculars?" he asked, his eyes nearly bugging out of his head behind those bangs that constantly plagued him. He stared at her for a second. "They are all watching right now?"

"Most likely."

He paused briefly. "Come here," he finally said

imperiously, and she snickered. His lips pinched together and his green eyes narrowed as he shifted his weight to the other leg. Then, his mouth quirked upward, ever so slightly, and his expression softened. He looked into her eyes and jerked his head in the silent universal playful gesture "come here."

She shook her head and smiled wider. His smile lifted a little more, making her stomach somersault. Pulling his gloves off and tossing them on the chopping block, revealing the ever present leather bracer on his left wrist, he quirked a finger at her, beckoning her closer.

"Come here, Jenni." He used her favorite bedroom voice, and despite her resolve not to give in to his wishes, she found herself rising and walking toward him.

But she couldn't make it easy for him, and stopped five feet away. "Yes, Elliott?" she asked innocently.

He snorted and closed the distance with slow determination, his gaze never wavering from hers. He lifted his hands and cupped her face, tracing her jaw with the pad of his thumbs. Despite the urge to place her hands on his chest, she tucked each index finger into his back pockets, drawing him closer.

Her breasts pushed into his ribcage, and she felt his heart thundering against her erratically, totally sexy and completely at odds with his cool exterior. His head slowly lowered, and in anticipation she tilted her head back for easier access. Just before their lips met, he gently caressed his nose against hers, his warm exhale washing over her face. She moaned.

"Welcome home, Jenirva," he whispered, making her heart thump wildly and her bones turn to pudding, despite using the full name she loathed.

He finally kissed her, sending the familiar shockwave through her system. She abandoned rational thought, immersing herself in her husband's scent, the feel of his mouth against hers, his teeth nipping her lips gently, his hands caressing her neck, his breath warming her face. Finally, he released her, placing his forehead against hers as he caught his breath.

"So much for making friends." She sighed, melodramatically. "They'll all hate me now for wrecking their fantasy."

"I had to do *something*," he answered. "*I'm* the one getting into trouble if Sarah, Jenny, or any of the others ever decide to act on their fantasies."

So he knew his fan club by name. Interesting.

"You are not the type of woman to mark your territory and fight for your man."

Jenni lifted an eyebrow at him. "What makes you think I haven't done exactly that?"

His jaw dropped for a second before he laughed. "You played me?" he asked, obviously impressed.

"Well, just a little," she admitted and received another kiss. "If I walk around all protective and jealous, I simply look insecure, which is an invitation for the vultures." She wiggled her eyebrows. "I wanted them to see you look at me. If they kept their binoculars on us, they now know none of them ever stand a chance."

"I'm whipped, huh?"

"Only in the best possible way. But I made you breakfast to make up for using you so shamelessly."

His eyebrows shot upward. "Wow."

"I really missed you," she said, explaining her

aberrant behavior. "I think this is the longest we've ever been away from each other."

"Close," he said, grabbing her hand and heading toward their house. "You forget the summer they sent me to Uncle Malachi's ranch without you, and sent you to your cousin Guinevere's to learn how to be a proper lady."

Jenni snorted her laughter indelicately. "Talk about an exercise in futility."

"I know, right? One of your greatest charms is your ability to belch the alphabet."

"That separation lasted longer? It didn't seem like it."

"By sixteen hours. This time only felt worse because you actually like me now."

"Well, you were a jerk back then," she said as he pulled her through the door of the cabin and closed it behind them.

"And you were a stuck up snob," he answered, pulling her into his arms. "Now that we don't have an audience…"

His lips returned to hers and this time, his kiss held nothing back. Her legs instantly dissolved, but he picked her up and set her on a small table near the front door. She heard a crash, and vaguely remembered a lamp resting on the tabletop, but classified it irrelevant. Nothing else mattered right now but the feel of her husband. His lips and teeth moved to her throat.

Another thought intruded. "Your breakfast is getting cold," she gasped, not wanting him to stop, but feeling obligated to give him the option.

He mumbled something, and though she couldn't understand the words, she understood his intent when he increased the pressure, causing the storm raging in her body to overload. Oh, how she missed him. These two months felt like forever. A physical ache took root in her body the day he left, agonizing at times, and with every touch, he smothered the pain into a dull memory. Desperately needing to express her relief, she leaned over and nibbled on the muscle above his collarbone as she hooked her feet around the back of his legs. Possessively, she combed her fingers against his scalp and grabbed fistfuls of that gorgeous hair.

To her gratification, he moaned and slid his hands under her shirt, caressing her lower back and climbing higher with slow promise as his mouth continued to work the sensitive spot on her neck. The stray thought that maybe this time, after a two month absence, they'd finally conceive, flashed through her mind and long dormant hope surged through her heart. She groaned and felt his lips lift upward against her skin, even as his ragged breathing washed over her neck.

Harsh pounding on the door broke through the hazy fog, and she felt a whimper escape as Elliott hissed a very impolite word.

"I tried to," she gasped, while he chuckled darkly against her temple. The visitor pounded again. "We'd better get that, it doesn't sound like they will go away."

"So help me," he growled, "If that is Ellen or Barbara with another casserole, I'm going to—"

"Tell them I'd like the recipe," she finished for him. She could stand to be magnanimous right now; she might get pregnant soon. Today, even. She smiled cheekily at him, thinking about how happy he'd be, how excited. Nearly two years ago, she threw out her birth control and every month without getting pregnant weighed heavier and heavier on her heart. But today might be their day. The crib Elliott made would need dusting.

He rolled his eyes at her. "Can you get the door? I need to put on a shirt." He started heading upstairs without waiting for her response.

Shaking her head, Jenni hopped off the table and opened the door. Before her stood a man seemingly frozen in shock with his mouth slightly ajar. His tousled blond hair topped a salon tan, and his blue gaze roamed up and down her body, pausing at chest level before finally stopping at her eyes. He smoothed his features into a suave smile. "Hello," he said. "I'm Ben Hanover." He held his hand out for a shake. "And you are?"

"My wife!" Elliott's disembodied voice shouted down the staircase.

"Or you can call me Jenni," she told their visitor as she stepped aside, amused at her husband's reaction. "Would you like to come in?"

"No, he wouldn't!" Elliott appeared in a clean flannel shirt, doing nothing to hide his irritation.

Ben stepped over the threshold anyway, his mouth still curved in a polished smile. "I didn't think you really existed."

"I'm real," she answered.

"Ben, what do you want?"

"Please excuse my husband," Jenni apologized. "He's frustrated you interrupted us in the middle of making out. It's been a long time for both of us."

She almost heard Elliott's teeth slam together as he locked his jaw shut, but she had a point to make. Now she waited to see if this "friend" caught it. Plus, she couldn't pass up the chance to tease her lover a little bit. He wouldn't miss his opportunity, if roles were reversed. He never did.

"I completely understand," Ben said in assurance, eyeing the shattered lamp beside the table next to the door. "If you were my wife, I'd be pretty eager, too." His gaze flicked back to her chest for half a second before he turned his attention to Elliott, missing her frown. "I came to invite you to a game of racquetball, but I guess I'll take a raincheck."

"Another time."

The creep turned and winked at her before sliding out the door with a wave. She closed it harder than necessary and frowned at her husband. "I don't like him."

"Ben's all right," he said, heading for the kitchen and their congealed breakfast. He looked up and saw the expression on her face, and broke into laughter. "He's a good racquetball player, and I needed a partner while you were gone."

"Why did he think you fibbed about your wife?" she asked, trailing after him.

Elliott picked up the plate with the cold rubbery omelet and dumped the yellow substance in the trash. Opening the fridge, he pulled ingredients into his arms.

"Because I wouldn't talk about you."

"Really?" That hurt her feelings.

He peeked over his shoulder and must have realized his mistake. His shoulders slumped; his eyes closed a second before plunking the eggs and cheese on the counter. "Sweetheart, if I told him my smokin' hot wife was so smart she's pioneering the AP math program at the high school next semester, I'd wave a red cape in front of the bull. I didn't feel like dealing with him, all right?"

She couldn't stop herself and smiled impishly as she asked, "Does he have a math teacher fetish, too?" Jenni knew she bored Elliott when she rambled about exciting math problems, he sometimes chose to kiss her to shut her up. But he always pretended otherwise.

Lighting the burner under the frying pan she used earlier, he plopped some butter in to melt. "Hey, when you spout those formulas, it's like you're speaking French, baby. You get that voice going and I can't help myself. And I bet every single one of your teenage boys at Brockelhurst High cried their eyes out last week when they found out you were leaving."

"They threw a party."

"I wanted to be here when you arrived."

"You could have woken me up this morning when you got off shift."

He shot her a sardonic look, not even qualifying the absurd statement with a reply. Her body simply did not function before seven in the morning, and the fact she managed to get up in time for the Hot Paramedic Show meant miracles could still happen.

"So what would you like to do today?" he asked as he cracked several eggs into a bowl and started whisking with a fork. "Tour of the town? We could go for a hike if you'd like, I've scouted out some great trails. Or we could go for a ride on the motorcycles—I finished overhauling the engines last week."

"Don't you have to sleep? You just got off a 24-hour shift."

"Naw, slow night. I'm good to go until this evening."

She reached over to grab a pinch of shredded cheese. "In that case, I want to get pregnant."

"Right now, or should we eat first?"

"We'd better eat first, we'll need the energy."

Before she could place the wad of cheese in her mouth, Elliott's fingers circled hers, flipping her hand over and drawing it closer to his face. "You're glowing again." Sure enough, the tips of her fingers on her right hand shone brightly, illuminating his face like five tiny flashlights. "It's happening more often. We need to get you to a doctor."

"And tell them what? That I randomly glow sometimes? They'll lock me in the loony bin."

"Well, we'd be there together, because I can vouch for you. Any pain this time?"

"No, only a tingly-tickly feeling that starts in the fingertips and shoots up my arm. But that could be because you're touching me."

He smiled and shook his head. "You need to see someone about this."

"You know, for someone following me around since we were kids, constantly tormenting me to see this again and again, you're being awfully pushy."

"Give a guy a break, okay? At six years old, the sight of your glowing fist headed straight for my nose won the 'coolest thing ever' award." He kissed her palm, then let go of her hand with a sigh. She shoved the cheese into her mouth and pulled herself onto the counter next to the stove, dangling her legs over the side like a five year old.

"You never told anyone," she said quietly as he poured the egg mixture into the pan.

"No, I didn't."

They watched in silence as the massive omelet cooked, and he added a hefty helping of cheese, just the way she liked it.

"Why not?"

"Why didn't you tell anyone about my poetry?" He shrugged. "It wasn't my secret to tell. I wanted to irritate you and make you mad. I wanted to drive you crazy, and I wanted to knock you down from that pedestal and make you wallow with the rest of us mere mortals." He paused and looked at her. "But I never, ever wanted to hurt you."

His gaze darted to her hand where the illumination now spread over her hand and wrist.

"You still love to torment me."

"You know it, Glow Girl." He flashed a smile before flipping the eggs and then slid them onto a plate.

Tossing his bangs out of his eyes, he turned off the burner and pulled two forks from a drawer. Holding the plate in one hand, he wrapped his free arm around her waist and pulled her from the counter. She circled her arms around his neck, and he walked backwards with her in his grip until he bumped against the small table in the kitchen nook. Kissing the end of her nose, he spun around, plopped her into a chair and sat across the table.

She reached up to take the fork he offered, and they both realized the glow had spread up her arm to her elbow. He took a breath, but she raised an eyebrow and he shut his mouth. Instead, he cut a chunk of the eggs and chewed silently for a moment.

"It's happened my entire life," she said in answer to his silent objection before taking her own bite of breakfast. "I think if nothing horrible has happened after twenty-four—"

"Twenty-five."

"Twenty-*four* years, nothing will. And I'm not twenty-five, yet."

"Close enough."

She harrumphed, and the incandescent glow spread higher, up under the sleeve of her pink t-shirt to her bicep. Elliot smiled, almost reluctantly. "I admit, I still think that is the coolest thing ever, but I worry about you."

"You didn't used to."

"I didn't used to love you," he said casually with a shake of one shoulder, and she smiled as she continued eating.

By the time she popped the final bite into her mouth, the glow had spread up her neck, covering the bottom half of her face and halfway down her other arm. "It looks like a full on attack."

"Which means no going outside today, unless we want the neighbors to call the local alien hunters."

"Darn."

"I know, right? I wanted to track down some of those women in your fan club and get those casserole recipes—"

He interrupted her with a kiss. Instantly, every square centimeter of her body, including the strands of her hair, lit up, incandescent. A thousand volts of electricity zipped through each molecule.

"Doesn't this freak you out at all?" she asked breathlessly, realizing he knelt on the floor beside her chair. He should run for dear life.

"Coolest." He kissed her. "Thing." He kissed her again. "Ever."

With each additional kiss, he laced his fingers through hers. An invisible flame scorched them where their flesh connected, and they looked down to see a clear bubble appear around their joined hands.

"Elliott," she called out, her heart racing, panic threatening. This had never happened before. "Elliott, let go of me!" She tried to jerk her hand away, but he held on tightly.

"No."

The bubble grew bigger, filling with heat as it enveloped their forearms.

"I'm going to hurt you, let go!" She struggled harder, but he refused to release her, wrapping his other arm around her waist.

"No." He pulled her off the chair and onto his lap, holding her tightly and pinning her against his body. "You're okay," he whispered, but his voice sounded ragged and as scared as she felt. "We'll get through this."

The clear bubble filled with light, growing bigger and bigger until their kitchen dissolved and the universe consisted of the two of them and searing heat and blinding white. Electricity. Fire. Jenni held onto her husband with all her strength, burrowing her face into his neck and hating herself for not backing away and saving him from her fate. His arm constricted tighter around her back, his hand gripping hers fiercely. His face burrowed into her shoulder.

A sonic concussion slammed through her body. Elliott ripped away, and she felt herself flying through a void of white. She couldn't breathe. She couldn't see. She couldn't feel.

Nothing.

Chapter 2

Jenni did not exist. Her body disappeared, and she floated suspended as pure consciousness in a white void. Alone. No lungs to breathe. No eyes to blink. No mouth to call out for her husband. What happened to Elliott? Her heart should be racing, but that did not exist either. Fear, joy, hate, love—none of it held any meaning. Only white nothingness.

Another shockwave pounded into the body she no longer possessed, and all sensation returned at once, bringing with it the terror of the unknown. Limbs flailing, her stomach lodged in her throat with the horrible sensation of freefall. She hated roller coasters. The floor slammed into her, knocking out her breath and reminding her of a belly flop she once endured at the neighborhood pool the summer before high school.

Elliott pushed her off the diving board, and then had to turn around and rescue her when she went into shock underwater and nearly drowned. She managed to hold onto that grudge for over two years.

"Jenni," his voice called to her urgently, sounding eerily similar to the swimming incident.

Moaning with pain, she rolled onto her back and opened her eyes to see him leaning over her, brows scrunched in concern. A blinding white backdrop hurt her eyes.

"Oh my gosh, we're dead."

"I don't think so." Falling into habit from years of training, he checked her pupils and pulse.

"We're dead—"

"No, sweetheart."

"And our bodies are back in the cabin and—"

"Honey."

"No one will miss us until I don't call my mother in a few days and by the time—"

"Jenni."

"She calls the cops and convince them to come check on us we're desiccated and gooey and—"

"Jenirva."

"Everyone will say the hot paramedic's psycho wife snapped and burned them both alive and—"

His mouth against hers stopped her babbling tirade long enough to disconnect her from the panic attack.

"Thank you," she said when he released her, "for not smacking me coherent."

Only a couple inches from her face, with his bangs tickling her forehead, she barely saw his wide grin. He seemed relieved. "This way is always much more fun. And you'll be happy to know that for a ghost, you have a strong pulse."

"So we're not dead."

"No."

He leaned back slightly, and she finally realized fluffy white clouds swirled around them, blotting out the view of anything farther than a few feet away. "And I'm not glowing anymore."

"Nope."

"So where are we?"

"I don't have the foggiest idea."

"Are you hurt?"

"Nothing I can't handle."

She sat up, suddenly angry. "You should have let me go." He shook his head, frustrating and irritating her to a level only he could accomplish. "You wouldn't be here if you'd just listen to me."

"Precisely."

Male chauvinist, she grumbled internally.

He must have seen her tirade building because he elaborated, cutting her off before she could get started. "Even if I could have let go of you, which I couldn't, I wouldn't have. Do you really think you were the only one hurting the last couple months?" he asked, sounding as frustrated and angry as her. "I missed you too, you know." He glared at her.

She glared back at him.

His words finally penetrated her ire. "You couldn't let go?"

"We were fused together. I tried to let go of your hand so I could wrap both arms around you, but I couldn't."

She moaned, dropping her head to her chest. "I am so sorry to get you into this."

He put a hand under her chin, lifting her face so she could see his eyes. As quickly as his anger ignited, it burned out.

"Are you kidding me?" he asked with an odd smile. It seemed now that he confirmed they were basically all right, his naturally adventurous and optimistic spirit decided to take over. "Remember what I said? Coolest. Thing. Ever."

Standing up, he held out an assisting hand to lift her off the solid cloud surface they landed on.

"Maybe, I never woke up this morning." The idea

grasped hold, filling her with hope. "Maybe, this is some elaborate dream and it's not actually happening at all."

"I hate to tell you," he said, looking around at the swirls, "but I am here, too."

"Wouldn't my dream version of you say that very thing?"

He shot her a look of patient irritation, and she wondered how he accomplished that. "Okay, Jenni, would your dream Elliott tell you that you have a pimple directly above your left eye?" he asked, pointing at her eyebrow.

She let out an epithet, and his lips twitched upward, eyes gleaming.

"You can be such a donkey's hind end sometimes."

"Which is how you know it's really me. Come on." He flicked his hair out of his eyes with a quick head toss and started walking.

"Where are you going?" she asked, following him. The substance they walked on felt fuzzy to her bare feet as the clouds squished between her toes with each step.

"I have no idea, but we can't just stand around forever doing nothing." He ran a hand through his bangs and grumbled slightly. "When we get back, will you please give me a haircut? This is driving me nuts."

"I like your hair like that. The little head-toss thing is sexy."

"I'm going blind."

"All right. If we get back, I'll—"

"*When*, sweetheart. *When* we get back."

"Ever the optimist."

"If I didn't have hope, I'd have never suckered you into marrying me."

"I wasn't exactly at the top of my game that afternoon, you know, and you sure took advantage."

"It's not my fault you decided to take my proposal as anything but genuine."

" 'Proposal' my eyeball, you dared me."

He turned his head and flashed an unrepentant smile. "It worked, didn't it?"

Shaking her head, laughing, she changed the subject. "Elliott, how do you know we're not going in circles?"

"I don't, but we're making great time."

She stopped walking and put her hands on her hips. "We don't even know—"

"Everything is as it should be," a gentle, soothing voice floated through the clouds. It sounded slightly familiar, but distorted.

"Hello?" Elliott called out. "Who's there?"

He took a step closer to Jenni, positioning her behind him in a protective stance, holding his hands out from his sides by a few inches. Though she couldn't see his face, she'd bet five bucks he was scanning the clouds and strategizing. She refrained from asking him what he'd do if their visitor came from behind, since they couldn't get a bearing on the origin of the voice.

"All will be explained," the disembodied voice assured them. "You are safe." Where did she know that voice from? It gnawed at her, on the tip of her consciousness.

Obviously not trusting the messenger, Elliott stepped carefully around her, keeping her to his back at all times with his arms out protectively. Through the cloudy swirls, a tall form slowly approached. It might be a man, but Jenni had a hard time seeing a face clearly over her protector's shoulder.

Standing on the tip of her bare toes to get a clearer view, she saw the imposing figure gliding forward majestically, gracefully, ghostlike, and her stomach curled inward. Yes. Yes, a man after all—a man dressed in blue shimmery robes, and a matching hat. An obnoxious hat, if she were perfectly honest about it. Made of the same shimmery blue material, the bullet-shaped concoction stood from the man's head by at least two feet. Thin, silvery, curly tendrils draped down over his face and neck, trailing across his upper torso.

"What do you want?" Elliott asked gruffly, eyes narrowed, peering into the mist.

"We are here to help you," the stranger said with stiff formality. "The first time is always the most difficult." As the man spoke, he took several steps closer, his voice slowly regulating to its normal tones.

"Dad?" Jenni asked incredulously, shocked into immobility.

Elliott's head whipped to her for a split second, then back around. Both men squinted, leaning closer to each other. "Edgar?"

"Jenirva? Elliott?" Her father's hand reached up, pulling away the ugly headpiece, causing his white hair to swirl around. "Oh boy."

"Okay, now I know I'm dreaming. This is some insane, trippy dream and any minute now, I'm going—"

"Honey."

"To wake up and find out I never really did wake up this morning because, let's be realistic now, how many times in my life have I *ever* been able to wake up that early, and certainly—"

"Dear-heart."

"*Never* without outside intervention so I'm either back in bed at the cabin or I'm sleeping alone at the old apartment and, oh my gosh, then I'll be stuck waiting for two more days before I see Elliott again and—"

Elliott's hand covered her mouth as he kissed her temple, stopping her incoherent litany. He now stood behind her, one arm around her stomach, the other holding her words at bay. "You aren't alone," he assured in her ear. "I'm right here. I swear it to you." His arms surrounding her, she felt his chest against her shoulders, his stomach against her back. The panic abated.

They both turned to the man before them as Elliott released her mouth. "Dad, is it really you?" her husband asked. "What on earth is going on here?"

Edgar stared at them, his mouth slightly ajar for a second. "Oh boy."

"Dad?" Jenni asked.

"We didn't think…" Her father stopped. "I've never…" Shaking his head, he took a deep breath. "Oh boy. Come. Follow me."

"Where are we going?" she asked.

He seemed to know the way, leading with confident strides while she and Elliott followed behind like baby ducks following their mama. They didn't go far before their guide stopped and gestured with his hand to seats. Their shape reminded Jenni of concrete benches, but made of a solid version of the cloudy mist. She and Elliott sat down experimentally on the surprisingly comfortable seats and she leaned forward, placing her elbows on her knees. Beside her, her husband leaned back slightly.

"Dad, where are we?"

Her father chose a seat across from them, plopping his ugly hat on the bench near his leg. He sighed deeply and rubbed his hands through his hair, making the white mess stand up worse. "This is the In Between."

"The what?"

"The In Between. We're between realms right now." He paused, pursing his lips. "We had no idea you would come today." He frowned at her accusingly. "After nine years, who could blame us for thinking you weren't going to transmorph?"

"Dad, what are you talking about?" Jenni asked with mounting frustration. She hated it when her parents talked in riddles.

Edgar sighed, his face smoothing out. "It's a long explanation. And you should know more by now than you do. Your mother…" he paused, seeming to reconsider his statement.

"Mom?"

"Yes, she'll be here shortly."

"Edgar, what is going on?" Elliott asked.

"Jenni is a gate," he answered, as though the statement explained everything. "She finally came into her full powers."

"I'm a what?" Her flat voice relayed her lack of amusement perfectly.

"Powers?" her husband asked, his head tilting to the side slightly, his face brightening.

"A gate. You open doors between—Ugh. I'm going about this all wrong. Short version. The universe is much bigger than you ever imagined." He spread his arms wide, palms open, as though to illustrate. "Within our universe are different realms, different realities. Only one race of people has the power to travel between realms. You are part of that group. We are gatekeepers."

"I'm not *human*?" she asked in horror.

"Yes, you are," he answered. Relief started to flood through her until he said, "Mostly."

Dumbfounded, she stared at her haggard father.

"Look, I know this is hard to take in."

"Oh, you think?" she asked. "I have absolutely no clue what any of this is, or what any of it means. Why on earth didn't you tell me sooner?" Elliott patted her on the back, but it didn't calm her down, as he probably hoped.

"We have our reasons for keeping our secrets," her father said lamely, his gaze darting around, and Jenni wondered why he wouldn't meet her eyes.

"You have to admit," her husband said, "this explains a lot."

"You're taking this calmly," she said in accusation, as though he betrayed her with his easy acceptance of her heritage. He should be freaking out right along with her. Maybe more so, since he just learned the woman he shared a bed with for the last six years wasn't completely human.

"My wife glows, sweetheart. I embraced weird a long, long time ago."

"How long?" Edgar asked; his voice urgent.

"We were six," Elliott answered. "At least, the first time I saw it."

"Six years old?" her dad said, hurt laced his voice. "I wish you told us, we needed a sign of your activation before we could tell you."

Her head shot up, eyes narrowed. "I go to the movies; I know what happens to mutants."

Edgar groaned, and Elliott rolled his eyes. "I told you to tell your folks."

"I wish you had trusted me."

"Well, it's not like I could control it to show anyone. It never turned off or on when I wanted."

"Of course not, sweetie," her father said with pained frustration. "Especially for you." He shook his head. "Only you. In sixty eight years of doing this, I've never seen a gate and their key so at odds with each other."

"Wait…what?"

"Elliott. He's your key."

"My what?"

"He's the rough surface to your match. The flint to your steel. He's your trigger. Your key. He's what sparks the power inside of you. Without him, you don't work."

"You mean I *literally* turn her on?" The smirk on Elliot's face annoyed her.

Oh there would be no living with him now.

"Yes," her father confirmed. "Although, for the life of me, I can't figure out what took you so long."

A short burst of laugher broke from Jenni, despite being freaked out by the whole situation. Score one for Dad.

"Usually, transmorphing—the moment you transform into full gatekeeper maturity and your powers activate—happens at roughly fifteen or sixteen years old. When you two went so long unchanged, we thought it skipped a generation. It's incredibly rare, but there are legends of gates and keys being incompatible."

"Wait. You mean Elliott is the only key that will

work for me?"

"Yes. One key for each gate."

"You pre-arranged my marriage?" she asked in outraged shock. "You set me up?"

Her father sighed and ran his fingers through his hair, rearranging the mess. "No, Jenni. *You* chose him."

Silence. The three sat staring at each other. Finally, with a calm deliberately moderated voice, Jenni spoke. "I didn't *choose* to sit at the same table every year in school with him. I didn't choose to live a block from him and ride the same bus. I didn't choose to always get picked for the same teams. I didn't choose to spend two months every summer at his uncle's ranch—"

"Yes, you did, so you could visit with Ilsy."

"I didn't even choose to go to the same college as him. All of that happened because of choices other people made. And it's starting to sound like I didn't even choose to marry him either. Like someone placed a voodoo charm on me, or something."

A strangled noise caused her to glance over to see Elliott's mouth pinched tightly, hiding a grimace.

Darn. She didn't mean for that to sound like it came out.

"You visited us in a dream before you were born to reveal the identity of your key. So yes, you chose him and he chose you. We simply provided you the opportunity to find each other. That is always the way."

Which meant they chose each other before they were born, and then they spent the next eighteen years fighting. She shook her head; swamped with confusion and so many emotions she didn't even know where to start to sort it all out. Her husband didn't seem to have the same problem.

"So, I'm not completely human either," Elliott said.

Edgar shrugged with a small, conspiratorial smile. "Mostly human. With a couple added traits." He sighed again and leaned back on the bench, looking around for something or someone, distracted. After a moment, they regained his attention. "Every gate and key I've ever known couldn't bear to be apart from each other for any significant length of time. They are friends, first and foremost." He paused, his eyebrows scrunching. "Which is why you two baffled us."

"He broke every single one of my brand new crayons," Jenni said in defense, explaining the start of the twelve-year feud.

"You stole my lucky penny." Elliot's right hand folded over his left wrist, covering the leather bracer he always wore. "And you punched me in the nose for those crayons."

"My penny. We found it on the floor of my side of the desk and that made it mine. *You* stole it from *me*."

"I saw it first and called dibs on it, and you know it."

"Will you two knock it off?" Edgar scolded, shaking his head with paternal irritation.

"Wait," Jenni said as a new thought occurred to her. "You said Elliott is my key, and I don't work without him, right?"

"Yes."

"And most people kick off the whole adventure at fifteen, but not me?"

"Right."

She turned her face to her husband. "Fifteen. The Year of the Volleyball Team, right?" So much for foreordination. He had enough free will to chase half the skirts at Beaumont High for four years.

"Hey, don't blame me," he said, putting his hand to his chest in injured innocence and twitching his head, removing the bangs from his eyes. "You chased after Eddie Blauer that year." He batted his brown eyelashes in imitation of her teenage self, and affected a falsetto voice. "Oh, Eddie is soooooo cute and his smile—" He swooned and then jerked his leg aside to narrowly avoid being punched by the back of her fist.

"I did not look like that."

"Yes, you did."

"Well, he did have a nice smile. And he was a nice guy, too."

Elliott's mouth clamped shut, obviously disagreeing, but refraining from voicing his thoughts.

"Are you retroactively jealous?" she asked in dawning realization.

"No, I'm not jealous of a fifteen-year-old pipsqueak."

"Because I swoon much better for you, now. You know that, right?"

"Only because of some voodoo charm, apparently."

"Oh Elliott, I didn't mean it that way."

"It's fine," he said without his usual smile, sitting forward and crossing his arms in his lap, resting his elbows on his knees. "So Edgar, what's next? You expected a teenage couple here today. What's supposed to happen?"

"Orientation. Gatekeeper 101."

Her husband successfully shut down the conversation, leaving a wall between them. She hurt his feelings more than she realized and felt badly. Maybe it was beneficial she couldn't apologize now, her father didn't need to witness that conversation. A lump formed in her throat and a strange, sad energy slowly stole through her body, slithering through her veins.

"What's with the getup?" Elliott asked.

"This?" the older man asked, waving his hand in front of his robes. "We find it easier to keep the teens on task and focused when we add formality and pomp to the whole affair."

"What happens next?"

"Well," Dad said, standing up and stretching his legs, "we go find Jenni's mother. She must be waylaid by the council. And then we start your training. Come on, it's this way."

Without waiting to make sure they followed him, Edgar plopped the ugly hat back on his head and walked away. Elliott jammed his hands into the pockets of his jeans as he followed, and spared a glance in Jenni's direction. "I guess we're on the move now." He turned and kept walking.

"Wait." She jumped up from the bench and ran over to him, throwing her arms around his neck as the urgent energy vibrated throughout her system. "I'm sorry. Please don't be mad at me."

"I told you, it's fine," he answered without returning the embrace, but pecked her on the cheek with a chaste kiss. "Your father is leaving us behind. We're going to get lost again."

She narrowed her eyes at him, recognizing his lie. "Fine."

Letting him go, she turned, looking for Edgar in the mist. Her heart pounded, the energy growing to a consuming force threatening to burst out of her skin. Elliott's hand touched her arm, creating burning tingles at their connected skin. His fingers slid down her flesh, across her forearm until they connected with her hand. He entwined their fingers, squeezing tightly.

Thousands of volts of electricity pounded into Jenni's body, slamming her backward and blinding her, stealing her breath. And then the shock disappeared. Coughing and gagging, she blinked and tried to focus through bright sunlight. Waves crashed in her ears. Hard, sharp rocks bit into her bare feet. She tasted salty air. Elliott's hand still held hers in a death grip.

Stumbling as she tried to breathe, the rocky ground disappeared beneath her feet. The world slipped away and for half a second she freefell until she jolted to a stop. Pain shot through her shoulders, and she realized the iron bands of Elliott's hands held her wrists as she hung in midair.

"Jenni," Elliott called her name.

Her eyes finally acclimated; she looked into worried eyes scanning her and whatever lay below. She glanced down to see a purple ocean angrily crashing against rocks and boulders fifty feet beneath her dangling feet. Her hand slipped a fraction, and she looked up once again to see terror in her husband's face as he knelt on the cliff above her, holding on for dear life.

Her hand slipped again.

Chapter 3

"Jenni, hang onto me," Elliott said gruffly, through a clenched jaw. "Don't you dare let go." The veins in his neck strained to break through his skin, and his face turned red.

Knowing he couldn't last much longer, Jenni scraped her feet over the face of the cliff, trying to find a foothold. Her movement jostled them, and she heard the scuffle of his body slipping on the dirt and gravel of the cliff, closer to the edge. His fingers bit harder into her wrists.

Finally, she felt an outcropping and managed to squeeze the toes of her right foot onto a small, sharp ledge. Pushing upward with all her strength, she relieved Elliott of her weight for a split second, long enough for him to scramble for a better, firmer hold. The rocks fell away, crashing silently into the water below and once again she hung solely by her husband's strength.

"It's exactly like the climbing wall in the tenth grade, remember?" he gasped. "You got the record for the fastest climb. This'll be a cinch for you."

"I got the fastest climb," she informed him breathlessly as she resumed her search for a foothold, "because you threw a tarantula on me."

"So what?" he countered. "The potential is there. You can do this."

Her left foot found purchase, and she pushed herself up a couple inches. Elliott backed up, taking the slack with him. He pulled, she pushed, and inch by agonizing inch she scaled the side of the cliff with his help. At last, he hauled her over the edge, and they scrambled a few feet to safety on their hands and knees.

Panting, they collapsed side by side.

"Jenirva Merryweather Carter Hamilton, you are determined to give me a heart attack before this day is over," Elliott gasped weakly, throwing an arm over his eyes, covering them with the crook of his elbow.

"It hasn't exactly been a picnic for me either, you know," she said as she pulled her dark chestnut hair away from her face.

"Are you okay?" He lifted his arm an inch off his eyes, raising his head slightly to look at her.

"Yeah, I'm just—"

"Bleeding."

Jumping up, he squatted beside her and examined her injuries. "Multiple lacerations over your arms," he lifted the hem of her t-shirt, "your stomach," he pulled the tops of her black sweatpants up slightly to quickly look inside, then let them snap back into place with nothing to report and continued his exam. "And your feet. You shredded your feet."

"The rocks were sharp," she explained, watching with surprise as Elliott grabbed the edges of his flannel shirt and ripped it open, causing the buttons to fly in multiple directions as they popped off, revealing his white t-shirt underneath.

Stripping off his over-shirt, he tore it into strips. "Any headaches? Nausea? Dizziness?"

"No, nothing like that. And my feet didn't hurt

until you pointed them out. What are you doing?"

"Making bandages. You need soapy water and antiseptic, but this will at least keep the gashes from getting dirtier until we can find a place to take care of you properly. And for the record," he stated as he carefully and gently wrapped the flannel strips around her feet, "it wasn't a tarantula. It was a plastic black widow."

"Whatever. A big ugly spider, thrown by you, landed on my shoulder." She took a deep breath.

"I'm sorry, I'm trying not to hurt you."

"No, it's not that." She paused and he looked up at her with curiosity. "I'm glad."

Elliott's eyes scrunched together, the look he always wore when bewildered. "Did you knock your head on the cliff? You have a scratch—"

"I'm glad I picked you. And you picked me."

His half formed word sat frozen on his lips as he stared at her.

"I can't think of anyone else on the planet who could keep up with my mood swings, and out-stubborn my stubborn-ness."

He smiled gently and winked at her. "I'm glad, too."

Finishing his task, he wiped his hand against his jeans and sat back, looking around them. Pulling herself up to a sitting position, she followed his example. The rocky bluff they sat atop overlooked an angry purple ocean on one side, while the other sloped down to a rolling meadow filled with a carnival of colorful flowers stretching for miles.

"Oh Elliott, it's beautiful."

"It's very panoramic. Do you see any sign of

civilization? Because I don't."

"What happened to the romantic in you?"

"It's bleeding all over my favorite flannel shirt, and threatening infection." He continued to stare out at the expanse with intense concentration, as though he could conjure a village by pure force of will.

She sighed. "No. I don't see any sign of life either."

"Any clue where we are?"

"Know of any place on Planet Earth with purple oceans?"

"No." He finally turned to look at her.

"Then I'd hazard a guess we're not in Kansas anymore, Toto."

He rolled his eyes. "Brilliant."

"It's beautiful here."

"Yes," he relented, picking up a small rock and lobbing it over the cliff, tossing his head to the side, flicking his bangs out of his eyes. "Yes, it is."

"You think Mom and Dad might rescue us?"

"Do you think they can follow us?"

"Very good question."

"Ok, we are getting nowhere. Let's talk about what we *do* know."

She held up a single finger. "We are only 'mostly' human, and hit 'gatekeeper puberty' ten years late for unknown reasons." She promised herself a thoroughly satisfying freak out with the mother of all identity crises when they finally made it home.

Elliott held up two fingers. "We tripped the activation sequence twice now. First time, you lit up like a light bulb. Second time, nothing."

Jenni pulled up two more fingers to tick off the

third point. "Both times you touched me."

"Oh honey, if we jump every time we touch, making love will get really interesting from now on."

She rolled her eyes to hide her grimace as her hand dropped back into her lap. Jumping in the middle of that particular activity would suck. There had to be a way to control it. "Both times, we held hands and both times, I felt energy running through me before it happened. Like a low wattage electrical current. You?"

He shook his head. "I grab your hand, get struck by lightning and open my eyes to watch you fall down and get hurt. Twice."

"I'm sorry."

"You get hurt, and you're apologizing to me?"

She shrugged while he shook his head. "I nearly killed us on the last jump. Two more feet the other direction and we'd have landed in midair."

"Don't dwell on it, Jenni, it won't do any good," he stated firmly. "Let's think about getting out of here so we can learn how to navigate and then we can come back and check out all the flowers at your leisure."

She nodded, holding her arm in his direction. "Here, give me your hand."

"Are you feeling the electricity?" he asked before slipping his fingers into hers and weaving them together to squeeze tightly.

"No." They waited. Nothing happened. Jenni sighed. "But I figured it couldn't hurt to try, right? There has to be a way to trigger it on purpose."

"Let's try this."

He scooted closer, plunging his free hand into her dark hair and drawing her into an intimate kiss, setting her blood on fire. She breathed him in, pouring her fear, her desperation and the conflicting excitement into her response. She so needed this. Every nerve ending hummed, calling out for a physical connection to the man who set them ablaze. Reaching behind his neck with one hand and grasping the back of his t-shirt with the other, she pulled herself closer in an effort to eliminate the inches of air between their bodies.

Elliott moaned and started to pull away. She followed him, refusing to let him go, but he diverted his face slightly and their mouths only touched at the corners. He panted heavily for a second before asking, "Anything yet?" with a hoarse voice.

"What?" she asked, frustrated and equally short on her own oxygen supply.

"Is it working?" She felt his mouth moving against her cheek as he spoke, feather light and completely in the wrong place.

"Is what working?"

He chuckled, sending little bursts of air over her face. "Am I turning you on yet?"

"Absolutely," she admitted. "But not in the way you wanted."

"Damn." He moved to get up, but she tightened her hold on his neck and shirt.

"Don't leave me like this, you can't do that."

"Jenni, I'm sorry." He reached up and loosened her fingers on his neck. "I want it as badly as you do."

She snorted in disbelief. "Apparently not."

"You need medical care." He held her face in the palm of his hand, forcing her to look into his eyes. "Once I make sure you're okay, I'll take care of your other needs, all right? I promise. Because frankly, this is taking every reserve of chivalry I've got."

She harrumphed.

He harrumphed back.

She glared at him for a second, watching as he glared back unfazed.

"It's because of the zit over my eye, isn't it?" He burst out laughing, dispelling the tension. "I'm absolutely hideous, and you can't stand the thought of touching me anymore."

"It won't work, sweetheart. I'm not going to let you dare me into forgetting about your injuries, however briefly."

She shrugged. "I had to try."

"You get an E for Effort. Now," he said, patting her leg before standing up and surveying the skyline as he rubbed his hands on his jeans. "We can't stick around here forever. We have no idea if your parents know how to find us, and the sun is too hot to leave you on this bluff."

"So what do you suggest?"

"I think I see a patch of trees over there in the distance," he said, pointing. "There's probably water as well. If I can get you in the shade with some water, I can go look for help."

"You want to split up?" Irrational anxiety slithered through her veins, turning her blood cold now. "What if I start to activate while you're gone?"

"Well, you can't jump without me," he pointed out, "so it's not like you can leave me behind."

"All right," she agreed, pride not allowing her to admit her fear of being left alone. "Let's get going."

Struggling to stand up, she felt him grab her under her arms and help haul her off the ground. Sharp knives of pain sliced over the bottoms of her feet, radiating upward as her weight settled on them. Luckily, Elliott's face turned in the other direction gave her a moment to erase the tormented scowl and replace it with a bright smile. Mind over matter. If East Indian Gurus could walk over red hot coals, she could walk to the oasis with slightly injured feet. The cuts weren't too bad; her personal physician's assistant simply over-reacted. Ever since he earned his license, she could barely sneeze without him checking on her.

"Okay, I think I see an animal trail heading in that direction," he said, pointing. "Come on." Elliott stepped in front of her and scrunched down slightly, knees bent, with his arms held out a little on either side.

"What are you doing?"

"Giving you a piggyback ride. Jump on."

"You can't possibly carry me that far."

"Way to castrate me there, babe. Trust me. You're light. It'll be easy. Jump on."

"What if I refuse?"

"You won't."

"What makes you so sure? You're not the boss of me, you know. You can't order me around."

"Because you're the smartest person I know. And the smart thing to do is hitch a ride."

"I'm also the most stubborn person you know."

He sighed, dropping his arms and his head and stood all the way up. "Yes, you are. So let's walk."

He flicked his hair out of his eyes and, at a slow and meandering pace, headed off without turning around. Tentatively, Jenni placed all her weight on one foot to take a step. A thousand imaginary shards of glass ground into the soft meaty flesh under the flannel, and she had to clamp her teeth together to bite back the gasp of pain. Step one complete. Only four billion to go.

She shifted position and her weight, moving forward. A whimper escaped against her will and she took a few deep breaths. Slow, ugly realization crept over her—she could not make this trip in a timely manner. Her poor husband, hot and thirsty, finished a long work shift earlier today. He needed to take a break without waiting on her pride.

"All right," she called and watched as he froze in place a little down the path. "You're right, I'm wrong and I need a ride."

That almost hurt worse than walking.

Abruptly, he turned and jogged the short distance back to her. Eyebrows scrunched in mock concern, he held a hand to her forehead as though to check her temperature and she smacked it way. "Knock it off."

He only smiled mischievously at her and turned around, lowering his body so she could climb on. It took a moment to get comfortable, wrapping her legs around his waist and locking her feet over his stomach. Accidentally choking him at first, she had to adjust her arms around his shoulders, and rested her chin in the crook of his neck. Securing her with his hands under her thighs, he set off at a brisk pace.

She could tell he tried to make it look easy, but after several minutes, his breathing became labored and she listened silently as he regulated it to a rhythmic pattern. It took a moment for him to hit his stride, but she eventually caught on: *inhale through the nose*, step-step-step-step, *exhale out the mouth*, step-step-step-step. She found herself breathing in time with him, and since she didn't have the exertion factor became slightly lightheaded from the excess of oxygen.

She needed to refocus. The flowers they passed through were taller than they appeared from a distance, reaching as high as Elliott's knees and thighs. Purple cups, red petals, blue sprigs, orange fans. A beautiful place to get married.

A yellow butterfly as large as her hand flitted amongst the blossoms, landing here, stopping there. The soft whoosh of Elliott's systematic breathing lulled her as the cadence of his footfalls hypnotically thumped against her chest with each step. A sense of peace and calm floated through Jenni's system, ethereal and serene, causing her to feel floaty and disconnected from the world. Reality didn't matter. Being only "mostly human" didn't matter. Her aching feet didn't matter. All was well.

And then the butterfly winked.

What?

Blinking a few times in an effort to pull her thoughts together and clear her eyesight, she squinted and leaned a little farther over Elliott's shoulder to get a better look. The massive yellow wings flapped up, and she saw a pattern resembling a black and white target on the underside. Oh, okay. She laughed at herself silently.

The butterfly flitted away, but black and white catlike eyes blinked at her again. And... glowed? She blinked. They blinked. They disappeared.

"Um, honey?" She tried not to speak up to this point, so he could reserve his oxygen, but this warranted disturbing him.

"Yes, dear?" he asked with rough breath on the exhale.

"We're not alone."

He froze mid stride, one foot in front of the other. "What? Where?" Still breathing heavily, his head moved side to side slowly, probably trying to see for himself.

"A pair of eyes just blinked at me from the middle of those flowers over there." She pointed over his shoulder to indicate the tall violet clump she'd been watching.

"Are you sure?"

Jenni paused. Darn. Had it been her imagination? She was a little loopy there for a minute. "Sort of sure," she admitted.

He leaned forward after bracing his legs against the shift of her weight on his back. "I don't see anything."

"They were like cat eyes. And they sort of glowed."

He began walking again, slower than before. "Tell me if you see them again."

"You believe me, right?" She felt a little silly because she didn't entirely believe herself.

"Why shouldn't I?"

"Because glowing cat eyes are weird."

"I embrace weird, remember? What part of this day *doesn't* fall within that classification?"

She squeezed her arms tighter around his shoulders. "You can be cool sometimes."

"Yeah, I kno—" Elliott froze on his last word, no breathing, not a single muscle twitch.

Fear curled through Jenni's stomach, and she placed her mouth next to his ear. In a low, barely audible tone, she asked, "What is it?"

He didn't answer, merely inclined his head forward

infinitesimally. Twenty yards down the path, a terrifying beast stepped out of the flowers into full sight and Jenni gasped involuntarily. She'd never seen an animal like that before. The massive long saber teeth glinted in the sunlight. Each ear had three points reaching skyward. Its muscles rippled with the lithe body of a leopard, covered in the black and white stripes of a zebra. Claws of a lion promised to shred any prey in seconds. Black and white eyes stared at them intently. Hunkered down, it could pounce at any second.

Oh my gosh, oh my gosh, oh my gosh, oh my gosh.

Elliott's hands squeezed her thighs on his waist, and she realized he felt her hyperventilating against his back. The creature's tail flicked forward once then slowly, gracefully, swooped back and forth. A long pink tongue dropped out of its mouth, circled up over its nose and then gradually caressed one of its gleaming teeth before disappearing back into its mouth. Eyes narrowing, it sniffed the air with small huffs.

They couldn't escape with her on his back; he'd never be able to run fast enough. Little by little, she unhooked her clamped feet and started to lower them.

"Don't. Move." He hissed at her through clenched jaw and unmoving lips, tightening his grip on her legs and pushing them harder into his waist.

"When I count to three," she whispered, "run for the trees."

"Stay still," he insisted.

"Let me go."

He didn't bother to answer, only wrapped his arms under her legs and now she couldn't jump down without causing him to fall over as well. Darn chauvinistic man, he stood a better chance without her.

The animal reached a paw forward, taking a small step. Elliott took one step to the side, off the path and into the flowers. Opening its jaws, a ferocious, rolling snarl sent visions of jaguars into Jenni's mind and the hairs on the back of her neck to stand up. Her heart thundered violently, her husband's back pressed tightly against her the only thing keeping it in her chest.

The creature sprung forward, and Elliott bolted into action. Sprinting through the wildflowers like a jackrabbit, he zigged and zagged, his breathing eerily regulated as he achieved speeds only attainable through an otherworldly adrenaline rush. Colors flew past her as he pushed himself beyond the limits of any normal man's endurance, but to no avail. The snarling call sounded again from behind, closer, and she heard the animal in pursuit. Desperately wanting to jump down and relieve him of the burden of her weight, she held on tightly, knowing he would stop and come back for her.

He must still intend to reach the oasis. His path, though indirect and rambling, slowly inched closer and closer to the outcropping of trees. The creature pounced. Elliott dodged and gained a few extra feet.

"Hold on," he hollered, then shocked Jenni by dropping onto his side at a dead run, as though sliding into home base.

The ground chewed into her leg and arm as they traveled over the dirt, but she held on and seconds later, without missing a beat, he rose back onto his feet and continued his sprint. She looked down to see each of his hands holding a large, rough cut rock, the kind that sliced up her feet on the cliffs. In a move that reminded her of his old baseball days, he ran at an angle, looked over his shoulder and threw with bullet precision, hitting the animal on the front shoulder.

An angry snarling roar tore through the air and Jenni saw red liquid stream down the animal's leg for a split second before Elliott changed direction again and cut off her view. Would they actually make it? Would the impossible happen? Somehow, her husband managed to perform a miracle. The trees, only a few scant yards in the distance, surely provided the protection they so desperately needed.

Another snarl, lower and more guttural echoed in front of them and another black and white face popped through the flowers, with eyes narrowed and teeth gleaming.

Chapter 4

As smoothly as though it had been his intent the entire time, Elliott changed course, feinting to the right. The new arrival snarled again, angry and…exasperated? She felt its frustration mounting as her husband dodged, completing an amazing spin and backtracking, placing both creatures behind them as he made for the boundary of the oasis. They would make it. Nothing could stop them now.

Two distinct snarls called out to them, and she strained her neck to look behind. Both creatures followed at a dead run, but the animals would not overtake them before they reached the promised safety of the oasis. Their tails flicked. *Stop!* Their snarls rolled over each other, calling, insistent, desperate, screaming in her mind. *Wait! Danger! Stop! Idiots!*

"Elliott, stop," Jenni yelled with sudden, agonizing certainty. "Stop or we're going to die. Stop now."

He leaped into the air, planting both feet to brake. As his boots hit the ground on a skid, he spun around while falling, placing the front of his body against the ground to take the damage of the slide. She unhooked her feet and pulled her legs out of the way in time, but her arms burned, pinned between his body and the mulchy dirt and rocks. She looked up to see a path of destruction amongst the flowers as they rode out the momentum. The cry of the creatures changed in volume, incredulous and shocked.

The second their bodies ground to a painful halt, Elliott rolled over again, covering her with his body, shielding her head with his arms and tucking his forehead against her temple. Mere inches separated their toes from the bluish grass of the oasis. What had she done? Had she condemned them to a violent death because she heard voices in her mind?

Both zebra cats descended on them, the larger one sinking its teeth into Elliott's waistband and pulling on his jeans, but her husband held tighter to her and both of them were dragged several feet. A low growl of frustration rolled through the creature's throat, and she swore a sentiment similar to "screw it" vibrated off it before it opened its jaws wide and encompassed Elliott's waist within its teeth.

"Jenni," her husband hollered, grasping at her in vain as the animal pulled with its might, ripping him away.

The other creature pounced forward to wrap its teeth around Jenni's upper arm. Surprisingly gentle, it tugged and pulled, dragging her a long distance from the grass and trees. Ignoring Elliot's violent, curse-woven struggle against his captor, the animal standing over her opened its mouth widely, flicked its tail and puffed shortly.

Sit still.

Suddenly, she felt like a child scolded by her mother.

"Elliott," Jenni called with a voice she tried to modulate as soothing, but he didn't respond, continuing a useless, ineffective fight. "Elliott. I'm all right. It's all right. Calm down."

The animal holding him hostage kept its head at an angle, leaving her partner upright on his feet during his struggles. Though the creature did not bite down, her warrior strained against the sharp incisors leaving puncture wounds along his stomach, drawing small pools of blood over the filthy t-shirt. She scooted across the ground, and the female zebra cat snarled.

"I have to help him," she argued, ignoring the command. Reaching the man she loved, she rose to her knees and stretched up as high as her arms would allow, ducking out of the way of his flailing feet and arms. "Honey, I'm all right. I'm okay."

The instant her fingers touched his face, the panic induced rage dissipated and his body froze. Elliot's unfocused gaze met hers. "They aren't going to hurt us, they are trying to help."

He reached out tentatively, stroking her face with his fingertips, disbelief and confusion in his eyes. "Jenni?"

"Yes, it's okay."

He simply stared at her for a moment, taking deep gulps of air. The creature, realizing the fight had ended, opened its jaw and released its captive. Elliott held himself upright for several seconds until he dropped to his knees then crumpled completely. Jenni caught him with her body, but his weight dragged them both to the ground.

She found herself sitting on the ground, feet outstretched, with him lying between her legs. Holding his head against her chest, she ran her fingers through his hair to comfort him. His arms hung loosely around her waist as he gasped for air. He lay in her arms like a ragdoll.

"I can't move," he said with a gasp. Then, "I'm going to be sick."

She twisted her body slightly, leaning over as his muscles convulsed. Blood from her scratched, raw arms smeared the side of his face as he leaned against her, opening his mouth and liberating all the scrambled eggs, cheese and milk they ate only a few short hours ago. Over and over again, he heaved into the dirt next to her, bits splashing onto her clothes as it bounced off the dirt and flowers. With the extent of his violent upheaval, she worried eventually she'd see his stomach emerge.

Finally, his body purged, he weakly collapsed into her embrace. Using the hem of her t-shirt, she wiped the sweat off his forehead, and the yellowish-clear liquid from around his lips.

"You're not wearing a bra," he said, his left ear resting against one breast and his nose merely inches from the other.

"I wanted to get lucky this morning," she reminded him, reassured he'd be fine now and slightly giddy with the relief. "It would have only gotten in the way."

"Yeah, I wanted that, too. Jenni, what is going on? And why can't I move a single muscle in my body?"

She knew he didn't expect an answer for the second question, his way of vocalizing his concern and frustration. But the first deserved attention. With her thoughts drawn back to the cats chasing them, she felt the tug of the bloody flannel bandages yanking on her feet and saw the cats using their long, sharp teeth for the task.

"Why did you stop me from going into the oasis?"

"They said it would kill us."

"They *what*?" His head turned a fraction, landing his face in her stomach.

"Didn't you hear them? They shouted at us to stop."

"No, Jenni. I didn't hear anyone yelling at us to stop, I only heard their snarls." He sounded muffled against her shirt, and she repositioned his head to keep him from asphyxiating.

The male cat huffed, the final bandage finally ripped free. *Got it.*

"Oh." She paused.

The female started cleaning Jenni's feet, alternately licking them and nibbling at the rocks and pebbles with her surgical front teeth, scraping out the embedded foreign objects. The cat hit a sweet spot, and she jerked involuntarily.

Hold still.

"I'm trying. It tickles."

"What tickles?"

"They are doing something to my feet."

"How come they aren't eating us?" he asked wearily. "Not that I'm complaining."

"Why aren't you eating us?" she asked, and then listened for a moment. She couldn't stop the smile spreading over her face from their answer.

"What are they saying?"

"When they saw your mad-skills, they realized we were visitors and not hunters."

"So that marathon mattered?"

"Yes, we were going to be kitty chow."

"Oh, good. For a second there, I felt really dumb for running from the good guys."

She chuckled. "Too bad you never joined track in

high school."

"Protecting you never involved running before."

"You amazed me out there," she told him, ignoring the burning, itching feeling spreading across her toes and foot to her ankles.

"Pretty good run, huh? One time deal, though. I don't know if I'll ever be able to move again."

The male snarled. "He wants me to turn you over."

"His tone of voice sounds angry."

"He's really ticked at you for injuring his mate."

Elliott managed to lift his head off her stomach to look at the creature, and she bit back a cheer for the fact he regained a modicum amount of muscle control. "I'm sorry," he told the male. "I didn't want her to kill *my* mate."

The cat looked at Jenni for translation, and when she repeated the apology word for word, he nodded at Elliott with begrudging understanding.

"So how does this translation thing work?" Elliott asked as she heaved and hauled, laying him on the ground and turning him onto his back. "Is it like the science fiction shows, where you hear English in your head when they talk?"

"No," she answered, finally getting him into position and lifting his shirt to expose the cuts along his mid-section. "I hear the exact same thing you do. It just…makes sense to me."

"Huh." His response sounded like a grunt as the male zebra cat licked one of his cuts. "Are we sure this is sanitary?" he asked, raising an eyebrow.

"Check this out."

She maneuvered herself around and hovered her feet over Elliott's face to show him the miracle cure as the female started licking Jenni's scraped arms, dripping copious amounts of saliva. All her nicks and cuts disappeared; leaving thin, faint scars crisscrossed over and around each other. Her toes wiggling only a few inches from his face, her husband blinked, suddenly crossed eyed.

"Too close, babe, you need to lift them a little higher." A low rumbling shook the earth, knocking Jenni off balance and throwing her feet downward into Elliott's face. "Ow!"

"Sorry," she said, pulling her legs in, trying to catch her balance and kneel next to him at the same time.

"An earthquake?" he said over the noise. "Seriously?"

We have to move, the female called out to her. *Now.*

"He can't."

"I can't what?"

Get him onto Nithlam's back, he'll carry him. I'll help. Hurry.

Movement out of the corner of her eye caught her attention, and she looked up to see the blue grass and tall trees of the oasis rumbling across the plains, smashing flowers in its wake.

"What in the—" she sputtered. "The oasis is *moving*."

It is not what you think it is. It is a Gherebat, and it will instantly paralyze anything touching the blue blades. We have to move quickly.

The rolling earth shook under her as she tore her gaze away and speared Elliott with a determined look. "Crazy monster at six o'clock and headed this way," she said as she wrapped her arms under his shoulders and heaved with all her strength. "Gotta ride the giant zebra cat." She managed to haul him two whole inches. He tried to assist, succeeding in moving his legs a couple of inches, but couldn't seem to put any force into the effort.

"Leave me and run," he yelled, eyes narrowed, voice huffy.

Nithlam lay down next to her husband's body, and the female grabbed a belt loop with one of her giant teeth. With the cat doing the lifting and Jenni guiding, it only took a moment to get him situated.

"Can you hold on?"

He reached up to the black and white Mohawk on the cat's neck and grasped it with his fingers. "Yeah, I'm good. Let's go."

He had to be lying; no way could he hold on with sufficient strength to keep from toppling over if the animal decided to run. She narrowed her eyes at him, weighing her options on how to fix the situation.

Get on Shesta's back, Nithlam told her sternly. *There's no time.*

The female scrunched her body low to the ground and Jenni pulled herself up, straddling the furry back and grabbing the hairs on its neck. Her fingers shook and when Shesta stood to her full height, the ground loomed beneath her. Her head swam and she instinctively lay across the cat's back, closer to something solid.

Their rescuers didn't wait, but began a surprisingly gentle and graceful, yet brisk, retreat. Wind kicked up, throwing her dark hair into her eyes and whipping her face. The experience reminded her of riding her motorcycle and she relaxed, savoring the familiar adrenaline rush. For one crazy second, she remembered that had been one of the suggestions Elliot made this morning of how to occupy their day, and wondered if he made the same connection. The two animals jogged side by side, and she looked over to see her husband smiling widely at her.

"You are such an adrenaline junky," she hollered, feeling warmth circle through her system at his smile.

"Anyone married to you has to be," he replied.

"I'm the pinnacle of boring," she said. "You're the one who got me into rock climbing and motorcycles."

"I—"

A loud rolling boom interrupted whatever protest he planned, and they looked up to find massive, black and gray clouds on the horizon, tumbling over each other in a race across the sky.

Long streaks of lightning stretched overhead, flashing again and again, causing continuous thunder and reminding Jenni of a stampeding herd of cattle. A lavender wall of rain descended from the tumult, directly in their path. The air crackled, resonating with the exciting thrill rushing though her body. She couldn't help it; she sat up straight on Shesta's back, threw her arms above her head and let out a long, loud, "Woohoo!"

Elliott's laughter sounded over the mayhem. "Now who's the adrenaline junky?"

"You know I love a good storm," she shouted back.

It will be here soon, Shesta warned. *It is dangerous for you. We won't make it to the township in time.*

We can take them to the hunter's cabin, Nithlam said.

Yes, it's the only safe place.

The two creatures shifted course, and now traveled at an angle to the approaching tempest.

"It's only a little water," Jenni argued. "We won't melt."

The female cat gave an equivalent of a sigh. *Human, you are new to this realm. Do not make the mistake of thinking you know better than those who live here, you will die quickly. Your mission is too important, you cannot be careless.*

"You're right, I'm sorry," she apologized, feeling dumb.

"I take it the rain is bad?" Elliott asked.

"Yes. I'm being a stupid human, and I'm going to get us killed if I don't pay attention."

"Ah. So where are they taking us?"

"Someplace they feel is safe."

The storm drew closer, and the cats continuously picked up their pace. Jenni lost track of time, and eventually a small hut appeared in the distance. As they drew nearer, it slowly took shape, and she couldn't help but smile. With its tan walls, grass-like roof and front porch, it reminded her of something off *Gilligan's Island.*

You need to get inside quickly, Nithlam instructed. *Do not come out until the rain has stopped for at least three hours.*

When it is clear, travel east until you reach the settlement called Carvinger. Find Vhenterhinge. She will help you, Shesta said.

"Wait, are you guys leaving?"

We have offspring to care for. They are waiting for us.

"What about the people who live here?" she asked as they slowed to a stop in front of the porch steps.

The hunters will not return, Nithlam told her with an angry edge. *Ever.*

"Oh." Jenni decided she didn't want details.

Climbing off Shesta's back, she reached over to Elliott, helping him slide down the cat's back. He landed on his feet, managed to hold himself upright for a second, and then fell to his knees with a muttered curse.

"It's getting better," she told him, ignoring his glare at her optimism and shouldering herself under his armpit. Pulling his arm around the back of her neck, she made an awkward and unsuccessful attempt to help him to his feet.

Here.

Nithlam circled around until he faced them both and then squatted down, positioning his nose mere inches from Elliott's. She saw the animal's chest expand and heard a massive intake of air before it exhaled and a gust of wind blew her husband's hair back from his face. His eyes closed in self-defense, but his chest expanded as he breathed in deeply, almost against his will.

She actually saw the vitality and energy flow into him, through him, filling him. He stretched his arms out on either side, as though waking from a deep sleep and stood on firm legs and opened his eyes, looking right into Nithlam's.

"Thank you. Thank you a thousand times."

She repeated the message.

Don't. It's only temporary, and you'll be worse than before. Get inside while you can.

Without another word, the two zebra cats turned and ran, leaving them alone in a foreign world, on the cusp of a storm they didn't understand.

Jenni sighed. "You're not cured, this is only a reprieve. We better get inside." A loud crash of thunder punctuated her words, lightning flashing around them.

"Who lives here?" he asked as he passed her, stepping onto the porch and carefully opening the front door, body poised for anything lurking behind it. He held a hand out in her direction, telling her to stand back.

"Nobody anymore. They seemed very sure the hunters were never coming back."

Elliott glanced back at her with an eyebrow raised. "Kitty chow?"

"I didn't want to know."

"Wait here." He stuck his head through the doorway before disappearing completely into the depths of the small structure. She waited a few minutes on the porch, hearing his footsteps cautiously moving inside and listening to the patter of fat raindrops as they slowly beat against the grassy roof above her head. Finally, he reappeared.

"All clear?" she asked her ridiculously over-protective bodyguard. "No paparazzi lurking in dark corners?"

"No," he answered. "And no wild animals, armed hunters or booby traps, either. You may enter."

He pushed on the door with his fingertips, sending it wide open, backed against the door jamb and, with a flourish of his hand and a toss of head to get his hair out of eyes, waved her into the cabin. Stepping beside him in the doorway, she stretched up far enough to touch her lips lightly against his for a second.

"Thank you for all you do for me."

Without waiting for a response, she turned to fully enter the room…and gasped in shock and horror.

Chapter 5

The entire room assaulted her senses. Illuminated by a lantern Elliott must have taken the time to light, the red walls, reminiscent of dripping blood, only highlighted the scene of carnage decorating them. Eerie shadows fell over countless busts of animals, faces contorted in pain or rage, hanging mounted and deadly still. They stared at her with angry and accusing black eyes, blaming her for their fate. Knives of every shape and size, machetes, bows and arrows and firearms hung around them in an indiscernible pattern.

"Macabre, isn't it?" Elliott said beside her, laughing.

"You could have warned me." She felt sick to her stomach.

"And miss the look of disgust and horror on your face? You're kidding, right?"

She swatted his stomach and he clutched the area melodramatically, hunching over slightly, pretending it hurt.

"I can't stay here. I just can't."

The room flashed brightly as a loud crash of thunder pounded into her, stealing her breath and causing the hairs on the back of her neck to stand on end. The light patter of rain instantly morphed into a torrential downpour. Elliott swayed beside her. Stumbling slightly, he grabbed her shoulder with one hand, and his head with the other.

"I'm sorry, Jenni, but I think—"

He slumped against her, and she caught him around the chest. The shrine to brutality momentarily forgotten, she quickly surveyed the large room and located several beds pushed against the far wall. Together, they shuffled the distance, and he dropped onto the mattress.

"Dammit," Elliott muttered into a green pillow.

"Nithlam warned it would be bad," she said as she adjusted his body, feeling his muscles beneath her palms contract with weak effort that accomplished little. His moans brought creeping fear slithering up her spine. "Tell me what's going on."

"My head is swimming." He managed to convey the thought as a simple fact, void of any self-pity.

"What else?"

"Spikes of pain keep shooting through my legs and arms. And they are getting heavier and heavier." He paused for a second, grimacing as another spike of pain must have passed through his system. "The cat said this would get better, right?" he finally gasped.

"Yes," she said, lying. "You will be fine."

Nithlam didn't explicitly say those words, but she got the impression the animal intended for Elliott to make a full recovery and refused to believe anything else. She could stand to be lost in another realm of existence for an indeterminate period of time. She could stand losing her new job and life-long dream home. She could deal with being ripped away from everyone and everything she held dear. Because the only thing that really mattered lay on the bed beside her right now, trying to hide his fear and his pain.

His eyes glazed over, then rolled back into his head

mere seconds before convulsions overwhelmed his body, seizing control. Jenni cried out, unsure what to do. Should she try to hold his tongue? Should she try to hold him still? Knowing she didn't have the physical strength to do either, she knelt beside the bed, watching intently, making sure he didn't fall off and damage himself even more. To comfort herself, and in case he could draw any strength from her presence, she lightly touched her fingers to his forehead and smoothed his hair away from his face.

Every second felt like an hour as Jenni knelt on the wooden floor, helpless. The storm outside forgotten, she listened to the sound of the bed scraping against the wall and floorboards in time with his shaking. She heard Elliott's desperate, short gasps for air and felt her own lungs hurting for him, unconscious of the tears streaming down her cheeks.

"Hang in there," she said, begging helplessly. "You're going to be all right. You're a fighter." She paused for a moment before admitting, "I need you; I always have." She watched him for a few seconds, feeling as though someone reached into her chest and placed a vise-grip on her heart.

"I'm going to tell you something I never told you before. You'd never let me live it down. But remember our first day of college? Scared, away from home for the very first time, I felt so alone. Everything so big and so many new people. The two days in the dorm before school started were a nightmare. You remember my roommate, and that whole situation. I just got out of history, and as I walked to my literature class, I wondered how I would pass without you sitting right next to me like the last thirteen years.

"But when I opened the door and walked in the room, the first thing I saw—you sitting there staring at the blonde three rows over…" She choked up for a moment, watching him convulse, "and I knew everything would be all right and I wouldn't quit and move back home like I planned." A small watery chuckle escaped. "Not that I liked you yet, but having you there to torment me made all the difference in the world. I didn't feel alone anymore." She swallowed and swiped at her nose. "Please, don't leave me alone now."

Jenni didn't know if he heard a single word of her confession, or if he consciously processed anything at the moment, and hoped maybe not. Religiously in total control of every aspect of his body, this embodied his worst nightmare. She waited, whispering to him, and prayed to every deity she could think of.

Finally, after what seemed like an eternity, the spasms decreased then disappeared completely, leaving him sprawled over the mattress—pale, unmoving, unresponsive. Jenni felt for a pulse and couldn't find one. Her own heart stopped and then began to race. Desperate, she held a hand half an inch above his nose and mouth and waited, reciting in her mind the steps Elliott taught her about resuscitation.

Weak, but present, she felt a soft current of air pass over her flesh. A relieved sob burst from her gut, and she fell against the side of the mattress. She allowed herself a few moments to cry into the green pillowcase before employing her own special breathing techniques to quell the flow of tears. *Breathe in through the nose, two three, hold it, breathe out through the mouth, two three. Repeat. Again.*

She didn't have time to break down, too much to

do. With determination, she stood and stretched her legs, swiping at her eyes to clear away the last of the moisture. Feeling more in control, she rubbed her hands together and inspected their new, temporary, home.

The next few hours felt like one long science experiment, with the main question being: "What happens when I do this?"

Is this strange-looking device a water pump?

Is the purple water drinkable?

Is this food, and is it edible?

Is the hole in the floor over there really the toilet?

Where does this trapdoor lead?

How do you operate the clasps on these clothes?

Did I really see these boots shrink to fit my feet, or have I finally lost my mind?

Every new test felt like a game of Russian roulette with mortality. If a simple rainstorm killed humans on this world, what other innocuous object might be their downfall? But someone needed to test these things. Elliott would be mad when he woke up and discovered all the chances she took, but his immobility and her mobility meant, this time, she needed to protect him.

The trapdoor, to her delight, led to a massive cellar. And there, in the very far corner, hidden in the shadows and almost completely concealed by bluish moss, a door. Letting curiosity get the better of her, she tried the handle. Unlocked. Holding out the lantern, she peered in and found a passageway. The tunnel extended far beyond her lantern light, and she itched to find the other end.

No. She couldn't leave Elliott alone upstairs. Besides the fact he might need her assistance, if she went on that particular adventure without him, he'd never forgive her. Biting her lip, she backed out and closed the door, listening to the small click of the latch as it closed. Soon, she promised herself.

She needed to go back upstairs, but the thought of waiting silently in the Shrine of Death made her stomach turn. Jenni looked around at the cave-like room, listening to an invisible drip and thinking how vast and empty the space looked. Covered in blue moss, it provided the perfect set for a horror film. A brilliant idea struck, and a slow smile spread across her face as she planned and plotted.

****

On her hands and knees, head stuck in a cupboard, Jenni took inventory of unrecognizable supplies in an effort to keep her mind busy. In the first hours Elliott lost consciousness, she was too busy to think. But, the heavy lifting finally completed, she found her thoughts wandering to places she didn't want to go and for the last several hours she fought this internal battle. *Don't let your heart hurt over impossible things, now is not the time.*

A slow wolf whistle interrupted her count of yellow spongy-looking things. Dropping her head, she peered under her arm to see the upside-down sight of Elliott sitting on the edge of his bed, feet on the ground, elbows on his knees, arms crossed, staring at her rear end.

"Feeling better, I see."

She backed out of the cupboard to face him, smiling too brightly for a half a second before realizing she'd overcompensated for her depression and pulled it back a notch. He didn't answer at first, merely studied her through tired eyes, and she took the opportunity to search his face, gauging how he truly felt as opposed to the lie he would soon tell her.

"Somewhat," he finally agreed. "How are *you* doing?"

"Asks the guy who nearly died. I'm a whole lot better than you at the moment."

She stood up, stretching her legs and slowly walked over to him, kneeling between his knees. Brushing his bangs away from his forehead, she leaned forward and kissed him on the forehead. Wrapping his arms around her, Elliott pulled gently on her back with the palms of his hands to move her closer. She obliged him.

"Do you like what I've done with the place?" Looking around, Jenni tried to see the red walls through his eyes. The dead animal mounts now absent, the blank spots between the weaponry left gaping, darker red splotches. "It actually reminds me of your workout room at home now, if you ignore the horrible color. You will love several pieces. There's this one—"

"What happened to all the…" He lifted a hand and waved at the missing trophies.

"I moved them. I didn't know how long we'd be stuck here, and I couldn't live with them. Wait until you see some of the cool things I found." She wiggled her eyebrows, thinking of the tunnel. "When you feel better, I've got all kinds of things to show you."

His lips turned up at the sides in an effort to smile. "I can't wait. What's wrong?"

"Nothing's wrong, everything has gone brilliantly since you checked out. Other than your seizure, of course. You scared the snot out of me with that stunt." He looked into her eyes for a few seconds as she spoke,

Shanghaied

and then pursed his lips with a short huff of air through his nose. "And I nearly gave myself a hernia carrying all those horrible stuffed corpses down to the cellar by myself." Pulling his hands from around her, he crossed his arms, elbows on his knees again. "Some guys will do anything to get out of a little heavy lifting." She winked at him. "Wait until you taste the food. There's this one thing—"

His lips covering hers stopped her babbling, and all thought evaporated. She felt his hand in her hair, felt it trembling slightly against her scalp. The other hand rested softly against her neck, caressing her for a moment before traveling downward, across her collarbone, sending tingles through her flesh as it moved. Over her shoulder and down her arm, he left a trail of invisible sparkles until his hand connected with hers. As they kissed, she vaguely registered something warm and round pushed into the palm of her hand before he curled her fingers around the object.

Ripping away from him, ignoring their labored breathing, she opened her palm and felt her heart drop into her stomach at the sight of the old, bedraggled penny. She didn't even need to look at it to know melted crayon dyed Lincoln's hair purple, some unidentified blackish substance obscured part of the monument on the back, and a gouge erased the date originally stamped next to the president on the front.

"No," she said, shaking her head, holding out the coin, trying to shove it back into Elliott's fingers.

"Yes." He pulled his hand out of reach above her head.

"Not now, not here, not like this. There are more important things to think about right now," she insisted.

"Not to me."

She glared at him.

He glared back.

"And you say *I'm* stubborn," she finally said, snapping the penny into the center of a ring hung on the end of a long leather cord around her neck.

"Which is exactly why I resorted to desperate measures." He reached around and pulled her close to his body, resting her head against his shoulder and caressing her hair. She felt his cheek against her head. He didn't say anything, simply waited quietly.

Closing her eyes, she took a deep breath, reveling in the feel of her husband surrounding her. Despite his comfort, she choked up again for the second time, and hated her weakness. "It's about this morning, how this whole thing kicked off." She backed up and tried to smile to hide the sudden sharp pang in her chest. She'd been moderately successful at keeping everything at bay all morning. Darn him for forcing her to bring it out in the open. "I guess it's a good thing we can't get pregnant, isn't it?"

"Wait, what?"

"Our sudden disappearance this morning. Can you imagine if we had a baby in the house and left it behind? How horrible that would be? So I guess," she breathed deeply again, "I guess it's a good thing we can't have children."

"We don't know that."

"Elliott," she said, summoning patience. "It's been nearly two years. If we haven't gotten pregnant by now—"

He placed a hand on either side of her face and gently forced her to look him in the eyes. "Honey, listen to me. We aren't giving up. Your parents had nine children, my parents had twelve, so obviously, there's a way to make this whole 'secret life of adventure' work with a family. We *will* find a way. I promise you."

"It's a moot point," she reminded him. "Since we can't get pregnant."

"We don't know that either."

"Two years."

"One and a half."

She harrumphed.

" 'Mostly' human, remember? Maybe it works differently for us; we don't have the foggiest idea. Maybe we had to go through 'gatekeeper puberty' first. And it's not like we've actually made a concerted effort."

She snorted. "Let me remind you of the facts, lover. We stopped birth control twenty-one months ago, and we haven't exactly been celibate except for the last two months."

"We're not out of options yet, sweetheart. And if we do exhaust all of our options and still can't get pregnant, we'll adopt."

"Are you sure you won't mind?"

"Not at all. We will have children, I promise you. I give you a solemn oath as your key."

She couldn't believe he managed to do it again, somehow make her feel lighter, despite knowing how unrealistic his plan seemed. She shook her head and smiled weakly. "You and your optimism."

"It's one of my few redeeming qualities." He searched her face for a moment. "Did you tell me everything?"

"You already know. This whole…" she waved her

hand around, "*thing* is a lot to take in."

"All right." He hugged her, and she realized how much he still needed to recuperate when he didn't squeeze away all her air. "You said something about food?" She laughed and started to pull out of his embrace, but he held slightly tighter for a second. "I'm sorry about the whole… you know…throwing-up-on-you thing earlier."

Not "sorry I scared you to death," but sorry about the puke. She rolled her eyes and stepped out of his arms and headed for the food cupboard. "Don't worry about it. I found some new clothes."

"Yeah, I saw."

Something in the tone of his voice made her turn around and look at him. "What's wrong with my clothes?"

"Nothing." He turned his head, gazing intently at the exotic knife on the wall next to him. Reaching out, he pulled it down and studied the workmanship, turning it over and over in his fingers.

"Liar. What's wrong?"

He paused. "It's stupid."

She waited.

He sighed, looking up at her sheepishly.

"It's the first time you've worn another man's clothes. It doesn't feel right."

Oh. Yeah, definitely stupid, but she understood. Emotion frequently trumped logic. "All right."

Jenni reached down with arms crossed and grabbed the hem of her shirt, pulling it up over her head and tossed it on the bed next to her husband before attempting to undo the alien clasp of her pants.

"What are you doing?"

She looked up to see his gaze pointed directly at her bare chest and chuckled. "I'm giving you these clothes to wear for a while. You need to change anyways, that white t-shirt is a lost cause now. After you've worn them for a bit, they will be your clothes, with your essence soaked into them, and maybe you'll feel better about me wearing them."

He shook his head and finally looked her in the eye. "You don't have to do that, I'll get over it." One side of his mouth quirked up. "But by all means, feel free to keep stripping."

"Only if you join me."

He smiled fully now. "If you insist. But I have to warn you, I'm not exactly at the top of my game right now."

"I don't care."

She pushed him back against the mattress, barely noting the thud of his knife landing on the floor when he tossed it out of her way.

"Yes, ma'am."

She kissed him then, and the entire world disappeared. The killer storm raging outside, the mountain of animal corpses in the cellar below, the uncertain future all melted away. For the next few hours, her whole existence consisted of only him and her, finally reuniting at last.

Chapter 6

Jenni floated at the edge of semi-consciousness in soothing darkness until a butterfly landed above her eye, slowly crawled across her brow, and then meandered down her cheek. It jumped away then flittered across her forehead, gently scooting a lock of hair from her face and tucking it behind her ear.

Odd.

She opened her eyes to see Elliott's green irises a few inches from her own and realized his breath created the soft summer breeze washing over her face. They both lay on their sides, facing each other.

"Sorry, didn't mean to wake you," he said. "I needed to touch you."

She smiled, and he smiled back. "You've written some new poetry during my absence."

He shrugged the one shoulder not trapped under his body. "Two months without you is long and lonely. I didn't have anything better to do but read in the quiet hours. And play racquetball to work out the energy."

"Nuh uh, pal. I've been around you long enough to recognize Byron and Yeats. You wrote new stuff."

"You're delusional."

" 'My body, my soul, my heart, belong to you'."

His hand covered her mouth while he laughed and cringed. "Don't," he begged. "It sounds really cheesy if we're not making love."

She rolled over until her legs straddled his waist and propped her elbows on his shoulders, lacing her fingers together in his hair behind his head. Looking into his eyes, she continued,

I surrender my existence into your loving care willingly, gladly.

Let your essence surround me, fill me, consume me-

For you are my air, my sunshine, my lifeblood.

Let the world melt away, let reality dissolve.

While I have you, your fire, your tempest...

Your kiss...to feed my hunger,

I am immortal.

"You were supposed to be enthralled by passion and not remember a word."

"I always remember your poetry. *Especially* the ones used to enthrall my passions. Every time I think of those words, I will remember exactly how I felt and exactly what we were doing at the moment you whispered them to me." She leaned down and kissed him quickly. "So thank you. I love you, too."

Elliott's stomach rumbled loudly, and she laughed while he cringed again. "Okay, so your stomach wants something more tangible than my kisses. Let me literally feed you now."

Without bothering to cover herself, Jenni jumped off the bed and walked to the cupboard where she located food earlier. Grabbing a package and a wooden cup of water, she started back toward her husband's reposed form.

"How can you walk around in your nakedness?" he asked, sounding baffled. "Not that I'm complaining or anything. Trust me; it's one of my favorite qualities about you."

" 'Nakedness?' Really?" She laughed at him. "Is that even a word?"

"I'm a poet, it's artistic license. Just roll with it and answer the question."

"Because I'm not the prude you are." She climbed onto the bed and ripped open the clear package, holding a brown stick-like substance in his direction.

"I'm not a prude." He accepted her offering, pulling it up close to his eyes, inspecting it closely. "I don't like flapping in the breeze. What the heck is this stuff, anyways?"

"No breeze in here, I think I'm safe from flapping." Thunder rumbled overhead, and she sighed. "Darn, I thought maybe the storm finally ended. No wonder Nithlam told us to wait three hours before venturing out again."

"He did?"

"This looks like it'll taste like cardboard," he said, eyeing the item in his hand warily.

"It doesn't. Just try it; I think you'll like it."

Tentatively, he brought the stick to his mouth and nibbled at the edge.

"Oh come on, you big baby. Take a bite. It's good."

He lifted his eyebrows doubtfully, but accepted her challenge and ripped off a nice sized chunk with his teeth. She watched him chew for a moment, irritated his face remained expressionless and gave her no clue to his reaction. Personally, she found the flavors exotic and intriguing.

"Well?"

"Well, what?"

"What do you think?"

"There's nothing to compare it to, is there?" he asked, still not giving a straight answer. "For once, you can't say 'it tastes like chicken.' " He continued chewing. After a moment, he held the jerky-like substance in her direction. "You gonna eat?"

"No, I'm not hungry. Those things stay with you for a long, long time. I ate half of one and a green cube thing and felt absolutely stuffed. I haven't been hungry since."

"We'll have to pack some before we leave. We have no idea how long of a walk we have. Did the cats give you any kind of directions?"

"Yeah, we're supposed to travel east, and when we get to the township called Carvinger, ask for Vhenterhinge. She's supposed to help us." He nodded at her and she smiled, feeling the zing of excitement shoot through her veins. "But I've got something to show you before we take off."

She wiggled her eyebrows, and he eyed her warily. "I know that expression. It means trouble."

"Possibly. But honestly, how much more trouble can we get in than we are right now?"

"Don't say that. Because Fate will step in and show us."

"I found a hidden door. With a tunnel."

He stopped chewing, his eyes wide. "Seriously?"

She nodded.

He swallowed. "For real, you found a secret passage?"

"Uh-huh."

He leaned forward, kissing her briefly. "Why didn't you say something sooner? Come on, we're wasting time."

She laughed as he jumped off the bed and started looking for his jeans. "I knew that would get you."

"How did my pants get way over there?"

She shrugged. "Go flap in the breeze and get them."

He rolled his eyes and trudged across the room to pull them off a sword hanging on the wall. "Where's the bathroom in this place?"

"See the round man-hole cover in the corner over there?"

His head swiveled around to her. "You're kidding."

"Wish I was. But it's not like normal latrines. It doesn't stink, and when you stand up there's a weird 'whooshing' noise."

"I'm not sitting down."

"Neither did I. I got a great thigh workout squatting over it."

He laughed, probably visualizing her trying to balance over the hole. She threw a boot at him, but he ducked and it flew harmlessly over his head. She stuck out her tongue before climbing off the bed to search for the clothes he hated so badly.

Getting Elliott to the cellar took longer than Jenni anticipated. He made her pack a bag, of all things.

"Elliott, we're only checking out a tunnel for a little while, we don't need to pack for a three day hike."

"And what happens if we're down the tunnel and we suddenly zap into another reality? We actually have supplies on hand; we need to 'be prepared.' "

She rolled her eyes. "I thought you hated Boy Scouts. That's why you earned your Eagle at fourteen, to get it over with."

"Yeah, well, a lot of things Dad forced on me suddenly make sense since this morning."

She harrumphed, but he held firm. So while she packed a satchel with extra clothes, food, water, and a first aid kit, he turned himself into a one man arsenal. Strolling around the room, he inspected each weapon carefully, picking it up, holding it in his hands, testing the feel of it. After a while, he collected a small pile on the bed, and Jenni realized each one he selected looked very similar to a piece in his own collection.

When finished, he had knives strapped to each ankle and thigh, a gun hanging under each arm in a shoulder-holster, a sword on his back, extra ammunition and various weapons on a belt around his waist and a long staff in his hand. Lastly, his right wrist now sported a thick leather bracer holding a small dart gun and a volley of darts.

She could personally testify to his skill with a dart gun. He could hit a barrette with a pencil eraser from the opposite side of a classroom.

"What, no crossbow?" she asked. "What kind of barbarian warrior are you?"

"One that sucks at archery. My troop made many jokes at my expense."

She raised an eyebrow in surprise. "And you admit it?"

"If a man can't come to terms with his weaknesses, he'll get himself and the ones he's protecting killed. You gotta work with your strengths. Here."

He held a small silver dagger out to her, simple in design, without any special markings or decorations. Compared to some of the knives he had at home, this was as basic as it got.

She shook her head. "No way. I don't know how to use that thing, I'll hurt someone."

"That's the point. I suggest hiding it under your shirt, or under your belt at your waist. You might even get it to fit between your breasts in that bra you made, but you want to be careful."

"I don't want to carry it."

He sighed. "I don't ask you for very much, do I?"

"No."

"Then please. For me. Just take the damn thing, and keep it on you at all times. I'll feel better knowing you have it."

"Fine," she grumbled, grabbing it from him and shoving the item into her waistband. "Can we go now, Conan?"

"After we find some rope."

"Oh good grief," she complained. "Don't you think this is a little overkill?"

"Jenni, listen to me," he said while he searched for the rope. "One evening at the age of twelve, I wanted to play baseball with Eddie and Groucho and Dad wouldn't let me because I hadn't done my two hour sparring session with my brother yet." He found what he wanted, and draped the roll over her shoulder like a purse, then met her eyes. "I whined about his stupid training regimen and told him how idiotic I considered his rules.

"He turned to me, looked me straight in the eye," he pointed to his to illustrate his point, "and said 'Elliott boy, I know it's hard and I know it sucks. But someday, a three-headed wildebeest with long purple fangs and drooling red saliva will appear out of nowhere and charge you. And you'll have to stand your ground or die trying.' At first, I thought he spoke metaphorically about challenges in life, until he continued with, 'Nasty things, those wildebeests. They slip through the fabric of time and reality and jump you when you least expect it.'

"I decided then and there he was out of his ever-lovin' mind. Now? Not so much."

"How old were you when he started your training?"

Her husband looked away from her and headed for the cellar trap door. "Six," he mumbled as he descended.

"Six? You're kidding me." She scrambled to catch up, following him into the room below.

"Yeah, the day you punched me in the nose." He paused at the bottom of the stairwell, looking around at the piles of stuffed beasts. "I blamed you for many years for those daily torture sessions. Until I decided Dad went nuts somewhere along the line." He glanced back at her, lips twitching upward. "Turns out I was right in the first place."

"Oh, shut up."

He chuckled, then grabbed a lantern off a crate and lit the wick with the lighter she left next to it, generously refraining to comment on the fact she stole it from his pocket during his convalescence. Flicking his hair out of his eyes, he looked up at her. "Where's this secret door?"

She showed him and together, they pulled it open.

"How on earth can a dank tunnel smell like honeysuckle?" her companion asked, breathing in deeply through his nose, closing his eyes with a wide smile.

"I think the key phrase here is 'on earth.' Which we're not."

"Right. Onward?"

"Onward."

Watching Elliott slowly enter the passageway felt like watching a kid walk through the gates of Disneyland for the first time. Jenni saw excitement in his eyes and mischievous smile; he'd morphed into Huck Finn, about to float down a river, Jim Hawkins about to sail away to look for buried treasure, or maybe even Oliver Twist about to run off with the artful Dodger. He didn't need to say the words; she heard them echo in her head. "Coolest. Thing. Ever."

He held the lantern high with one hand and his staff with the other while they moved forward. She also noticed he glanced behind occasionally to keep tabs on her location. Luckily, neither of them suffered from claustrophobia. Standing tall with her arms out straight, she could touch either side of the tunnel with her fingertips. The ceiling dropped low enough it came within a few inches of kissing Elliott's hair.

As they walked, the yellow beam of light from their entryway grew smaller and smaller until it snuffed out completely. Left with only the light from the lantern, it created a bubble around her and Elliott, cocooning them within its embrace and consigning everything beyond its reach to a black void. Its color combined with the blue moss covering the walls gave the rocky surface a green hue.

Lost in the adventure of it all, neither of them spoke at first, absorbing the experience. Remote, unseen water droplets *drip-drip-dripped* in slow rhythm. A deliciously eerie scurrying in the distance gave her the impression they were not the only travelers in this dark tunnel, and at some point they might encounter rodent-like creatures. A weird whooshing noise she couldn't quite identify brushed against her flesh. Her more fanciful side wanted to identify it as deep, sluggish breathing—the pull of inhale and the measured release of exhale.

"You all right?" Elliott asked.

"Yup." Noticing her thumbs hooked in the straps of the satchel started to tingle, she pulled them out, wiggling her fingers in an effort to keep the blood flowing. The tingle remained, but it didn't get worse.

They continued silently through the dark passage for another half an hour before it branched in two directions.

"We have three choices, hon. We can go this way," he pointed ahead of them with the end of his staff, "that way," he indicated again to the passage on their left, "or, turn around and go back, see if the storm has let up and find the woman Nithlam described."

"I'm not ready to go back yet, you?"

His goofy smile told her she made the right decision. "Me neither. So, ladies choice. Forward or left?"

Popping the penny out of its ring on her necklace, she balanced it on the edge of her fisted thumb and flicked it into the air. Their heads moved in unison, watching it fly upward, then downward into her right palm. Slapping it against the back of her left hand, they both peered at the copper.

"Tails. We go left." She snapped the coin back into its ring, tucking the necklace safely into her shirt to rest against her heart.

He nodded, then handed her his staff and took out the large knife sheathed to his right thigh. The instant he began scratching an arrow into the moss, indicating which direction they needed to return, a high-pitched wail reverberated throughout the small cavern, engulfing them.

Pain sliced her eardrums and she dropped his weapon, grabbing her ears in a vain effort to mute the sound, doubling over with her eyes closed. Finally, the horrific sound faded, leaving only a small whimpering.

"I think," Jenni told him weakly, "you hurt the tunnel."

"What the blazes happened?"

She looked up to see him sheathing the knife and retrieving the lantern from the ground with shaking hands.

"I think the tunnel might be alive."

"Oh crap." He looked upward to the rock walls. "I'm sorry." They waited a moment, frozen and watching. Nothing happened. "Do you think it's mad?"

"How should I know?"

"You're the one who talks to cats these days."

"Doesn't mean I'm a mind reader. We can only hope."

"I'm sorry," he said again to the walls beside them. "I didn't know."

They headed farther into the darkness, the mood now subdued. After a few moments of silent walking, Jenni couldn't take it anymore.

"You can't blame yourself, Elliott. You didn't know."

"I know," he said flatly.

She sighed, wishing she could take away some of

the guilt washing through him. "We're new at this other realm business, there's no way for us to—"

"I know."

"Elliot, stop. Right there." He obeyed, turning to her with frustration written on his face. "You can't—"

The rocky earth disappeared underneath her feet, and her stomach flipped up into her throat as she smashed first into one side of the new hole, then the other in her descent, preparing her for the final crash at the bottom. Rocks and debris rained down on her, and she covered her head, tucking into the fetal position until the torrent finally abated.

"Jenni," Elliott called down to her. "Jenni, talk to me."

"I'm all right," she yelled back, choking on dirt.

The rocky grime reached into every crevasse of her clothing, and when she sat up, she immediately reached into her shirt to pull a dirt clod out of the bra she fashioned out of a tight tank top. Her teeth crunched unpleasantly when she closed her mouth, and she spit in an unsuccessful effort to clear out the silt.

"This is gross."

"Yeah, well, if gross is the worst of your problems right now, consider yourself lucky. Do you have the rope with you?"

Darn. She looked at the ground to keep from seeing his smug smile. "Yes."

She counted in her head. *Three. Two. One—*

"You know, the one we didn't need for a short walk." She rolled her eyes, despite the fact she knew he couldn't see her with her head bent slightly. "Throw it up here, and I'll haul you out."

"I'll climb up."

"Suit yourself."

She lifted her gaze to find him sitting at the edge of the hole, his legs dangling over the side.

By her calculation, it appeared a fifteen foot climb to the top.

"What is it with you and cliffs today?"

"Just shut up."

"Yes, dear."

Chapter 7

Climbing a rock wall, much to Jenni's chagrin, turned out to be as tough as she remembered. And if it weren't for her own sense of pride, and the fact Elliott sat at the top waiting for her to come to her senses and ask for help, she'd throw in the towel, toss up the rope and let him do all the heavy lifting. She couldn't let him have the satisfaction.

"There's a good hand hold about six inches above your head, to your left."

She grunted, saving her breath, and reached for the spot he indicated. Inch by agonizing inch, she slowly scaled the side of the pit. Her arms ached. Her shoulders screamed at her. Sweat trickled over her face, getting dirt and grime in her eyes she couldn't swipe away. The last time they did this, she had a helmet and a safety rope connected to a five-point harness rigged around her body. Falling off simply meant swinging in the breeze until she secured a good foothold again.

"You're doing great, honey, you're more than halfway there."

"You're enjoying this," she gasped with irritation.

"No, absolutely not. The sight of you scaling the wall like a world class rock climber is not a turn-on at all." He paused for a moment, she figured to give her a chance for a witty reply. When she didn't oblige, he finally broke down. "Can I help you if I promise not to

---

use the rope?"

"Only if you promise not to be insufferable, too."

He didn't answer, and she continued to climb.

"Fine," he said at last. Pulling his legs up, he lay flat on the ground, leaning into the pit and extended his staff as far as his reach allowed. "Grab hold."

She had to stretch, but managed to wrap a fist around the end. Breathing in deeply, she let go of the wall, and felt herself rising even before she wrapped her second hand around the oversized rod. Above her, Elliott now stood on the edge, pulling her upward, fist over fist. The errant visual of a Mediterranean fisherman standing on the bow of his boat hauling in nets sprung to her mind, which made her the floppy fish.

Her whole body buzzed with the strain of the climb and holding onto the staff. The instant she reached the lip of the hole, she scrambled to safety. Elliott helped her stand and brushed the grime from her clothes, his gaze roaming her body, his fingers gently pressing here and there.

"You'll have a few bruises. Too bad we don't have any bottled zebra cat spit, that would clear those right up."

She laughed. "Can you imagine using it in your ambulance?"

"That's not a bad idea, actually. If we ever run into them again, you'll have to ask them if they'll spit into a jar for us."

His hands, firmly but gently, traveled over her shoulders, neck, scalp and then trailed down her arms, causing a light buzz through her system. The dark cavern flickered around them, and she felt like a dying fluorescent light bulb. Two worlds sputtered, fighting for dominance. For a split second, they stood in the tunnel, then next to their kitchen table, then back in the tunnel. Over and over again, they jumped between the two realities.

She tried to breathe evenly, to keep her eyes open—to *will* the jumping to stop during the microseconds they existed on earth. Elliott slid his hands upward on her arms, and the scenes changed. The brilliant, blinding white of the In Between fought for dominance over an alley sandwiched between two tall red brick buildings, lined with green metal dumpsters.

The strobe effect turned her stomach, and the worlds tilted and spun as her dizziness grew steadily worse. "El-ott," she gasped, hearing the word slip brokenly from her mouth, missing a syllable with a flash. "I'm g—ing t- be si-"

"H-ng o- Je-i."

She felt Elliott's fingers tighten around her arms, pulling her closer until their bodies collided. She leaned into him, grateful for the connection to the only solid and real object left in her existence. Her stomach twisted and knotted. The worlds swirled. Faster and faster, the scenes flashed around her as she clung to her husband in desperation.

And then it abruptly ended.

White misty clouds surrounded them, and the floor, though solid under her feet, swayed slightly reminding her of the boat rides her brothers used to take her on during the summer.

"Wonder when we get our sea legs?" Elliott mumbled into her hair.

"Keep up, you two." Jenni's father's voice floated

to them through the mist. "It's too easy to get turned around in this infernal—" He stepped into view, his eyes growing wide the instant he saw them. "You jumped."

"Edgar—"

A sonic concussion pounded through her body and the In Between vanished, leaving them clutching each other in the long alley between two tall red brick buildings.

Elliott let out a short and benign expletive. "We were so close."

"Let's wait a minute, maybe we'll jump again."

They stood together, listening to muted vehicle traffic passing in the distance. After five minutes, she finally gave up and stepped away with a sigh. "Maybe we're on Earth. It *looks* like Earth so far."

"At least we didn't fall off another cliff."

"You mean me."

"Your words, not mine."

They started walking to the end of the alley side by side. "I can't believe Dad didn't even notice we were gone."

"Did you get the impression we were only missing for a few seconds?"

"Yeah. Hey, you lost your walking stick, didn't you?"

"Nope." He stopped their progression and pulled a small metal rod from his belt, tapping the edge of one side. Both ends snapped outward until the rod achieved its full seven foot length, smooth and without crease, or fold. "Neat trick, huh?"

"When did you figure it out?"

"I accidentally hit the end of it after I fished you

out of the pit back there, and it collapsed. Here, try it."

He held the staff out to her, and she grasped it firmly with one hand, tapping the end with her other. It snapped shut, startling her and making her jump. "That is so cool," she said over Elliott's laughter, tapping the end to watch it open again.

She opened and closed it a few more times before he took it away, collapsing it and hanging it off a loop on his belt. Draping an arm around her shoulders, he tucked her in close and walked toward the street once more. She ignored the gun in the shoulder holster pushing into her ribcage and wrapped her arm around his back, under the sword, hooking a thumb into his belt. The rope, hanging from one of the straps of the backpack she wore, tapped against the back of her thigh with each step.

"Are you insane?" a deep voice asked from behind them. "Or just really, really stupid."

Elliott spun around, shoving Jenni behind him while drawing one of his guns and aiming it at the man who stood several yards away.

"Whoa there, cowboy," the stranger said, holding up his hands to show he didn't hold any weapons. "Put the gun away before you hurt someone."

He seemed harmless enough, if a little odd; dark hair shorn close to his head, short beard trimmed to look like lightning bolts crashing down to meet together at his chin. With tight black pants, black knee-high boots and a red shirt under dark brown suspenders, he reminded Jenni of a space cowboy from one of her favorite television shows.

"We don't have any money," Elliott said. "So if you turn around and walk away, we can pretend this never happened."

"Stupid, then. I'm not after your money, you moron. I'm here to make sure you don't expose the rest of us with your idiocy."

"What are you talking about?" Jenni asked.

"What else do you call it when you jump into Allistance Alley during a patrol, drawing foreign weaponry and looking like you escaped the Jihvisten mines? Some of us take our jobs seriously. It's hotshots like you who put everything we work for in danger. People rely on you, and you act like—"

"Look," Elliott interrupted. "Who are you? Where are we? And how do we get back to the In Between."

"Or Earth," Jenni joined in. "We'll take Earth, too."

"You're kidding." He stared at them for a few seconds, judging their sanity and sincerity. "The Underground didn't send you?"

"Nobody sent us," Elliott said gruffly.

"Can you tell us how to get home?"

A loud crack at the end of the alley drew their attention for a second. "Follow me," the man said nervously, looking over their shoulders. "We have to get her off the street, it's not safe."

He scanned the area quickly to make sure they weren't watched, then pushed one of the green dumpsters away from the building slightly, revealing a black hole in the wall. "Let's go, the patrols will be here any second."

"You first," Elliott ordered.

"Fine." Their new guide ducked and disappeared into the opening.

Jenni moved to go in next, but Elliot's hand on her

arm stopped her progression. "Let me check it out." She stepped back and watched as he followed the stranger. A few seconds later, his head popped out. "It's clear."

Upon entering the building, she found herself in a cramped hallway. She had to press flat against a wall when the man in the red shirt squeezed by to pull on a rope connected to the dumpster, sealing them in. He squashed past her again, belly to belly, and she felt grateful for the pitch black, keeping Elliott from seeing.

"Give us some light, sugar."

"Her name is Ms. Hamilton."

"I don't have a light."

"I meant crank up the glow. We don't need much, only a couple fingers."

"I can't."

The man grumbled in irritation, his voice traveling away.

Jenni felt a hand on her waist encouraging her forward, and she squished past Elliott to follow the voice. Travelling blind, she dragged her fingers on the wall to guide her as she walked. Her husband's hand stayed on her waist following her lead and providing silent comfort and assurance.

One minute, they traveled through a black void, the complete antithesis of the In Between, and the next they emerged into a large, spacious room with blinding light spilling in from every direction. Blinking a few times, she slowly regained her sight. Rusty metal beams sporadically lined red brick walls and held a glass roof in place.

The large space seemed divided for functionality. One corner held a collection of bunk beds, another corner a kitchenette and a small round table. One area seemed like office space, leaving a large amount of the room vacant. Ten sets of eyes turned in her direction as someone let out a low, predatory wolf whistle.

"Well, well, well, look what we have here," a deep voice said. "She's a little rough around the edges, but beggars can't be choosers, right?"

Fear zipped through Jenni's veins. Her hands shook, and her breath came in short gasps as men of all sizes and colors unfolded themselves from cots, bunkbeds and chairs spread throughout the room and slowly stood, eyeing her speculatively. Elliott's back suddenly blocked her view and she took a deep breath, propping herself onto tiptoes to look over his shoulder. He stepped backward, nudging her closer to the door, and she realized his arms extended outward in front of him, his guns missing from their shoulder holsters.

"Stand down, men."

All of the men on the other side of the room looked ready for combat, ready to pounce. Red Shirt stood in the center, between her and Elliott and the others, with his arms extended, as though holding both sides at bay. Unable to maintain good balance in that position, she dropped to flat feet and looked around Elliott's arm. It left her slightly exposed, but she had a clearer picture of the events.

"She's a gatekeeper."

"That just makes her yummier," the same voice sounded.

All eyes shifted from the guns to her, shocked and speculative. Reaching forward without looking, Jenni pulled one of the weapons from Elliott's belt, gripping what felt like a stick tightly in her fist while breathing deeply in an attempt to calm her racing heart.

Jenni watched Elliott draw deep, even breaths, his trigger finger tense.

"Unless you want to eat your reproductive organs for lunch, Louie," Red Shirt continued sternly, "I suggest you stop antagonizing her key." He turned to look at Elliot. "Put the guns down, cowboy. I give you my solemn oath, no one will bother her."

Elliott didn't obey, keeping the weapons leveled.

"They're a little rough around the edges, but they are good men. We're all on the same team here."

"Who are you, where are we, and what the hell is going on?"

"You're on Earth Three, in lower Oklahoma. My name is Rick, and I'm a guardian. These men are under my command. I know things are disorienting right now, you're probably not used to being gated remotely, but—"

"We're not used to 'gating' at all," Jenni mumbled.

"What?"

"Louie needs to apologize to Jenni."

"Elliott," she hissed, "Don't make a—"

"Louie, you heard the man. Apologize." Rick waited a beat. "Now."

"I'm sorry, ma'am, for scaring you." Louie turned out to be a man in his early twenties with shorn blond hair, angular features and a wide smile belying any true sorrow on his part. "I was just funin' and didn't mean any disrespect." A very dark man standing near him smacked him upside the back of his head, and the smile faded. He coughed and stepped back, ducking his head slightly.

"Please don't judge us by Idiot Boy over here," the man who hit him said. "It's an honor to meet you." He bowed his head briefly in their direction. "My name is Mitchell. I'm looking forward to working with you."

"I'm Nellum," another man said.

"Craysock."

"Edinverge."

"Harry."

The names went on and on, Jenni nodding to each man as they continued their informal roll call, forgetting them almost instantly. While they introduced themselves, Elliott slowly lowered his arms and then holstered the guns, his eyes continuously scanning the room. She tried to return the stick to its origin, but as her hand met his belt, he flinched with a short grunt, his mouth in a grim line.

Looking down, she realized a spiked metal ball hung on a chain from the end of the weapon, and she accidentally bumped it against his leg, skewering his thigh. A small red dot of blood on his jeans marked the entry point.

"Sorry," she whispered.

"No problem," he gasped.

"Does this count as domestic violence?" she asked, distracted and ignoring the crowd of strangers watching them.

"I promise not to press charges for accidents. You start using the flail on me on purpose, and all bets are off, though." Carefully taking the item from her, he twisted the end of the handle, retracting the spikes and pulling the ball flush against the device.

"That's cool."

He nodded, half smiling through his grimace as he secured it to his belt.

"If you follow me, we can talk in peace," Rick

said.

"Just give us directions home, and we'll be on our way."

"It's not that simple. You've been sent here for a reason." The man eyed Jenni critically for a second, as though assessing her and finding her wanting.

"I already told you," Elliott said, following Jenni as she urged him closer to the table Rick gestured toward. "There's been a mistake. Nobody sent us. We took our first trip through the rabbit hole this morning, and before we got Lesson Number One, we tripped the activation, forcing us to run ever since. We're only trying to get home." He finally perched on the edge of a seat after adjusting the sword on his back and glancing over his shoulder as Jenni joined him.

Rick sighed as he sat across from them. The other men in the room went back to whatever they'd been doing before the intrusion. "I promise you, you've been sent here on purpose. Because of your…unique…situation, you are the only ones who can help us. Martha had to act quickly before the council discovered—"

"Martha?" Jenni interrupted. "You mean *Mom*?"

For the first time, their host looked supremely uncomfortable. "She and her husband—"

"Dad."

"Edgar, are sympathizers to our plight here. They've worked in secret to relieve our banishment."

"Woah, back up. Banishment? And where do we fit into all this?"

Elliott pulled one of his knives from a leg sheath and, without looking at his hands, flipped it through his fingers. Jenni felt the energy pulsating from him, knew from long experience his driving need to regain control of a situation careening out of all proportion.

"That is a long story. The short and immediate situation is there's a young woman close to transmorphing, but she is stuck in this realm while her key is in another. You two are the only ones who can reunite them. The council will not help. We desperately need you."

They stared at him. He stared back.

"Maybe you didn't hear Elliott the first two times he told you. We don't know what we're doing. We never even started Lesson Number One. We have no idea how to activate jumping, we have no idea how to navigate jumping and we have no idea how to land after jumping. And now you say we're supposed to take other people with us? Like we're some inter-realm bus system?"

"No, nothing like a bus system." He paused for a second. "More like an inter-realm commuter flight."

"You're kidding."

"With tighter security features than the FAA on your home world. The council likes to list entire realities as 'No Fly Zones.' "

Elliott took a deep breath, then spoke slowly, pausing between each word to get their point across once and for all. "We. Can't. Do. It."

"Not yet, you can't, which is why your mother sent you here. The council doesn't know about you yet, and so they cannot trace you. I have someone who can teach you everything you need to know to finish your mission and get home again."

"You're not making any sense," Jenni argued. "If my mom can gate people remotely, why doesn't she send this young woman where she needs to go?"

"Because she hasn't transmorphed yet. To jump a non-gater, you have to be in physical contact with them. Listen, we can help each other. I'll take you to the person who can teach you how to work your gift. In exchange, you take Milliscent to Porthinch so she can unite with her key."

"Where's Porthinch?"

"I believe it's sandwiched between Earth Five and Mexico, but I've never been there."

They stared at him for a few seconds, but the man didn't crack a smile. Jenni leaned closer to Elliott without taking her eyes off Rick. "Is he serious?" she whispered incredulously.

"I can't tell," he whispered back.

Rick didn't enlighten them. Instead, he eyed Jenni's ragged appearance again and stated, "I have concerns, though. I'm afraid Martha may have made a mistake."

"I think you're right," Jenni agreed.

"Your key looks competent enough, but the journey is dangerous, long and grueling. I'm not sure you can endure it."

"Oh no." Elliott groaned, dropping the knife on the table and covering his face with his hands, slumping in his chair slightly. "You have no idea what you've done." His fingers fell to the sides, his gaze darting to Jenni for a second, surely saw her determined glare, then shot back to Rick. "You just made my life a living hell."

He dropped his elbows onto the table, raising his voice slightly. The hum of voices lowered, and the men turned their attention to their leader.

Jenni opened her mouth to give this arrogant, high-handed, patronizing, donkey's hind end a piece of her mind, but her husband cut her off before she could utter a single word.

"So far today, this woman," Elliott said, grabbing the knife back off the table and ticked off the points on the fingers of his other hand as he made them, "has scaled the side of a cliff, walked barefoot over razor rocks, ridden bareback on a mutant, saber-toothed cat while chased by killer rain, nursed me back to health from the brink of death, re-arranged an entire cabin full of furniture, and fallen into a deep dark pit after it mysteriously opened up under her feet. Then, when the avalanche of rocks finished raining down on her, *she crawled back out*. And, thanks to the mother of all time zone differences, she managed to do all this before lunch. And all of *that* happened after the emotionally scarring revelation her parents lied to her for her entire life about her true identity as a person, and the very essence of her mortality."

Everyone in the room now stared at them.

"Don't ever, ever tell my wife she can't do something."

Chapter 8

A sharp stab of pain cascaded over Elliott's shin as Jenni's boot slammed into it under the table. Refusing to acknowledge her censure, he turned his wince into a scowl, and directed it at Rick. The bastard. Anger at the man rolled over him in waves, and he fought to remain in control of his temper. Taking a deep breath, he strategized ways and means of getting the two of them through the journey with minimal injury and argument, calculating how much goodwill he'd willingly sacrifice as opposed to how much fatigue or pain he'd allow his wife to endure.

The bugger of it all, the most frustrating part; Elliott could count on her to pay attention to both of their limitations if they made this quest alone. But add in strangers, with the man before them questioning her stamina and fortitude, and all bets were off.

"Good," Rick said. "Then she might stand a chance."

"Don't worry about her, she can make it. Jenni's the toughest person I know." Which is exactly what made his life so difficult.

He saw her out of the corner of his eyes, her expression. Surprise. Concern. Flabbergasted. Perfect word choice, flabbergasted. Not only did it describe her exactly at this moment, he had fun saying it. Kind of like juggling with your tongue. Fla-ber-gas-ted. Could he manage to shoehorn it into a poem at some point? It would make her laugh. Could he find anything to rhyme with it?

Two mercenaries staring at Jenni with incredulity stood to full height, and Elliott let the hilt of the knife circling through his fingers fall into his palm, grasping it firmly, at the ready. Resting that hand in plain sight on the table, he subtly adjusted his position on the chair for easier lunging, should the need occur.

Mastershafted.

Annermasted?

Nagerjasted.

He might give Dr. Seuss a run for his money.

"We have some time before our courier returns with our instructions. You should use it to rest and eat." Rick eyed Jenni again. "There're showers if you want to get cleaned up."

"Do you have a first aid kit?"

His wife rolled her eyes, but he ignored her. She had scratches all over her face and arms again, and they were fresh out of zebra cat spit.

Their host looked over his shoulder, toward his men. "Mitchell, retrieve the medic bag." He turned around to continue talking to them as Friendly Mercenary went to a cupboard and rooted around. "I'm afraid we're not really equipped for privacy around here, but we'll do the best we can."

The man didn't exaggerate. Elliott found himself standing guard in front of the blanket a couple of soldiers pinned over the entrance to the shower room.

"Are you there?" Jenni's voice softly called from behind the thin barrier.

"Yeah, baby. Don't worry, I'm not going

anywhere."

The shower turned on, and as he watched the room, he saw her in his mind removing each article of clothing. He heard her moving around in the water, and instead of relying on imagination, he pulled out some of his favorite memories to follow her movements.

One of the men broke away from the rest and slowly approached him, hands up. Not taking any chances, Elliott adjusted his stance slightly, and rested his dominant hand on the collapsed staff hanging from his belt. "Crabfoot, isn't it?"

The man smirked. "Close. Craysock."

Elliott nodded. "Don't come any closer."

Craysock halted. "We're not going to hurt her."

"I know." He'd make sure of it.

The man paused for a moment, gathering his thoughts. "What's it like?"

"What is what like?"

"Sharing your living space with a woman full time."

Really? Elliott raised an eyebrow, and shrugged. This kid needed to get out more. "I have four sisters, so I've done it my whole life. I don't know what it's like to *not* share a bathroom with a woman." Unless the last two months of hell he just finished counted.

The soldier's eyes widened. "Doesn't that lead to discord?"

"Frequently."

"So why choose that?"

He looked the man in the eye, trying to gauge his sincerity. He saw no humor in them. "Because I'd rather be near her than not. Besides," he smirked, "for the most part, arguing with Jenni is highly entertaining."

"And yet you are protective."

"Yes."

Craysock considered this for a few moments. "I guess it's different for gatekeepers and their key. They are biologically compelled to unite which must make it easier to cohabitate and the relationship less disruptive—"

Elliott burst out laughing at the thought of his and Jenni's relationship being "less disruptive." He couldn't seem to stop as memory after memory flitted through his mind in microseconds, causing him to laugh harder. Should he tell him about the time…no.

"Kid, we fight like cats and dogs sometimes. So what?" he finally stopped laughing enough to elaborate. "It's this simple." He chuckled again, but maintained control. "Picture the most beautiful woman you have ever seen." He waited a second until the soldier nodded. "Now, picture waking up and seeing her next to you every single morning." He waited another second. "Wouldn't your beautiful woman be infinitely more preferable than waking up to *that*?" He pointed to a hairy man scratching himself. "You simply have to learn how to compromise a little. They make it worth your while."

"Men and women are not biologically engineered to be monogamous."

Elliott shrugged. "Different realities, I guess. A lot of cheating goes on in my world, yeah. But a lot of people manage to stay loyal for entire lifetimes."

"My world has cured itself of cheating. It's no longer a problem."

"How?"

"Cohabitation is outlawed. Monogamy antiquated."

He stared at the soldier for a moment, trying to absorb what he heard. "What?" he finally asked stupidly.

"Cohabitation is against the law."

He paused again, coming to terms with the fact he heard correctly the first time. "How does your government even control everyone? How do they know if two people choose to be faithful to each other?"

"Oh you *can* be faithful, you just can't live together." He smiled ruefully. "Not that it's a real issue anymore; most folk follow the true path and don't try to force themselves into a stifling relationship."

"What about marriage? How do you handle that?"

Craysock shrugged. "We have no marriage. Men and women never cohabitate. The cities are divided into male and female sectors. Trespassing is punishable by castration, and taking any vows of permanency is punishable by banishment, which pretty much equals death."

Elliott choked. "So how do you guys...you know...get any action? And how are your children raised?" And then another thought occurred to him, and cold fear swept through his veins. "And what will happen to Jenni if she's caught here?"

"She won't."

"But if she were?"

"She won't. I promise you. We have a strategy in place to sneak her into the women's sector where sympathizers can smuggle her out of the city. We're only waiting for the rendezvous instructions."

"But that means—" The water turned off to the shower, and Elliott clamped his mouth shut.

Turning, he carefully peeled back the blanket just far enough to slip inside. Making sure the cover fell back into place and no peepholes were created by his entrance, he turned to find a long tiled room. Shower spigots hung at intervals on the wall, and several small drainage grates lined the floor. At the farthest end of the room, near a set of sinks bolted against the opposite wall as the showers, Jenni stood naked with her feet planted shoulder width apart, bent upside-down at the waist, wrapping a towel around her hair.

"Jenni."

She yelped, jumping up and backwards at the same time, slipping on the tiled floor and landing against the wall. She managed to catch herself before falling completely and shot him a dirty look. Leaning heavily on the wall with one hand and putting the other hand over her heart while she breathed deeply, she scolded him. "Don't DO that to me."

"Jenni, we have to get out of here. Now."

"Can I get dressed first?"

He rushed forward, grabbing her shirt off the corner of the sink where she stacked the clean change of clothes from the backpack she teased him about, and started pushing the neck hole over her toweled head. "We have to jump." The cotton stuck to her wet skin as he tried to pull the fabric down over her body, and he managed to trap her arms in his hurried efforts.

"What is going on?" she asked, batting his hands away as she extricated herself. He reached for her pants to hold them out. "Ten minutes ago, we had a plan and now you're freaking out." Her words became muffled as the shirt covered her face. "What happened?" Her head emerged, and she pierced him with her brown-eyed gaze.

"We have to try to jump. Now."

She humored him enough to step into the pants while he held them up for her, and after tying the cord at her waist, grabbing his hands and interlacing their fingers. She stepped close, and he felt her soft curves pressing into his chest and her head lean against his shoulder, the towel rubbing against his chin. Her stomach pushed into his nether regions, but anxiety for her safety stripped away any of the lustful thoughts normally accompanying close contact with her body, and he waited for the lightning to strike so they could find themselves anywhere else in the universe.

And he waited.

And waited.

"Dammit."

Jenni stepped back a few inches and looked up at him, ignoring the towel wrapped around her head falling awkwardly to the side. "Cold feet?"

"The grand plan Rick presented to us? He failed to mention it involves our separation."

Her mouth fell open, her eyes bulging for a second. "What? No!"

He nodded, his gut churning. "No way around it."

"Yes, there is, you tell him we go together or there's no deal. Period." She chopped the air in front of her with a flat hand to illustrate the punctuation. "I'll wait here with you until the next cycle, and we'll take our chances with the unknown. Besides, separating won't do them any good, we have to be together to jump. We know that much, at least."

"I don't know the details of their plan, but you can't stay here. Every second you're here, you're in danger."

"That's what I've got you for, my own barbarian warrior. And we'll leave together."

"Yeah, well, I appreciate your confidence in my abilities, but even I can't fight off a police force. And I can't go with you."

"What did you learn?" she asked somberly, and as he explained his discussion with Craysock, her face drained of all color. "I'm going to be sick," she finally said when he ran out of words. She doubled over slightly, holding her stomach. "I can't believe my mother pushed us here. No wonder the council banned this rotten place."

"It's not exactly gatekeeper friendly, is it?" he said, pulling her into his arms, wrapping them tightly around her, barely noticing the water from her shower soaking through his clothes. "We can do this. You can do this; you're the toughest person I know."

He felt her thump his chest lightly with a flat hand. "Why did you exaggerate so badly earlier?"

"I didn't."

"Oh, please, I did *not* do all that stuff you said."

"You did everything I said. You simply brush off your own awesomeness sometimes."

"I thought you called it obstinacy."

"Potato, pahtahto."

She laughed shortly. *Much better.*

"I don't want to go without you," she mumbled into his chest, causing pain to lodge there.

"I don't either."

They held each other for a few moments longer, and he let her warmth seep into his body, filling him. He breathed in her scent, ignoring the foreign soap she used and concentrating on her essence. The poet in him reared its head, and he forced himself to refrain from opening his mouth and letting the words start falling out.

"Come on, we need take care of your scratches," he said a little more gruffly than he intended. Pulling away from her, he scanned the room for the medic bag Mitchell kindly gave them earlier and located it on the sink near her clothes.

Blessedly, she allowed him to fuss over her without argument, patiently standing still while he removed her towel and inspected her head, face, arms and body, applying antiseptic where he felt necessary. Handy, these people used the same brand he favored at home. A little eerie, too.

At last, when he couldn't find anything else to minister over, he tossed the tube of clear gel back into the bag and stepped back. "You're done."

"Are you sure?"

"Yes."

"You didn't check my armpit, there might be a—"

"Just shut up," he said over a chuckle. "You'll appreciate my thoroughness someday."

"My hair probably looks horrendous," she complained, gathering her few belongings into the bedraggled backpack.

He eyed her critically for a few seconds. The blackish mass partially dried while trapped under the towel, creating a cowlick near her forehead, and at the back, causing a large clump to stand out half an inch before flowing downward. Another clump swooped out at an awkward angle near her ear.

"Yeah," he agreed, doing a very good job of hiding

his smile. "You look pretty scary."

"Bastard," she mumbled under her breath as she stormed past him, one hand holding the bag securely over her shoulder, the other combing through her hair in a useless attempt to undo the damage.

Jenni flung aside the blanket with gusto to enter the Den of Women-less Soldiers, probably so irritated she forgot her nerves. And probably not stopping to consider the fact her damp blouse and pants clung to her in ways he normally appreciated, at home alone.

"Honey," he called as she stepped halfway through the barrier. She turned her head, and he pulled at the front of his shirt, looking at her breasts pointedly. Her head dropped to look. As her eyes registered his meaning, her face turned red and she tugged at her blouse to peel it away from her skin.

The instant the blanket fell down behind her departure, he caved in to the hollow feeling gutting him, and he bent over, grabbing his knees with his hands and breathing deeply a few times. He could handle everything they learned during the past however-many hours since this insane adventure started. His whole life finally made sense.

But this, ripping him away from Jenni, was simply cruel. He could survive. He would survive. He always did. But for the love of all things holy, he didn't want to have to do this without her. Selfishly, he wanted her intelligent, adventurous and, let's be honest, competitive spirit egging him on to climb higher, be smarter, faster, stronger.

And, on a whole different level, his need to protect her exploded into a consuming madness ever since their first jump. His entire life, he watched out for her, even when being forced to sit next to a snobby, uptight, self-righteous princess felt like the worst kind of cosmic punishment. He learned over the years to deal with it, to find balance between his life and hers. But now, since the transmorph, his very existence depended on her safety.

How could he send her away with total strangers, on an alien planet, into a world that could never understand them?

He swallowed once. Twice. Breathe. Blink. Breathe.

Standing to his full height, he continued his deep breathing exercises and grabbed the medic bag off the counter beside him to follow his wife out of the shower room. Pulling back the blanket, he froze for a second at the sight in front of him. In the few moments, he stole to compose himself, the men made their move.

Jenni sat at the table in the kitchen area like a queen surrounded by peasant lackeys attending to her every whim. One placed a glass of clear liquid on the table next to the plate of food another man set before her, while yet another supplied a fork and knife. One fiddled with an antique boom box, adjusting the station while looking at her for approval of the choice. One stood by offering to loan her some slippers for her bare feet and several others hovered, awaiting instructions.

Keeping her arms folded awkwardly over her chest, she cast her eyes up to meet him pleadingly.

"Are you cold?" Nellum asked before diving headfirst into an old army locker, and Elliott had to admit that while her crossed arms were probably to protect her modesty more than anything, goosebumps covered her flesh. "I have a sweater you can have." The young man emerged, holding up a bright blue sweater triumphantly.

"Um, thank you, but—"

"Thanks, Bellum," Elliott interrupted, crossing the room to take it from him and hold it out to Jenni through her entourage. They parted to let him through, like Moses and the Red Sea.

The soldier didn't correct the mispronunciation of his name, merely nodded.

Jenni narrowed her eyes at Elliott as though to say "play nice" and snatched the sweater from his hand and slid it over her head. The static electricity made her hair stand up, and his amusement caused his lips to twitch as he leaned in close to whisper in her ear.

"I'll get over the fact you're wearing another man's clothes. Be warm." He felt her nod against his cheek, and he quickly kissed her temple before backing away, searching for Rick to get some answers.

Chapter 9

"Give her some space," a vaguely familiar voice broke through the din of voices surrounding Jenni. "You'd think you never saw a woman before."

The hovering men disbursed, leaving Mitchell leaning a hip against the surface, arms crossed and smiling at her with amusement. "Please forgive them. This is the first time a woman has ever set foot in this sorry place. You're a bit of a novelty. Just tell them to back off if they start to get stifling."

"Thank you."

"Do you mind if I sit?" he asked, indicating the chair across from her. "I promise to behave myself."

"No, I don't mind. I didn't mind the others, either, to tell you the truth. They were only…"

"Overwhelming."

"Precisely." She laughed, and picked up the fork to dig around a plate of what looked like pot roast, mashed potatoes and carrots with brown gravy.

"Where's your key?"

"I don't know." She shrugged. "I think he's looking for Rick."

"Not very wise of him to leave you with the wolves like this."

"Are you saying I'm in danger?"

"No, not at all. But in my world, everyone is fair game for pursuit."

Distaste coiled through her stomach and her nose and mouth scrunched up in an involuntary gesture. "Elliott knows he has nothing to worry about."

Mitchell's dark eyes softened and he smiled wistfully. "Watching you two interact, it reminds me of my parents. I haven't seen anything like that in a very long time."

"Like what?"

"Tenderness."

A lump formed in her throat and she had no idea how to respond to the simple statement. Plopping a carrot piece in her mouth, she chewed slowly, enjoying the buttery flavor before swallowing.

"Your presence here means a lot to us."

"Why?" They planned to take a young woman to another realm, not start a revolution.

Mitchell opened his mouth for a second, then snapped it shut again. He pursed his lips tightly and folded his hands together on the table, twiddling his thumbs absently.

"Milliscent is a sweet kid. She deserves happiness."

"You've met her?"

"Yes. She's Rick's niece."

"But I thought…someone told Elliott the city is divided." Hope surged through her. Maybe some jerk had yanked their chain.

"It is."

Her heart dropped back into her stomach.

"But there's neutral sectors for commerce and industry where we work and play together. We just don't live there."

"Oh." She slowly ate without enjoyment. Finally,

she couldn't take it anymore, and she dropped the fork, listening to it clatter against the plate. "How did you guys get to this? This is *America* for crying out loud. Land of the free. Home of the brave."

"Do you really want a political history lesson?" he asked with a raised eyebrow.

She thought about his question for a moment and realized she didn't. So she shook her head and picked up the fork again, stirring the food.

"It didn't happen overnight," he explained, despite her answer. "Very good and valid reasons existed for the laws made in the beginning, ones not as restrictive as they are now. But special interest groups got involved, extremists in power, and after a few decades; the country was stuck in a trap the people voted for and never saw coming. And there aren't very many of us who actually want change. Most everyone is fine with the status quo."

"But not your group," she said, waving her hand in the air to take in the room at large.

"Actually, a lot of these men are very happy with the way things are. They believe the teachings of Hoam Tin Smith as far as it is convenient for their own purposes. But they are radicals because they feel if two people want to live together, they should be able to do so... somewhere else where their evil and misguided actions will not bring suffering on the righteous.

"But some of us remember when we were very little, and we didn't have to visit our mothers and sisters in a park, or a restaurant." His dark eyes lifted and his brown lips quivered slightly. He cleared his throat. "Before we had to watch our mother and father cry when they kissed each other goodbye every week." He paused, swallowing. "No one cries for want of each other anymore. No one lets themselves get too attached."

"I find that very sad."

"So do I."

They sat together in comfortable silence for a few minutes.

"What happens to people who accidentally fall in love?" she asked.

He shrugged with a smile that seemed to hold secrets. "Hopefully, they find us."

"And what can you guys do for them?"

"Offer them hope. If they give up everything, we find a way for them to be together."

Elliott slid into the seat next to Jenni, letting an arm rest on the back of her chair. She pushed the half-eaten plate of food in his direction and, despite the fact it had to be cold and rubbery by now, he dug in with enthusiasm. "I've gotten more details," he said between bites. He chewed and swallowed before continuing. "In two hours, we're taking you to meet the woman's coalition leader. You'll stay with them for two days—"

"Two days!"

"Until the next caravan leaves the city. You'll be smuggled out the women's gates, I'll go out the men's side and we'll meet up on the trail, where our guides will take us to Milliscent and the woman who will teach us how to jump out of this place."

"You're going to be late for work."

He laughed and kissed the side of her head.

"Yeah, I guess I will."

"The caravans are monitored by true believers," Mitchell told them. "I don't know if Rick told you yet or not, but that means after the two groups meet on the trail, you two cannot talk to each other until you're given the signal."

Elliott froze with the fork halfway to his mouth. "It just never ends with you people. Why can't we at least talk to each other?"

"Casual connections are acceptable and encouraged. 'It helps to reduce the backflow of hormones,'" he quoted. "But one glance at you two standing next to each other, and you will 'out' yourself as long-term lovers. It's too risky. No matter what happens, do not engage in conversation; do not go near each other. And if you can help it, don't even look at each other."

"That's ridiculous," Jenni blurted, seeing Elliott's jaw clench.

"That's realism. If you want out of here with all body parts functioning properly, you'll do what I say."

Elliott mumbled darkly under his breath as Mitchell left them alone at the table.

"Only a few more days," she told him, patting his knee. "We can do this. A week at most."

"Don't take this the wrong way, honey. But I hate your mother right about now."

He stabbed a piece of meat and shoved it in his mouth, chewing forcefully. She watched him work through his initial anger as he finished off the plate. At last, he let the utensils drop and he rested his elbows on the table, his face in the palm of his hands. Breathing deeply a few times, he rubbed his face and then turned to smile at her as though they hadn't a care in the world.

"So, Jennirva," he said with a teasing smile, barely

pulling his leg out of the way of her knuckle punch in time. "What do you want to do for the next two hours?"

"I'm sorry to interrupt." A young man who looked like he belonged in one of her math classes stood nearby, supremely uncomfortable by the expression on his face.

"Yes?" Elliott asked with good humor, causing the boy to relax slightly.

"Um, in order to get Ms. Hamilton past the gates, she's um, gonna to need to change her clothes. Not that there's anything wrong with what you're wearing, ma'am, but boys around here don't dress like that and the guards, they'll spot you real quick, for sure."

"They don't dress like this where I come from either," she informed him.

"Once we get your clothes figured out, um, Dalton's gonna need you in the other room to deal with the implant."

"The what?"

"The implant. A gender chip. Well, it's not gonna be a genuine one, of course, but we've got a fake one which'll pass the checkpoints a few times."

"This just gets better and better," she grumbled.

Elliott patted her leg. "A few more days. A week at most."

"And a few surgical procedures along the way."

"He's not going to cut into you, ma'am. For us natives, the docs insert the chip into our gums at birth. He's gonna fit you with somethin' to put in your mouth to imitate the right frequency."

"All right," Jenni said on a sigh, getting up from the table. "Let's go turn me into a boy."

****

"I'm having horrible flashbacks," Elliott said, eyeing her warily.

"It can't be that bad, can it?" she asked, trying to adjust her lips over the temporary braces holding the gender chip on her teeth. She forgot how uncomfortable all the metal could be.

He held up a large mirror, and she inspected her reflection.

Yup.

That bad.

Sighing, she shrugged. "Guess you should have kissed me goodbye before he put them on and brought back memories of junior high, huh?"

In answer, Elliott leaned forward and gently touched his lips to hers for a moment. "It's the next part which might be the deal breaker. I'm sorry, but I like you as a woman. I'm not into teenage boys."

"I need your help wrapping up."

They eyed the pile of clothing on the counter next to them. "I don't know if I can do that to you."

"Should I ask one of them for help?" she asked, nodding toward the door Dalton and the teen disappeared through.

"Don't get snotty." Snatching the long white material from the mound, he twirled a finger. "Strip."

She pulled her shirt off and held up her arms. Handing her one end of the cloth, she held it under her armpit while he wrapped her torso. "Tighter," she instructed. "It's not doing any good."

He adjusted the fabric, pulling tight, and she involuntarily gasped in pain as her breasts cinched down and her lungs constricted. Elliott's head shot up, his eyes filled with worry.

"Keep going," she ordered.

Setting his mouth in a grim line, he finished his task in silence. Jenni tried to hide her discomfort, knowing every whimper only upset him more. Finally done, he stepped back, eyeing her. "No good," he said. "Your hips are still too wide, and your waist too thin, let's try something different." He reached for the wrap to let her free and she sidestepped him.

"They've done this before, Elliott. Let's trust them, okay?"

Bending hurt so she held onto his shoulders as he helped pull down her pants and put on the new ones. Baggy jeans engulfed her, the waistband managing to sit on the widest part of her hips, cinched tightly by a black leather belt. An oversized green t-shirt hung low to the pockets, providing the optical illusion her waist actually started at her hips. A pair of sloppy high tops, skull hoodie and backward baseball cap later, she made the complete transformation. When she dropped her head and shoulders slightly, imitating the boys in her classes, Elliott's eyes widened and he backed up, hands out.

"That's creepy."

She lowered her voice a notch. "D'ya think I'll, like, you know, fool them?" She shrugged her shoulders and rested her weight on one foot, slipping her fingers into the pockets of her jeans.

Her husband shuddered, and snatched the ball cap off her head, shoving it against her stomach. "Put it back on when you're leaving. This completely freaks me out."

"So I'm selling it." Jenni snatched the hat away from him, wadding it tightly in her fist.

"Yeah, you're selling it."

"Good," she said as he tucked the now familiar small dagger behind her belt and then shoved his hands in his pockets, looking away from her.

A sharp rap on the door interrupted them and after they bid him enter, Craysock stepped through. "We've gotten word. It's time."

Elliott turned to her. "Does your mouth hurt?"

"No. They aren't real braces or anything, just slip-ons. Like fake Dracula teeth, only better."

He swooped down, drawing her roughly against his body, kissing her as though it would be his last opportunity in this lifetime. Passionately. Intimately. She felt his desperation and his love pouring into her, shoring her courage for the upcoming trials. Jenni tried desperately to do the same for him, tried to detach a piece of her own soul to implant in his so he wouldn't have to be without her. At last, he pulled away and she felt his nose caress hers, felt his forehead against hers for a moment.

"Here," he said, gently taking the hat from her fingers.

He wouldn't meet her eyes as he carefully placed the ball cap on her head backward and spent a couple of seconds meticulously tucking her hair under the cover. Finally satisfied no dark tendrils would fall out and betray her, he cupped her face in his hands for a moment. He didn't speak, but lowered a hand to pat where he knew their penny hung from the necklace. "Remember."

She swallowed. "You, too."

He nodded, frowned for a second, then took a deep breath and smiled wide. "All right, *James*. Time to go."

She narrowed her eyes, punched him on the shoulder with a fist in the most boy-like manner she could imitate, and stalked past him and Craysock who stared at them with open confusion.

The next half hour passed in a blur of activity and anxiety. Escorted out of the building by Mitchell, with Elliott following close behind, the bright sunlight nearly blinded her for a second. She didn't have time to absorb her surroundings before she found herself engulfed by a rowdy group of young teenage boys, all joking, laughing and pushing each other around, catching her in their tide as they travelled down the sidewalk in mob formation.

"Hey, new kid," a boy with blond hair and acne called out to her as he tossed a baseball in her direction. "What's your name?"

"James," she answered in a lowered voice, miraculously catching the ball and trying not to lift a victorious gaze at Elliott. She attempted to throw the ball back to the kid, but completely missed her target, sending it to a plump boy with red hair and freckles.

He caught it easily and tossed it to someone else. "I'm Bean," he said with a smile.

"That's Dupey, Snokey, Rico, Handy and Manny," the boy with the acne said, pointing to each boy as he identified them. "I'm Shark."

She snorted in her attempt to hide her laugh, and Snokey slugged her in the shoulder, laughing. "Yeah, they're dumb names, I know. But Snokey is better than Fitzgerald any day of the week. What on earth was my mother thinking?"

The other boys howled in laughter, while Jenni internally disagreed with him.

"What's up with the escort?" Handy asked, pointing over his shoulder to the two men following at a discreet distance. "You need babysitters?"

"Naw, my brother has to register me for school today, being my first day and all," she told them, remembering the cover story.

"What district did you come from? I have a brother over in Hellion," Shark said amicably, tossing her the ball again. "I'm gonna stay with him next month, if I can get my mom to agree to the transfer." He spit on the sidewalk. "She's got this thing about meeting up every Wednesday night for dinner, and if I go there it'll be too far away."

Dupey rolled his eyes. "Moms."

"I know, right? Cut the strings, woman," Manny declared.

"How'd you talk your folks into letting you transfer?" Shark asked. "Maybe I can use the same angle."

She shrugged, tossing the ball and hitting Bean in the back of the head. "Sorry," she said as the entire group started laughing. "My brother is my guardian," she explained. "He started working for Mitchell, so we moved."

"Mitchell's all right," Bean said as he rubbed the back of his head. He glanced over at Mitchell and smiled. "He helped us get our Dinga team into the league."

Dinga team? She nodded as though she understood, feeling clueless. "That's pretty cool."

"You play?"

"Single file," a voice hollered at them through a bullhorn, saving her from having to answer.

She looked around to find a tall chain link fence in front of them, with uniformed officers posted on either side of a wide gate. Men and boys of all ages stepped through a scanner one at a time, which bleeped and showed a blue light as they emerged onto a wide sidewalk on the other side. Some of the men entered busses, some walked, while others proceeded to a parking garage across the street.

Obediently, they fell into line, but as they approached the gender scanner, Mitchell leaned over and whispered something into Bean's ear. Affronted with whatever the older man told him, Bean reached over and smacked Dupey upside the back of his head. When Dupey spun around to confront the assailant, Bean pointed to Fitzgerald and before the boy could refute the accusation, he got knuckled in the arm. Shark stepped in with a "What's your problem?" and got elbowed on accident as Bean, Fitzgerald and Manny really started to get into a tiff. All seven boys now involved, Jenni stepped out of mayhem and through the scanner, holding her breath.

The guards didn't even pay attention to her exit, running over to break up the fight. Her two escorts jumped in to help, and Elliott managed to get body slammed through the scanner into the neutral zone without having a gender chip of his own and no one the wiser.

But how on earth would he get back in?

Chapter 10

Jenni looked at the woman across from her and tried not to fidget. Feeling like the fourteen-year-old boy she'd emulated for the last forty-five minutes, she gulped, and reminded herself as a mature adult, she had no reason to feel intimidated by the scowling principal. This woman wore the mantle of a stereotypical professional woman with precision and thoroughness, down to her crisp gray suit, black hair tamed into a tight bun and the half glasses perched on the end of her nose. Her dark-chocolate skin flawless of any blemishes, she seemed anywhere between thirty and fifty—one of those ageless types who never showed their years.

The door stood open to the receptionist outside the office, and all staff traffic.

"Do you have any idea what time it is?" she asked her and Elliott.

"We—" Elliott began.

"And where is your sponsor?"

"He's on his way. A delay—"

"As you know, coed schools can be much more selective of which students they accept, and being thirty minutes late to your administrative registration does not bode well with—"

"Sorry I'm late," Mitchell said as he rushed into the room breathlessly. "Had to deal with some paperwork over a fight at the border crossing."

"Shut the door," the principal instructed ominously.

The receptionist outside grimaced and looked at Jenni with compassion as she rose from her desk and closed the door between the room and the staffing area. The door barely clicked when Mitchell reached out and turned the lock while the scowl melted away from the woman's face. Ignoring Jenni and Elliott, she rushed into the soldier's arms and embraced him in a tight hug.

"Are you okay? What kind of fight?" she asked.

"I had one of the boys provide a distraction," their sponsor told her, returning the embrace, "to get the key out. Elliott, Jenni, this is Yvonne Larkin. She's my sister."

Jenni saw the family resemblance now. They both had high cheekbones, and the same eyes.

"You don't have much time," Yvonne told them as she let go of her brother and returned to the other side of the desk. "You need to change and get out of here." Pulling out a small pile of clothes from her desk, she handed them over and Jenni once again found herself in a blur of activity.

Mitchell discreetly turned his back while the principal and her husband quickly extracted her from the painful wrap. One extreme to another, she donned the push-up bra, then a form-fitting, but somehow demure, skirt and blouse and three-inch heels without comment.

"Hand me the braces," Yvonne instructed and didn't even grimace or flinch when Jenni plopped the soggy wires into her palm. After handing them to Elliot with, "You're going to need these to get back into your sector," she combed, fluffed and spritzed Jenni's hair and applied a layer of makeup with skilled precision. She stood back to inspect her work and nodded with satisfaction.

"Welcome back," Elliott said from across the room and winked at her.

"Since when do I wear three-inch heels?" she asked with a raised eyebrow. "Or this much makeup for that matter?"

"The night of senior prom. You accidentally made yourself taller than your date."

She stuck her tongue out at him, and he chuckled. "He ditched me before the end of the dance, remember? You watched me throw those heels in the garbage and your date insisted you give me a ride home."

"He didn't ditch you because you were taller than him."

"Oh really? I suppose you know the 'real' reason?" she asked making air quotes with her fingers.

"He ditched you because I calmly and rationally explained to him he would not get lucky that night, despite what he said to the entire track team."

"You are such a liar. Brad was not like that."

"Okay." Elliott quirked his mouth up with unconcern.

Darn.

"Your 'calm and rational explanation'…did it involve your fists?" she asked, suddenly suspicious. "He had a black eye on Monday."

"From the way I heard it, he ran into a door. Twice. Must have gotten very drunk."

She shook her head in disbelief. All these years together, she still managed to learn new details about their history. She opened her mouth to ask him why he chose to defend her virtue while still mad about her liberating her penny from his overly-cologned clutches not two hours previously on that long ago night, but a cough interrupted her thoughts.

Jenni looked around and realized Mitchell and Yvonne stood watching their conversation with amusement. "I could stand here and watch this all day," Yvonne told them. "Seriously, this is a lot of fun. But I have an assembly to attend in ten minutes." She held up a pair of small pearl earrings. "You need to put these on and keep them on. They have your gender chip in them."

As Jenni slid them into her ears, a sharp knock sounded on a door at the back of Yvonne's office she didn't notice before. "Come in," the principal said in her stern voice and a woman with short pink hair, tight jeans, and a baggy pink sweater burst into the room.

"Sorry, I'm late," she said breathlessly, holding the doorknob with one hand and her heaving chest with the other. "I got caught up in the—Oh hi," the woman said, interrupting herself and grabbing Jenni's hand with an energetic shake. "You must be Jenni. My name is Starflower—"

"My roommate," Yvonne said with an amused smile. "She'll keep you company during your vacation while I'm at work."

"I have a ton of things planned; you are going to have the vacation of your life. I promise you. Too bad you only have three days, but I'll get in as many of the sights as I can. By the way," she said, grabbing Jenni's arm and pulling her out the door, "do you have any allergies to kumquat?" Jenni shook her head and took a breath to answer, but Starflower didn't notice. "Oh good. It sucks highwaymen stole your luggage, but at least you didn't get kidnapped and forced into marriage to an outlander."

Starflower shuddered, obviously horrified at the awful fate. Jenni looked over her shoulder as they turned a corner and lifted a hand to wave, one last time. She thought she saw Elliott trying to hide a laugh as he waved, but the wall almost immediately blocked her view.

Hours later, Jenni kicked off her shoes and sank into Yvonne's flowered couch, closing her eyes in an attempt to ward off an impending headache. Her feet hurt. Her legs felt sore. The scratches Elliott ministered to earlier burned slightly, itching. Her arms felt like lead. But her problem lay elsewhere.

Could she handle the culture shock?

Walking down the street with Starflower, being shown the opera house, the fish market, a monument to Edison Markwell, the inventor of electricity, and a hundred other tourist sites made her head spin. So much looked almost familiar, but not quite right. And it didn't help they were technologically backward by twenty years.

Her hand moved to her side and the unyielding fabric of her skirt glided over her fingertips, reminding her she not only had no pockets, but no cell phone to sit in the non-existent pocket, and so she could not call Elliott to tell him about the old man playing Beethoven under a tree in the city park—a common reaction all day long.

She sighed deeply, irritated.

"Starflower getting on your nerves?" a voice asked, and Jenni opened her eyes to see Yvonne walking through the living room, headed for the hallway to the bedrooms.

"No, she's all right," Jenni answered with a smile. "She had an appointment. I thought I was alone, so I allowed myself to indulge in moping."

Yvonne disappeared down the hall, but her voice called back, "I can imagine. This must be really hard to be away from your key like this."

"Well, it's not like we're glued together at the hip," she said, wondering if all gates and keys were codependent or something. "It's just…" Yvonne emerged from the hallway wearing jeans, a stylish blue pullover and fuzzy yellow socks. "He's my best friend. Do you have a phone I can use? I'm afraid I'm in the habit of texting him. And we Skype a lot."

"All the phones are monitored, so using them is risky. What's texting?" Her host wiggled her eyebrows. "And what's Skype? It sounds intriguing."

"Texting is typing messages to each other on your phone instead of talking, like electronically passing notes in class. And Skype you can see each other on the screen and talk face to face."

"Oh."

Jenni laughed. "You look disappointed."

"Well," her host said on an exaggerated sigh, "that sounds incredibly convenient. But it's not nearly as fun as where my imagination could go with it." They shared a smile. "Here, I'll show you where you'll sleep and get you something more comfortable to wear. Unless you want to go fishing tonight?"

Jenni raised her eyebrows. "You guys have somewhere to go night fishing around here? Elliott would really love that, he likes all—"

Yvonne's laughter interrupted her. "No, sweetie. That's our term for going out and hooking a man for the night."

"Oh," she said, feeling the blush creep up her neck. So much for not being a prude. *Good thing Elliott isn't here, he'd laugh his head off.* "No. Thanks."

"So you really are monogamous?" Yvonne asked with wonder in her voice as she led the way down the hallway.

Jenni nodded. "Yes."

"I've heard the stories about gatekeepers and their keys." Her new roommate paused beside a door and opened it to reveal a small, homey bedroom. "It's just so foreign. Though, my parents loved each other very much."

"Mitchell told me about them."

"They were one of the last of their kind," she said wistfully, walking to the tall dresser and pulling some clothing from the drawer. She held them out to Jenni, her eyebrows drawn together.

"What's wrong?" she asked, accepting the clothing and beginning to strip.

"You can't really expect he is too, can you?"

"Who is what?"

"Your key. Monogamous."

"Elliott. Yes. I can." Jenni stepped into the sweatpants and tied the string at the waist. "And he is."

"How do you know? Honestly, how can you really be sure?" Yvonne sat on the bed and leaned back on her hands. "I'm sure he has plenty of chances to go fishing on his own, and you'd never know."

She couldn't help but smile, amused. "Because of who he is. He lives by a code," she continued, forcibly shoving the memory back to an abyss of days past. "I've known him for twenty-five years; he will never break his code."

"That's an awful lot of trust."

Jenni climbed onto the bed, tucking her feet under her legs. "Yes, it is."

"How long have you two been together?"

"More than six years. Married for most of it."

"Don't you ever get…bored?"

She considered the question for a moment. "We're both too stubborn to have enough peace to get to the point of boredom."

"I meant in the bedroom."

"Oh." She paused for a second. "Well, I haven't yet."

"He's that good, huh?" Yvonne asked, a note of longing in her voice.

She wondered how to explain it's not about the sex, but the bond? The affection? Showing him how much she loved him, how he's *everything* to her while he showed her the exact same thing in return?

She finally settled for, "Yeah, he is. And he makes great morning-after omelets, too."

Yvonne laughed. "I have to admit, seeing him watch you leave today nearly broke my heart. The look in his eyes as you walked out the door…my dad used to look at my mom like that."

"So explain it to me," Jenni asked, desperate to change the subject. "How do family ties work in a community where the men live in one sector and the women live in another?"

"It's tricky," Yvonne answered, and Jenni settled back into a socio-economical lesson.

****

Elliott lay on the couch, feet propped up on an armrest, one arm flung over his eyes, the other over his stomach, pretending to sleep and wishing he could. Insomnia plagued him ever since he let Jenni get dragged away by the typhoon named Starflower three days ago. Despite his relaxed exterior, his ears stayed alert to his surroundings, so the footsteps approaching didn't startle him. They stopped for a moment nearby, then turned and slowly started to move away.

He lifted his elbow to peek underneath and found one of the younger soldiers quietly leaving.

"Did you need something?"

The boy turned, he had to be in his late teens or barely twenty, with his mouth scrunched in a chagrin. "Sorry. Didn't mean to wake you."

"Not sleeping." Elliott moved his feet out of the way and pushed himself up into a reclined position. "Paul, right?"

The kid nodded, eyebrows raised slightly with a look of surprise. Elliott smiled to himself, wondering if any of them realized yet there were only certain names he couldn't manage to remember properly, and every single one of them hit on Jenni during her short stay in their bunk house. Yes, childish. He didn't care. Besides, most everyone either called him "Key" when addressing him or "the key" when discussing him, so they were even.

"Yes, sir."

"How old are you, Paul?" he asked out of idle curiosity, waving to the end of the couch telling the kid to sit down.

"Nineteen." The soldier carefully lowered himself

to the cushions

"You know, I'm not a whole heck of a lot older than you. 'Sir' seems a bit excessive, don't you think? My name is Elliott."

"How old are you?"

"Twenty-five."

"You seem older."

He had to laugh. "I wish my wife heard you say that, it has to be the first time in my life anyone accused me of being more mature than I should be."

The soldier fidgeted slightly. "Actually, the gatekeeper is why I'm here." Elliott sprung forward as adrenaline shot through his body, but Paul raised a hand to waylay him before he could react further. "No, no, not like that. She's fine, last I heard, and there've been no new reports since then."

"Then what is it?" Elliott asked, sitting back again and employing deep breathing exercises to dispel the fuel dump to his system.

"The caravan has been delayed. The weather is bad and the highwaymen have been very active, so the company rescheduled departure for next week."

A short and violent explicative shot from Elliot's mouth before he could stop it, and Paul grimaced.

"Sorry."

"Is it your fault?"

"No."

"Then don't apologize."

The young man nodded and continued to sit on the edge of the couch.

"Is there something else?"

"Well…um…is it all right if I ask you a few questions?" He met Elliott's gaze for a second, then looked away. Paul leaned forward in his seat, elbows resting on his knees and his fingers twisted together nervously.

"Depends." Why not? He needed a distraction.

The kid nodded and took a breath, paused, breathed out and started over. "Do you love her?"

Uh, what? Since when did men sit around discussing their feelings about women? Especially on this Godforsaken version of Earth.

"What I mean is," Paul rushed to explain, his face turning red, "Do you love her because she's your gate and you two are assigned to each other, or do you think it's possible to love her without that connection?"

Elliott paused, studying the young man in front of him for a moment, trying to figure out the real question. "We weren't assigned to each other," he said. "We picked each other, according to her dad. Before we were born."

"But still, with the link pre-ordained and sealed, you didn't really have any other choice but to follow through. Of course, your relationship is successful."

Paul sounded much older than his age. Elliott sighed.

"You guys keep trying to find a magical explanation and ending to all this. It's not like that. She and I…" he searched for the right word "…quarrel. A lot. Couldn't stand her for twelve years growing up, and she still drives me insane half the time. We didn't feel some cosmic connection, ever. We're a normal couple. Eventually, we matured enough to stop antagonizing each other, which led to a weird kind of silent truce. Then we went off to college and slowly turned into friends. Friendship grew into something more—"

"Love."

"Yes, love. I wanted to be with her, she wanted to be with me. We got married; it's as simple as that. Then the real trials started, but we work through them. That's what you do in a relationship. It's simply a matter of working through the crap to make it work."

"You make it sound so easy."

"She's the hardest thing I've dealt with my entire life."

"You make no sense. Why bother, if it's so hard?"

"Because she's worth it." Good grief. This info should have been handed out by a father. Elliott's father gave this exact same advice to him at nineteen, when he and Jenni went home during their first year of college to break the news to both sets of parents they eloped. He watched Paul nod, thoughtful instead of doubtful, and he wondered. "Is there someone in your life you want to make permanent?"

"Me? No." The young man denied it quickly, shrugging. He studied the picture of squares on the wall as he continued. "Of course not. That's wrong."

"What's her name?"

After a long pause, he said, "Alicia."

"Tell me about her."

"How did you know you were in love?" Paul asked instead. He glanced for a second at Elliott, then back to the squares.

Ah, the age-old question, handed down from generation to generation. Universal, apparently. "When she became more important than anyone and anything else in my life."

Silence stretched out as his statement sank in, but finally the young man asked, "How did you know she loved you?"

Elliott laughed. "I didn't. In fact, I don't think she did until I made my move."

"Your move?" Paul shook his head. "I can't risk that. If I out myself and she doesn't feel the same way, I could end up in serious trouble." His face changed from contemplative to curious and he turned to Elliott.

"What kind of single move makes a woman fall in love with you just like that?"

"Oh, not a single gesture, but an entire battle campaign, breaking her down. But the one move put the nail in the coffin of her resistance, and she finally broke."

Paul seemed amused. "What was it?"

"I gave her a penny." Elliott smiled, thinking back to the look on Jenni's face as he held it up to her.

"A penny for your thoughts," he said, holding it in the palm of his hand where she couldn't see.

"Inflation pal, my thoughts are worth at least a dime."

"What about this *penny?"*

He held it up and her mouth dropped open, her gaze shooting to his in shock. "You're lying, there's no way you'd ever give that up."

"I will. But if you take this, it's with a solemn oath you will tell the absolute truth about your thoughts. My penny is priceless, you know."

"You mean my *penny," she said as she always did. But her eyes softened. Her mouth widened into a slow, wobbly, small smile. She breathed in deeply, holding out a trembling hand, and he knew—he won.*

The young man raised his eyebrows in doubt, obviously unimpressed. "A penny. You're a big spender, aren't you? Seriously, what did you do?"

Elliott shrugged. "It's personal. But the point is, I figured out what meant the most to her, and I provided it at great personal sacrifice. She realized what I did, and that is what pushed her over the fence into my camp."

"Sacrifice, huh?"

"Yup."

"This whole 'permanent' thing sounds hard."

"Sometimes. Other times, it's as easy at breathing."

In his mind, Jenni sat across from him at their old table, in their old kitchen, in the broken down, crappy apartment they shared for most of their marriage. The pale light from their overhead lamp shone on her dark hair, and she looked up at him and smiled, then laughed and wiggled her eyebrows.

Damn this kid, Elliott didn't want to feel homesick for Jenni. "I'm tired; I think I'll sleep now." He slid down a little, closing his eyes, and Paul took the hint. Elliott heard him quietly leave.

He forced his mind to blackness, then slowly painted the horizon blue, adding in the green of the trees and finally the brownish yellow of the mulchy dirt beneath his feet. The weight of his favorite ax rested in his hand, and he lifted it a few times, testing the weight. The bite of morning chill flowed into his lungs as he breathed in deeply, absorbing the pine into his very essence. Then the systemic rhythm of the ax. Up, over, down, *Bam*, up, over, down, *Bam*.

He managed to chop half a cord of wood before sleep finally embraced him.

****

"Let's see what you've got," Rick said, standing

casually off to the side in the training room. He nodded to Mitchell, who stepped onto the sparring mat.

Elliott breathed in deeply, his mind focused, his body tense and ready. They bowed to each other, and circled. He vaguely noted other guardians entering the room, surrounding the mat, but he blocked them from his mind, intent on his opponent. Mitchell lunged, Elliott dodged, dropped and swept his leg out, but the other man jumped, spun and tried to counter-attack. They continued this dance for roughly two minutes before his opponent moved increasingly faster, using more elaborate moves. Elliott kept pace, watching and learning his fighting style.

Another guardian stepped onto the mat, and he allotted enough attention to track the man's movements as he glided behind the sparring pair. The new combatant silently, stealthily, moved behind him, and Elliott counted the precise moment when the enemy's hands would grab him from behind. He let himself get hit and fell to the ground in defeat.

Glancing at the leader of this group, he saw the consternation on the man's face as the other men laughed and cheered.

"Some key this guy is."

"I waited all these years for this?"

"Rick, you said keys were tougher than guardians."

"Again," Rick commanded from the side.

Elliott shook his head as he pushed himself to his feet. "Thanks, but no thanks."

"Don't get cocky," Rick said. "You just transmorphed, and you have no idea what you can do. Let me teach you."

"What about them?" he asked, nodding to the

crowd of men around them, still smiling and joking with each other. "I don't want to hurt them."

Rick raised an eyebrow. "Louie, front and center."

Elliott rolled his eyes. "I've got nothing to prove."

"No, but maybe you can teach them something."

Fine.

The blond-haired man antagonizing Jenni the first day stepped onto the mat, his smile cocky and sure of himself. He stood loose, dancing around slightly. Elliott bowed. The other man bent slightly at the waist, and then lunged. Elliott easily dodged to the side, spun while sweeping his leg to kick out Louie's. While the man stumbled, Elliott punched him in the side of the throat, using minimal force and the young man dropped to the floor. The skirmish lasted all of three seconds and Louie rolled on the mat, gasping for air while Elliott stood above him, holding out a hand offering to help him up.

The crowd of men quieted. Mitchell shook his head while Rick smirked. Scowling now, the young man jumped to his feet without assistance and took a few seconds to think about his attack before moving in. More controlled this time, Elliott parried with him for a minute. Rick made a motion with his hand, and once again, a second assailant tried to sneak onto the mat.

Elliott directed the fight to the corner he wanted, and then kicked backward, ducked, rolled and came up behind the new invader, in time for Louie to run into his new partner's fist. A few seconds later, they both lay on the mat.

"Why are you going easy on them?" Rick asked.

"I use the amount of force necessary to neutralize the situation."

"Who taught you that?"

"My dad. When sparring partners range from eight years old to thirty, all at the same time, you learn to only do what's necessary."

"Eight?" Mitchell's eyebrows shot up.

Elliott smiled. "She's a mean little sucker, let me tell you. She's harder than some of her older brothers and sisters."

"How many can you take at a time?"

"Some," he answered vaguely.

"All right, let's find out."

"Let's not."

"Elliott?" a familiar voice called from another room, and his blood turned to ice. Why did she return?

"What is going on?" he asked, but Rick only stared at him.

"Elliott?"

"Jenni," he called loudly, "I'm coming."

He started in the direction of the distant door, but one of the men stepped into his path. He tried to move around them, but they blocked him still.

"Elliott," she called, and he heard fear in her voice.

"Get out of my way," he growled.

Instead, the man reached out to grab him, but he ducked out of the way, punching him square in the chest and sending him flying several feet. More men stood in the path between him and the door, several moving toward him. Red hot anger swirled through his veins, and he glanced around the room, making sure his earlier inspection of this battlefield had been complete. Running and sliding across the slick floor, he jumped up beside a table, grabbing several weapons and while still in motion, pulled his staff out, ready for use.

Swallowing the rage, he forced himself to think, to plan, to strategize, even while they came after him. No longer caring about damaging them, every move calculated for the quickest drop, he fought his way to the door. Bone crunched beneath his staff. Blood sprayed onto his clothes. One and two at a time, they fell to the wayside until at last; he reached the door and threw it open to run out to an empty bunk room.

"Where is she?" he yelled back to Rick, who stood on the other side of the room, surveying the damage with astonished chagrin.

"She's with Yvonne," came the hoarse response over the moans. "She's fine."

With forced control, Elliott reined in the pulsating need to tear the man apart and walked through the carnage, toward their leader and his sidekick. "Prove it," he ordered, shoving the end of his staff under Rick's lightning-bolt beard.

The man's eyes darted to Mitchell, and the dark man pulled an antiquated cell phone out of his pocket and dialed a number, keeping wary eyes on Elliott. "Yeah, hi, hon. I need you to put Elliott's sister on the phone; he needs to talk to her for a minute."

He held the device out and Elliott grabbed it roughly, keeping the staff lodged against Rick's jaw.

"Hello, Elliott?" Jenni's voice carried to him over the device, and relief washed through him.

"Jenni?"

"Yeah, it's me. Are you all right?"

"Yeah, I'm fine swee—uh, yeah. I'm good. Are you all right?"

"For the most part."

"What does that mean?"

"It means I'm upset the caravan has been cancelled. And my birthday is in four days, and you're going to miss it."

"Are they treating you all right?"

"Yeah, everything is good. Nothing to worry about."

"Hey, Jenni?"

"Yes?"

"What did you want for your birthday again? I can't remember."

She paused on the line, and he knew his question surprised her. "I wanted Cricket," she said quietly.

"Oh, right. I'm going to be a little late giving that to you. I have to go now, but make sure you keep my penny safe."

"My penny," she answered back. "Always."

He hung up the phone, tossed it toward Mitchell and then reared back, landing one hard punch in Rick's left eye. The man's head snapped back and he stumbled a few feet before catching himself and recovering.

"Don't ever use my wife again," Elliott said in a low, menacing voice. He turned around to inspect the damage he inflicted.

As the anger slowly ebbed away, a new kind of pain entered his heart. He hurt people before, in minor capacities. Given a few black eyes, a couple of bruises when the occasion warranted, but never had he caused this amount of damage. The crunching of the bones echoed in his head over the moans of the men.

Elliott earned his medical license to help people, and to keep from being a monster.

Swallowing, he knelt next to the first man he came to, and inspected the injuries. "Craysock, hold still," he

137

said. "I can help you."

The young man grumbled and flinched away.

"I'm a licensed PA," he explained as he gently explored the injuries. "I prefer working ambulances, but I know what I'm doing." He glanced up at Rick for a second. "This is your fault, you know. You knew how I'd react when you brought my wife into the equation."

"You have to learn control."

"I had complete control," Elliott answered. "I calculated every single move. And I'll do it again." He raised his eyes to pierce Rick with them. "Without hesitation. Don't ever try to test me again."

Rick nodded. "This is my fault. It's been too many years since I had to deal with the pull of a key to their gate." He smiled sardonically. "My brother wouldn't have been as nice as you. These men were lucky."

"You have no idea."

To his horror, Elliott felt the energy drain from his body as though someone pulled a plug and he collapsed to the floor, immobile next to his patient. *Aw crud. Not again.*

****

Confused, Jenni hung up the phone and turned to her host with concern. "Yvonne," she asked. "Why did Elliott need confirmation I'm all right, and why did he have to verify I'm actually me?"

"What do you mean?"

"He asked me a question no one else could have guessed the answer to. Why did he do that?"

Her roommate sighed. "I have no idea, but I bet you twenty bucks Rick is behind it. He's probably messing with his mind. His training practices can be…brutal sometimes."

"He better not push him too far," Jenni observed. "He might not like how hard Elliott pushes back."

Half an hour later, when the newscast showed multiple men being carted away from a training facility in ambulances due to "a training accident," she bit down on her knuckles and tried to swallow her worry. Elliott would be heartsick over what he did, and she couldn't be there to help him.

This place so sucked.

****

A strange mixture of anger, irritation and excited anticipation swirled through Jenni. Irrational? Yes. Unfair? Absolutely. But it had been three weeks. Three. He missed her birthday for the first time since preschool, but she could forgive that. Okay, he hadn't technically missed it; he sent a present via Mitchell via Yvonne. And his letter with a new poem went a long way to smooth over the fact he couldn't be physically present to celebrate her quarter-century milestone.

The first time the company cancelled her caravan, she felt disappointed. Starflower took her out to the local creamery and bought her a Floove to make her feel better. Much to Jenni's surprise, a massive double-fudge ice cream sundae with maraschino cherries and nut shavings appeared on the counter before her. She ate every bite.

The second time they cancelled the caravan, she was frustrated. Starflower countered with a trip to an art museum for her intellectual side, and then appealed to her feminine and latent frilly side with a shopping trip to the local shoe store, in which Jenni obtained a new pair of leather knee-high, low-heeled boots. The wonderful kind, with many buckles and zippers.

The third time, mounting anger surged inside her. Starflower prudently stayed quiet and merely sat on the couch watching action movies in the dark, eating chocolate bars like they were an illegal substance and cheering on the good guys as they blew up half of Delaware to protect the world from their evil machinations. Jenni couldn't understand the plot, but it served her mood well enough.

And then finally, *finally*, The Powers That Be operating the overland troop decided weather, marauders, equipment and planetary alignment all coalesced into suitable conditions for travel.

And here she sat. Alone. Traveling in a foreign land, a foreign *planet*, on an unfamiliar train hoping against hope a sixteen-year-old girl at the end of the line would take her to her husband so they could eventually get home.

"Silver City in three minutes," the conductor declared, and she started to hyperventilate.

Closing her eyes, she pictured Elliott standing in front of her with an amused smile. "Relax, honey," he'd say as he ran his hand over her hair. "She'll be there. You won't be alone."

Jenni breathed deeply a few times and ignored the battalion of butterflies assaulting her stomach as the train slowed and then came to a stop. Time to depart.

Chapter 11

Jenni stepped down from the train onto a wooden platform reminding her of an old western movie set. A single wooden building stretched out on either side of her, painted simple white. She almost expected steam to huff out of the engine several cars ahead, but the sleek metal tube merely sat quietly, patiently waiting to move again.

Hitching one bag higher on her shoulder and grabbing the handles of the other bag tightly in her fist, she stepped closer to the building and surveyed her surroundings. Women jostled around her, intent on meeting friends and family or getting to their destinations. Business executives, touristy-looking types and a great many which looked as though they stepped out of Huckleberry Finn all co-mingled together in an eclectic mixture of humanity. She felt right at home in jeans, t-shirt and sneakers.

"Jenni? Jenni Carter?"

The name threw her momentarily; she hadn't used her maiden name in years. But she turned to find a young woman, escaped from a Japanese anime movie, looking at her expectantly. "I'm Milliscent. I'll take you to the caravan."

Relief flooded her as she took in the young woman's appearance. Her neon-green-tipped brown hair defied the laws of physics and stood out in clumps around her head about six inches in one direction, with one long purple braided rope hanging down behind her ear and over her right breast. The youth's only makeup, thick black eyeliner, spiked out on the sides creating a mask-like look. Her neon-green top stopped a couple of inches above her belly button, and her black jeans hung below it by two. Green high tops covered her feet, and colorful, woven, leather bracelets rose partway up each black-gloved arm.

Jenni instantly liked her and held a hand out to shake. "Nice to meet you, Milliscent. I've heard quite a bit about you."

The girl rolled her eyes and hefted Jenni's second bag over her shoulder. "All from Uncle Rick," she said, stretching and wiggling the fingers on her right hand a few times at her side. "I can imagine what he's said. He still thinks I'm eight years old."

She couldn't help but laugh as she followed her guide through the crowd. "Uncles can be like that. Uncle Malachi still takes us out for ice-cream cones every time we visit, and he still brags about the time I won first place in the state math competition back in seventh grade. You'd think he was *my* dad's brother instead of Elliott's."

They reached the end of the platform, the crowd thinning the farther they traveled. Stepping down, they followed a dirt path around the side of the building until they reached a busy dirt road.

"I feel like John Wayne might step out of the general store any minute now."

"He'd get shot," Milliscent warned, now casually flexing her other hand beside her hip, twisting her wrist in a circular motion. "This is a women's sector."

Jenni sighed. "Yeah."

"Do you have a thing for this John Wayne guy?"

She laughed, remembering the twinkle in her grandmother's eye, gushing like a teenager, and it took a moment before she could answer. "No," she explained, still chuckling as she followed her guide through the small town. "He's an actor from my world. A real heartthrob around my grandmother's time. Played in a lot of westerns."

"Oh."

They walked in silence for a few minutes and even though Jenni tried to soak in everything around her, shamelessly looking like a tourist, she noticed Milliscent occasionally flexed and flipped her hands.

"Is it bad?" she asked sympathetically.

"Is what bad?"

Jenni waved a hand vaguely in the general direction of the teen's arms. "This attack. Is it a bad one? I remember they really hurt sometimes. Like sticking your finger in a light socket."

"No, it's only a little tingly and numb. Like when your leg falls asleep."

"You want me to rub them for you? Elliott figured out a really good trick to help make it feel a little better."

"Elliot's your…" Her gaze darted around for a second. "You know. Key?"

"Yeah. He's my…key."

They now passed the outskirts of the town and headed to a group of wagons and horses in the distance. "You seem like a fairly smart woman," Milliscent observed.

"Thank you."

"Why on earth did you do that to yourself?"

"Do what?"

"You know, get…the 'M' word."

"Because he dared me," Jenni mumbled and then saw the look of shocked disbelief on her companion's face. "And because I'm not afraid of commitment," she clarified.

"Commitment has nothing to do with it." Her guide stopped walking, turning to her and waving her hand in the air to emphasize her point. "It's about slavery."

"What?"

"Slavery. Men have used marriage as a form of slavery for centuries, and it's only been within the last several decades women have finally been able to shake off the shackles and—"

"I'm not a slave, Milliscent."

"Yes, you are, but you're brainwashed into thinking you aren't."

Jenni's eyebrows shot up as the incredulity swarmed her. "Wow." She paused for a moment, speechless. "Just…wow." Shaking her head, she walked past the young woman and headed for their obvious destination.

Milliscent followed. "Frankly, I have no interest in going to Porthinch, or meeting Jeremy. The thought of being stuck with one man my entire life, one that thinks he owns me, makes me wanna puke."

"So don't go."

"Yeah, cause like, I really wanna die." She snorted and shook her head. "Whatever."

"Die?"

"Uncle Rick says if I don't transmorph, the attacks will get worse and worse until I eventually die of a seizure."

"Holy crap." And the council refused to let this girl meet up with her key? How on earth could they sentence a teenage girl to death simply because she'd been unfortunate enough to be born in the wrong reality?

"I know, right? So it's either stuck with a shmuck, or death."

"Must be a hard choice," Jenni observed wryly.

"Exactly."

"Well, at least your uncle told you what's going on. My parents never told me about gatekeepers, and I spent my life scared to death someone would find out about my freakish glowing problem."

"Holy crap."

"I know, right? They never told Elliott either, so neither of us knew."

"How did you keep it from him? Rick says during sex you can light up like a giant glow-stick sometimes."

"I didn't keep it from him. I'm just lucky he has a thing for freaks."

"Wow."

"Yeah. Tell me about it. He's a good guy, my Elliott. Not all men are into the whole 'slave' thing. I mean, can you picture your uncle treating anyone like that?"

Milliscent shrugged. "He can be an overprotective pig sometimes."

"Not the same thing. So where are we supposed to go?"

"This way. The Overland Caravan manager is with those women."

They approached a woman with long brown hair

and a nice smile. She wore jeans, a black t-shirt and a white cowboy hat. Busy supervising several women similarly dressed as they hitched horses to three wagons and loaded supplies, she broke away to approach Jenni with an outstretched hand.

"Hello, you must be Jenni Carter, Rick's cousin. I'm Jennifer."

"Um, yeah. Thank you for taking me on."

"No problem, I'm sorry it took so long to get going. Even now, we're chancing it, what with the highwaymen being so active and all. But I hired extra security, so we should be all right. That your gear?"

Jenni nodded and Jennifer pulled the bags from her, handing them to one of her workers. "Go find a good seat. We have the most comfortable bus this side of the Appledock border."

Milliscent laughed. "You have the only bus this side of the border."

"Then I guess it's a good thing I believe in comfort, isn't it?" She smiled at Jenni again. "Don't worry. We'll get you home to Beaver City safe and sound."

The teen grabbed her arm and led her to a massive wagon actually resembling a bus. Steps near the front for entry and exit, a center aisle between rows of padded seats. After a quick calculation of rows to seats-per-row, Jenni realized the bus accommodated twenty people for the trip. The vehicle had no roof, but dome-shaped metal braces made her think a top could easily be attached.

"So here's the thing," Milliescent whispered, pulling her down into a seat and making room for other women boarding. Her voice dropped even lower, and

Jenni had to lean in close to hear. "We're not going all the way to Beaver City. Follow my lead, and when I tell you it's time to cut and run, you follow, got it?"

Not without Elliott, she thought, but merely nodded. No use getting into an argument right now. "Does Jennifer know?" she asked.

The girl shook her head. "Say nothing to anyone."

"All right, listen up, I have some instructions," Jennifer said from the front of the vehicle, reminding Jenni of a flight stewardess. "We leave in about five minutes. In roughly thirty minutes, we will exit the protected zone. Remain calm, but keep your eyes open. My staff is highly trained and can protect you. Anyone with a black t-shirt is your friend. The other two wagons you see are the supply wagon and the portable chow hall. Tomorrow, we will meet with the male contingent of this party. Separate tents are provided for the men and the woman, and be reassured I will have patrols every night for your safety.

"Are there any questions?" She looked around expectantly, but no one said anything or raised their hand. "All right, let's get this roundup moving."

Jenni sat back in the seat and propped her feet up on the small foot rest in front of her. The wagon lurched forward, and to her amusement, the departure seemed anticlimactic like any other bus.

Now to fight boredom.

****

They loomed in the distance. One large wagon bus with ten outriders on horseback, all wearing black t-shirts and cowboy hats, surrounded the old vehicle waiting in the shade of a group of trees. Piranhas chewed at the lining in Jenni's stomach as she scanned the male crowd, searching. Hoping. The sharp teeth of the metaphorical fish gnawed harder and harder with each profile in the wagon she studied and rejected until she finally admitted the truth.

The bastard didn't show.

Swallowing a lump newly lodged in her throat, she breathed deeply a few times, blinking to keep the tears at bay. The weight sitting on her chest for the last three weeks grew heavier and she rubbed the sore spot, trying to ease some of the pain.

"There's Uncle Rick," Milliscent said happily beside her.

The young woman waved and one of the outriders returned the gesture with a wide smile. A man on a brown speckled horse next to Uncle Rick turned in his saddle and all the air in Jenni's body instantly evaporated. Elliott. They locked eyes across the distance for one short moment, three brief seconds. Long enough for him to wink and for wide, uncontrollable smiles to spread across both their faces.

Then they both looked away. Mostly.

She kept him in her peripheral vision as the wagon slowly approached their new escorts, and his gaze seemed intent on the wagon, if not directly on her. The weight on her chest disappeared, and she felt light for the first time in weeks. Bouncy, even. She hummed to herself.

"Is that him?" Milliscent asked in a low whisper. "The one beside Uncle Rick?"

"Yeah, that's him."

"Huh. For an old guy, he's pretty hot. I can see the attraction."

Jenni snorted, then laughed outright. He did look

incredibly sexy on the horse, riding it as though he'd been born on it. Summers at Uncle Malachi's ranch really paid off in this instance.

A low buzz of excited conversation in the wagon grew louder with each progressive minute and as the two groups finally merged. The outriders opened and swallowed the women into the circle of their protection, surrounding both vehicles now. Rick and Elliott guided their horses to the right side of the wagon, merely a few feet away.

"Hey punkin', I see you made it," Rick called enthusiastically.

"Yeah, so far so good. How's this trip lookin'?"

Their conversation faded out of her mind as she kept surreptitious watch on her husband from the corner of her eye and pretended to pick at her fingernails. Elliott held his reins with one hand and casually propped his other on his thigh with the pinky finger out and his pointer and thumb in the shape of an "L," never looking directly at Jenni. Her heart skipped a beat as she recognized the sign for "I love you" and she tapped her chest briefly with the same. His smile stretched as widely as hers.

"Hey, cutie-pie," a woman called from the row in front of her, waving at Elliott.

"Are you talking to me, ma'am?"

"Yes. I need to use the facilities and I'm hoping you'll help me down? I'm afraid I'll fall getting out of here."

Jenni rolled her eyes in irritation, but refrained from expressing her opinion as her husband dismounted and then let the red head in the skimpy shirt, tight pants and high heeled sandals fall all over him as she clumsily stumbled off the wagon into his arms, laughing at herself.

"I'm so sorry," she said insincerely. "I can be so clumsy sometimes. My name is Amber. What's yours, cutie?"

"Mr. Hamilton," he said as he extracted himself from her tentacle-like embrace and held her by the shoulders an arm's length away. "I believe the facilities are that way." He pointed to a couple of plastic port-a-johns located a few yards off the path.

"Thank you, Mr. Hamilton. You are a life saver." Amber batted her eyes at him a few times before heading the direction indicated.

Jenni coughed, but he ignored her. It seemed everyone used this time for a brief break and her wagon slowly emptied as women chose to disembark by the perfectly good stairs at the front of the vehicle. Jennifer handed out sandwiches from a cooler in the back of the supply wagon and as everyone ate, the two genders mingled.

"Must be a neutral zone," she mumbled under her breath.

"Actually, the whole trip is gender neutral," a man beside her answered her rhetorical observation, taking a bite of his sandwich. Dark blond hair. Blue eyes. White teeth. Nice smile. Tall. He swallowed after chewing a couple of times and continued. "I'm surprised they didn't explain it to you. The sleeping and sitting arrangements will be sectioned off, of course."

"Of course."

"Name's Trevor, good to meet you." He held his hand out.

"Jenni," she replied, putting hers in his to shake.

He lifted it to his lips and kissed her fingers, looking into her eyes intently and causing a creepy slime to ooze down her back. Pulling her hand away roughly, she wiped it on the side of her jeans before stuffing it in her pocket. Ugh. Her reaction didn't faze him; he merely smiled a little wider.

"Am I too bold in saying you have exquisite eyes?"

"Yes."

"They draw a man in."

"I'm not interested." There. She couldn't get any more brutal than that, could she?

Trevor smiled, undaunted. "Not yet." He wandered away; obviously confident in his ability to change her mind.

A shudder passed through her. Elliott laughed from a few feet away, and she glared at the ground. Glad he found this whole situation amusing. No longer hungry, she chose to wait in line at the toilet, and then escaped back to the wagon.

"Why'd you disappear?" Milliscent asked a while later, plopping next to her onto the padded bench.

"Not hungry." A sandwich fell into her lap, and she looked at the youth in confusion.

"Elliott said to tell you he asks very politely, with please and puppy-dog eyes, for you to eat, or he'll worry all day."

Jenni harrumphed, but she peeled off the wrapper and took a bite, chewing slowly.

"He comes across as a pretty decent guy."

"You mean for a slave owner."

Milliscent rolled her eyes. "You know, he told me if the puppy-dog eyes didn't work to tell you he'd, and I quote, 'go first year on you,' whatever that means."

Jenni laughed at the exact same second she tried to swallow, and her bite of sandwich lodged in her throat. It took longer than it should have to dislodge the soggy bread and tears streamed down her face before she could draw in clean air.

"He did, did he?" she finally said, chuckling.

"You tell me he's this awesome guy and how devoted he is, but out of all the messages he could send, he chooses that one instead of something like 'Tell her I miss her,' or 'Remind her I love her.' Doesn't sound besotted to me."

"He already took care of the mushy stuff himself."

"When?" the teen asked, in apparent disbelief. "You two haven't even spoken yet."

"Didn't need to."

Even though her companion stared at her expectantly, she didn't bother to elaborate. Some things were private.

"All right, what did he mean 'go first year'? Did he threaten you?"

"Yes."

Milliscent glared and tensed, appearing ready for a fight.

"He'll go on a hunger strike until I eat properly." Now her companion looked baffled, so Jenni continued.

"The first year we were married, we were dirt broke. Didn't have two nickels to rub together. We had very little money for food, so we didn't keep much in the apartment. Every single morning, Elliott woke up and made breakfast and tried to get me to eat it. And I told him he needed to eat it. We both had our reasons why the other one needed it more, and we'd fight. Every single morning. I refused to eat. He refused to eat, and we got angrier and angrier at each other over how the other person wasted precious resources."

"Sounds like a really stupid argument."

"I agree. So yeah, if I don't finish this gourmet sandwich, he's going on a hunger strike. He knows I won't let him work all day on an empty stomach."

"How did you guys finally resolve your problem?"

"We agreed to each eat half a meal and shared out of the same bowl or plate. That way, we could watch how much the other person ate to make sure they didn't skimp."

"That's disgusting."

Jenni shrugged, smiling. "That doesn't even make the list of disgusting things we've done for each other."

Milliscent shuddered. "I don't think I want to know."

"I'm not telling you anyways. Wouldn't want to ruin the surprise."

"You're doing a lousy job of convincing me marriage is the better way to go."

"I'm not trying to. I couldn't care less if you ever get married or not."

"Don't let Uncle Rick hear you say that, he'll have a coronary."

She laughed. "Just...promise yourself you'll give Jeremy a chance to be your friend."

"I have friends," the young woman mumbled. Other women began finding their seats, so Jenni lowered her voice.

"But you still feel hollow inside, right? Even when you're with a crowd of the people you like best in the world, you still feel a chunk missing somewhere in the back of your mind. A hole in your heart you've always had, and you are positive will never go away. You've accepted it's part of who you are, and you wonder if you're deficient."

Milliscent shrugged and looked away. "I don't know what you're talking about."

"It hurts not having him around, and that really ticks you off because you don't want to need some stupid boy in your life. You want to be completely independent and self-reliant."

The girl didn't respond.

"It took me a long, long time to discover opening up frees you instead of stifling you. Think about giving the kid a chance to help you. Because he needs you, too."

Milliscent snorted, and Jenni decided to drop the subject. The wagon lurched forward and the sounds of horses and creaky wagon wheels and men and women calling to each other momentarily distracted them from further conversation.

Chapter 12

No possible way this day could drag on any slower, or be any more tedious. Completely impossible. Riding in an enclosed, air-conditioned, shock-absorbed vehicle at 65 miles an hour felt monotonous on Earth, but nothing compared to the mind-numbing dullness of this trip. She could walk to Beaver City faster.

That's it. She could walk.

"Um, excuse me," Jenni stood and called to the driver, attracting the attention of all the women around her, and several of the men in the wagon in front of them.

"Yes?" the driver hollered back.

"I feel a little carsick. Is it okay if I jump out and walk for a while?"

"Yeah, you can." The bus slowed to a stop. "But stay close, and within the perimeter of the outriders."

"Thank you, I will."

"What are you doing?" Milliscent hissed beside her.

"Getting some air."

The look of incredulous disbelief on the youth's face illustrated the absurdity of her statement, but she didn't care. Not bothering with the stairs, Jenni sat on the edge of the wagon, swung her legs over the side, flipped onto her stomach and then jumped backward. The wagon being higher than she anticipated, her landing lacked somewhat in graceful dignity, but she didn't fall on her posterior, and counted it a "win" as she stumbled and caught her balance.

She stole a moment to stretch her legs, stretch her arms over her head and complete a few toe-touches before following in the wake of her bus already moving forward again. Freedom. Absurdly happy now, a warm hum of electricity flowed through her muscles as she explored the wilderness within the confines allowed.

Bright orange flowers dotted the countryside and looked so much prettier close up than from the wagon. Lizards with brown spikes on their backs scurried to the underbrush, their tongues flicking in and out. A green snake watched them suspiciously from under a clump of rocks. If Elliott stood beside her instead of riding his horse ten feet away, he'd make up a poem about the poor guy. He'd name him something, too. Bernard? Cassidy? Something easily rhyme-able. She pointed to the animal, hoping her husband caught the motion and understand.

"That's a pretty mean-looking snake," said a voice, not Elliott's. "You might want to back up a little bit." She looked up to find Trevor standing beside her, smiling. Her stomach dropped.

"Hello," she said courteously, once again resuming her journey near the wagon. Picking up a stick, she trailed it in the dirt beside her. The newcomer kept pace.

"It's a beautiful day."

"Yes, it is." She noticed several other people chose to exit the vehicles to walk, and a sigh of relief escaped her.

"This is a good idea, getting out and stretching

your legs."

"Thank you." They walked in silence for several minutes as Jenni tried unsuccessfully to come up with a way to shake him.

"So," he finally asked, "is Beaver City a layover, or do you live there?"

"Business."

He waited a moment before asking, "What kind of business?"

"What about you?" she countered. "What takes you to the city?"

"I'm on vacation." He smiled at her.

"Interesting choice."

"I like a challenge."

Oh brother.

As she rolled her eyes heavenward, a solid immovable object connected with her ankle, catching her mid-step. Her stomach flipped, the world spun, her arms flailed. The fall only lasted a few brief seconds before she slammed into the ground with full impact, knocking the breath from her lungs as though punched. Throbbing pain shot up her leg from her foot and she groaned as she rolled over, utterly humiliated. Voices shouting, she heard Jennifer yell for the medic.

"I'm fine," she gasped as loudly as possible, sitting up to prove her point while ignoring the dull throb around her ankle. "Just hurt my pride."

She tried to stand, but Trevor's hand on her shoulder shoved her back onto her butt in the dirt. "Let the medic check you out before you get up."

Rage exploded and she opened her mouth to tell him exactly what unpleasant body part she now viewed him as, and what he could go do to himself, but Elliott's amused face appeared in her line of vision, kneeling before her. "Hello, Ms. Carter. My name is Elliot Hamilton, and I'm the medic for this journey."

Oh.

"Ms. Duran, the manager of the company, asked me to examine you to make sure you're all right. It's a liability issue."

"Oh. Right. Okay."

Trevor squatted down behind her, crowding her personal space and watching the medic's every move.

"Any pain?"

"No, not really," she lied, still embarrassed and hoping to get this over with as soon as possible.

"You hit your ankle and your elbow pretty hard, mind if I take a look at those?"

Of course, he saw her fall. "Yeah, sure," she grumbled, and Elliott's lips twitched. Then he magically transformed into the epitome of "medical professional," gently and carefully inspecting each area, poking and prodding and asking her to move this way and that.

"You'll be fine in a couple of hours," he finally declared. "I don't think you even sprained it, though you'll probably have a really nice bruise."

"Thank you, can I get up now?"

"No." He scooped her into his arms bridal style and started walking toward the women's bus, not meeting her eyes. "You need to stay off it for a few hours, keep it propped up if you can."

She looked over his shoulder to see Trevor watching them with narrowed eyes, his mouth set in a grim line. "I think Trevor hates you," she whispered, barely letting her lips move.

"I'm devastated."

She smiled slightly. "You smell really good." She breathed deep, closing her eyes to savor the moment.

"I smell like horse, leather and sweat."

"Well, it's working."

"Flirt."

"Tease."

"You still have the dagger on you like I asked?"

"Tucked into my belt at my waist as promised."

"Thank you."

He ascended the steps of the wagon then, pausing at the front of the center aisle to gently let her down from his arms and help her limp to her seat. The bus mostly empty now that people chose to use the unexpected break as a rest stop, she still overplayed the ankle a tiny bit for those remaining. It didn't really hurt very much anymore, and she suspected Elliott only banished her to the wagon to keep Trevor away.

He helped her into her seat and left without looking back, pretending to ignore all the adoring stares of the women surrounding him as he weaved his way through the milling crowd. She saw his breath of relief when he remounted his horse, and Jenni laughed to herself.

"He's the strangest man I've ever met," Milliscent murmured, and Jenni laughed harder.

The next few hours dragged by. The teen gave her a book to read, which only made her sick to her stomach. The passengers all found different ways to occupy themselves. Some slept. Some listened to music on old-fashioned-looking walkmans with cassettes tapes. Some read. Jenni occupied her time by watching the woman across the aisle knit a cotton-candy pink blanket.

The traveler's hair, probably once raven black, now liberally salted with white and gray. She wore modern clothes, faded jeans and a red tank top, with a tattoo of a penguin on her right shoulder. The aura of serenity surrounding her fascinated Jenni, drawing her in by a kind of inner peace the knitter emanated as her hands flew, directing the needles to create the work of art.

"That's really cute," Jenni finally said, and the woman glanced up with a soft smile.

"Thank you. It's for my niece. She's two weeks old."

"Oh, how precious," she said wistfully, the blanket reminding her of Cricket, the baby Elliott promised her. She pictured wrapping her own chubby little girl with a pink bow on a bald head in a similar blanket and sighed.

"Do you knit?" the woman asked congenially.

"No, I never learned."

"Do you want to?"

"I never thought about it before. It looks hard." She'd never been any good at anything artistic. Her mind simply didn't function like that.

"Not if you practice at it. Here, I have a spare set of needles and some yarn. I'm Amanda, by the way," the woman introduced herself as she rummaged through a large canvas bag.

"Jenni."

Amanda explained the basics, and Jenni's heart soared to learn how much math it involved. She could do this. She spent the rest of the day's journey learning how to hold the needles and yarn correctly and making a misshapen, pathetic-looking scarf out of a bright yellow ball of shim-shim wool, whatever animal that might be. The patience of her instructor knew no bounds, giving kind and gentle tips and reminders. She didn't even laugh once with the resulting mess, instead delving out liberal praise.

"Why is it skinnier up here and wider down there? And it's all crooked in the middle," Milliscent said with the grace and tact of a teenager.

"Artistic license," Jenni proclaimed, undaunted.

Visions of matching family scarves and sweaters and cute baby booties danced through her mind, and she happily occupied herself for the rest of the day listening to the click-click of the needles and commiserating with Amanda.

To her vast astonishment, she felt keenly disappointed when the wagons slowed and circled for the evening, marking the end of the day's travel.

"Thank you very much," she said as she handed the needles and yarn across the aisle.

"Oh, no, those are yours now," her new friend insisted, waving her hand. "We can pick up where we left off tomorrow."

Jenni beamed at her and carefully packed her new treasures into the bag at her feet, wishing she could jump up and show her partially completed scarf to Elliott like a five year old declaring, "Look what I've done!"

The next several hours more than made up for the boredom of earlier. She spent the time helping erect the women's tent, assisting the dinner cook, dodging Trevor and ignoring his winks, smiles and attempts at personal conversation while doing her best to not use her hiking-booted feet to trip Amber as she followed Elliott around looking helpless and beguiling.

The bimbo took siege, cornering him at dinner, plopping down on a log right next to him and batting her eyelashes, giggling delicately. If she planned carefully, Jenni figured she could walk behind them and trip again, accidentally spilling a bowl of chili on the woman and her flowing hair. If she aimed it exactly right, she could probably get some down her ample and barely-covered cleavage as well.

Grabbing her bowl and consigning herself to a hungry evening, she started to stand only to freeze halfway up as Elliott opened his mouth and let out a massive belch which echoed through the surrounding trees while he punched a fist to his chest a couple times. Seemingly oblivious to the shocked silence of the immediate group and all eyes now staring at him, he casually placed a finger to one nostril, leaned away from Amber and blew hard and fast, sending a wad of snot to the ground beside his log with bullet-like precision. He then wiped his nose with his hand with a slight sniff, then his hand on the side of his jeans. He picked up the spoon and kept eating.

Jenni barely contained herself long enough to drop her bowl on the log beside her and run as far away as possible before dissolving into uncontrollable, gut wrenching, snort-laden laughter. Milliscent discovered her on the ground with tears streaming down her face, hiccupping and guffawing as she held her stomach, trying to ease the ache in her muscles.

"The…the look…the look on her face…" Jenni could barely talk or breathe through her giggles, and Milliscent started to laugh too, sitting beside her in the mulch. "I've never…seen anything funnier in my entire life, I swear to you."

"I think that is the loudest, wettest burp I've ever heard," the teen snickered.

"It's one of his best. He must have saved it up all afternoon."

They both burst into giggles again.

"The nose thing, that's pretty gross."

"I know, right?"

They sat there trying to stop laughing, employing deep breathing exercises in their effort. But no sooner did they start to gain control, one of them imitated Amber's expression and they both broke down again. At long last, when the sky turned pink and orange from the setting sun, they controlled themselves enough to head back to the camp.

"Here, I want to show you something," Milliscent said, leading her on a path through the forest.

"So you've been this way before?"

"Yeah, my mom used to live in Beaver City until she had to relocate last year. I went to visit her every summer."

The path opened up and Jenni found herself standing on the edge of a short cliff, boulders behind her and a beautiful lake below.

"Oh wow."

"I think this is my favorite spot in the entire world," her companion admitted.

They sat on the ground, feet dangling over the edge as they watched the last of the sun slowly descend behind the mountains in the distance.

"Can we go swimming?" Jenni asked, itching for a bath.

"If you don't mind losing a toe or two. The lake is the home of Old Sam," the teen said. "He's a creature four feet long with two inch razor sharp teeth. No one's ever been able to catch him, and you never know when he's going to strike."

"Sounds like an urban legend."

"That's what a lot of people say." Milliscent shrugged. "Kids dare each other all the time."

"You ever know anyone attacked?"

"One of Uncle Rick's men one time had a chunk of his left calf eaten. Sam's never killed anyone I know of, just takes a bite or two of expendable pieces."

Jenni shuddered.

The teen sat forward suddenly, peering into the darkening night. "Hey, is that Elliott down by the lake?"

She squinted, trying to make out the features of the silhouette. "Could be. Hard to tell from up here."

"Come on," her companion said, jumping up and pulling on Jenni's arm. "You can go see him."

"We were told not to talk at all. Mitchell said not to even look at each other," she protested as she rose to her feet and brushed off her pants.

"Mitchell can be a drama queen sometimes. Besides, no one's around to see." The youth dragged her down the path. "And I'll keep watch, so you don't have to worry about anyone seeing you."

"I don't know…"

"Do you want to talk to him or not?"

"Of course I do."

"This could be your only chance for a long time. Are you really going to pass it up because some guy in the city is paranoid?"

"Aren't they missing us back at camp?"

"We still have a little bit of time before lights out.

They know you're with me, and they know I explore. You have an alibi. It'll be all right, I swear. If anyone comes along, I'll signal."

During the entire argument, they wandered down the path, ever closer to the water. "How will you signal me?"

"I'll hoot like an owl." Milliscent demonstrated her owl impersonation.

"I don't know," Jenni repeated, still nervous. But then they broke through the trees, and she caught sight of him. He stole her breath. She didn't even register her companion slink away into the trees

The night felt silent, though crickets chirped against the backdrop of water gently lapping against the shore of the lake. The sun completely set now, moonlight shimmered on the water, creating the illusion a person could almost walk on the serene surface. Elliott stood at the edge, staring out into the depths with a peaceful smile. Jenni simply stood, watching him for a moment.

" 'I travel five hundred miles and you're still around, Dorkface. What's a girl gotta do to get some peace in her life?'" Elliott's voice floated to her, though he didn't turn his head to look at her.

She recognized her own words, the ones she said to him in lit class back on the first day of college when she slid into the empty seat beside him.

" 'Hey,' " she quoted back to him, slowly strolling closer. " 'You walked into *my* class, Short Stuff. Shouldn't you be off working formulas with your little nerd math buddies?' "

He shrugged, imitating her on that long ago day. " 'I'm here to liberate *my* penny again, you thief. Don't think you can keep it hidden behind your Frost and Shakespeare. I'm fearless.' "

Stopping beside him, close enough for their shoulders to graze, she shoved her fingers into her pockets and stared out across the water. " 'You say that now, but wait until the research paper, Darlin'. Leave now, while you still can.' "

"For half a second, I was terrified you might actually listen to me for once," Elliott admitted. He hesitated for a second, then continued. "I wasn't staring at Angeline, by the way. I watched for you through the reflection of the class window. She just happened to be in the way."

So he heard her confession back in the cabin.

She didn't answer, but turned her head to study his profile in the silvery light, letting the familiar buzz work its way through her system. His face reminded her of a beautiful sculpture, becoming more interesting and intriguing the longer you looked at it; and these foreign shadows made the familiar new again. The crescent-shaped scar at the base of his jaw from the trebuchet incident. The faint laugh lines at the edge of his eyes. The tilt of an almost imperceptible smile on his face.

"Enjoying the view?" he asked as he shifted slightly.

"You're pretty easy on the eyes."

"Oh please," he denied. "We both know you prefer blonds."

"Whatever." She bumped her shoulder against his arm and felt his answering counter-bump.

They stood in companionable silence again, watching the moonlight glimmer on the water. The never ending current of electricity flowed through

Jenni's blood, and she felt a weird sort of Zen happiness. The look on Elliott's face intrigued her, and she popped the penny from its resting place in her necklace and slipped it into his palm. He flipped the copper in his fingers a few times, smiling down at it before sliding it into the secret slot on his bracer.

"I'm thinking this place, this lake, is a metaphor of you, of what you do to me."

"What?"

"Yeah. Everything about it reminds me of you," he explained as he stared out at the water. "It's calm here. Peaceful. The water is warm, and I could float in the middle and close my eyes and listen to the crickets and just…exist."

"They tell me a flesh-eating creature lives in there and has been known to occasionally take chunks out of unwary swimmers."

His face didn't move, but his gaze darted to her for a split second and she watched his lips twitch, as though fighting a smile.

"But you already knew that." She shook her head, chuckling quietly.

"It's a good thing I'm an adrenaline junky."

"I love you too, Elliott."

They watched the moonlight dance among small ripples for a moment in silence.

"Want me to take care of Trevor for you?" he asked.

"No. Thank you."

"You sure? It's no problem."

"I'll handle him."

He sighed in frustration.

"Are you all right?"

"No. Not really," he admitted. "But I'll deal."

"You're not jealous…are you?" she asked incredulously.

"No. I'm possessive."

"Of me?" she asked in shock.

"Yes."

"Since when?"

"Since always." He snaked his arm around her waist, pulling her around to face him and tucking her in close, their bodies flush against each other, leaving her nowhere to rest her arms other than his biceps. "It's been easy to hide and keep under control." His forehead dipped down, gently touching hers. "But ever since we transmorphed, it's blown all out of proportion, and I'm having a hell of a time remaining rational."

"Huh." Warmth spread throughout her body, separate and distinctly individual from the gating power.

"Don't get mad. We both know you'll put me in check if I go too caveman. But it's driving me nuts."

"Well, if it makes you feel any better, I've become more possessive, too."

"Surely, not you."

"If you waited thirty more seconds, Amber would have taken a shower in my bowl of chili."

He snorted as he tried to hold back a laugh. "Oh dear."

"Thank you for saving me from having to do that." She moved to step away, but his arms flexed, keeping her trapped against his body. "Someone might see us." She didn't hear an owl hoot, but there's always a chance Milliscent could miss something or someone.

"We'll say we're hooking up."

"Dearest, no one in any realm would believe that with the way you're looking at me right now." Her knees felt weak and she didn't know how much longer she could hold out before throwing her arms around his neck. Or her fingers into his hair. Which would only lead to catastrophic events. Pleasurable, yes. But catastrophic nonetheless.

"See, the problem is I know it's going to hurt when you walk away."

"You are such a girl sometimes."

He pulled her tighter against him, smiling. "You are so full of it," he whispered. "Because I know if I were to dip my head like this," he brought his face closer to hers, "and touch you like this," his lips barely caressed hers, feather soft, and then didn't lift as he continued "you won't walk away from me."

"No," she breathed in his air. "No, I won't." She swallowed heavily. "But you're going to do the right thing and let me go."

"Why do that?" he asked, his voice raspy, his lips tickling hers.

"Because I could get in trouble if you don't."

Elliott's arms fell away and she stumbled slightly as he stepped backward twice, shoving his hands into his pockets and looking over her shoulder to the lake. "I'm sorry," he said with his voice raised louder than needed for the quiet night. "You're right, Ms. Carter, my actions were totally inappropriate. I will not bother you in the future."

Her heart started to crack and she felt angry he'd react so meanly, simply for reminding him of their precarious situation. But then he looked at her and winked, and her ire disappeared as a puff of smoke in a breeze.

She narrowed her eyes at him. "See that it doesn't." She couldn't help it, as she stormed past him she smacked him on the rear.

"Hey, that's sexual harassment," he protested with nearly-believable indignation.

Jenni didn't bother to answer, only smiled to herself and continued down the path in an attempt to find Milliscent. She found the young woman sitting on a boulder, staring into the air before her, face pensive and lost in thought.

"Are you all right? The transmorph acting up again?" Before the teen could reply, she pulled a gloved hand into her own and began to massage.

"He really loves you," Milliscent's ragged voice reached her.

"Yes."

"I've never seen that look on anyone's face before."

"He doesn't always look at me like that. He's particularly sentimental tonight."

"My dad loved my mom." At a loss for words, Jenni remained silent, using her thumbs to work the muscles under the gloves. "At least, that's what Uncle Rick said. Dad was his brother. Dad was a key, too."

Was a key. Past tense. A lump formed in Jenni's throat.

Milliscent shrugged. "I have a very faint memory. I hear a man's voice singing to me, like a lullaby, and I feel strong arms holding me, rocking. I think I might have been three or four, but it's all very vague." She wiped a tear from her cheek, smudging some of the dark mascara across her face. "The images don't really matter, though. I remember feeling so calm and serene. In this moment, I feel completely safe, and so completely loved. I don't need anything else in the world, I have my daddy."

Jenni climbed up next to the teen and pulled her knees in close to wrap her arms around them. "Yeah, dads are good for that. I can still close my eyes and breathe in his cologne and feel his arms wrap around me in a hug."

"Uncle Rick tries, but it's not the same."

"What happened to your father?"

"One day he disappeared. Mom, Uncle Rick, and Uncle Kevin, he's my mother's brother and a guardian too; they all insisted he wouldn't leave on his own, but found no trace of him. He went out hunting and never came back. Uncle Rick is sure a bear or the slavers got him, but Mom and Uncle Kevin think some group called the Rogues kidnapped him."

"The Rogues, what are they?"

"I don't know; they won't talk about it."

"Well, I can tell you this," Jenni said, thinking about her own dad and Elliott. "He is a key. And if he is anything at all like mine, he'd never leave of his own free will, and he will never, ever stop trying to get back to you and your mother, no matter if the slavers or the Rogue's took him."

"That's what Mom says. But what if he's dead?"

"Don't think like that. Always hold out hope."

"Hope hurts."

"The alternative is despair. That hurts worse."

The teen fell silent, and Jenni didn't know what else to say. She wrapped an arm around Milliscent's shoulders, and the two sat watching the stars. After a few moments, the young woman broke the silence.

"It's always been just me, my mom, and my two uncles. What about you? What's your family like?"

Jenni smiled. "More of a tribe actually."

Milliscent's eyebrows drew together. "What do you mean?"

"Well, I'm sixth of nine children. I've got five brothers and three sisters. But my mom is best friends with Elliott's mom and my dad is best friends and coworkers with Elliott's dad, so we spent every holiday, birthday and all kinds of vacations together. I spent two months every summer at his uncle's ranch. His family is my family, too. He's fifth of twelve children."

Milliscent gasped. Jenni couldn't help but laugh.

"Yeah. People find us intimidating. Especially when you start counting the aunts, uncles and cousins. We keep a flowchart."

"No way."

Jenni nodded. "We're up to about twenty-something nieces and nephews so far."

"Wow." The poor young woman stared in front of her with wide eyes, mouth slightly agape. "I can't even imagine."

She laughed and jumped down from their perch, pulling her young friend with her. "Come on. It's been a long day. Let's head back."

Together, they started down the trail, silence stretching between them. Apparently, she managed to shock the teen speechless—unlike her mind, now replaying memory after memory and triggering a longing in her heart for her own world. She sighed.

Surely, the worst was behind them now. Smooth sailing from here on out.

Chapter 13

Jenni stared in disbelief, mouth slightly agape, at the creature standing a few scant yards in front of the lead wagon. Reflexively, her gaze darted to Elliott for a second, but returned to the fifteen foot tall snarling *thing*, eyeing them hungrily.

Lizard? Cyclops? Big Bird?

A low stream of obscenities flowed from Milliscent's mouth beside her while Rick shouted orders. The outriders, following his command, all shifted strategically to a battle formation eluding Jenni.

"What is that?" she whispered to Milliscent, unable to look away from the creature and unconsciously pulling the knitting needles in her fingers from the yarn and holding them like daggers in her fists.

Because knitting needles could save her life, apparently. She inwardly rolled her eyes at herself, but grasped the pathetic weapons tighter, swallowing in an attempt to calm her racing heart. Low buzzing energy slithered through her veins.

"A hummingbird," Milliscent answered, grasping the seat with a death grip. "You don't have these?"

"Um…yes and no. Mostly no."

"They live in packs, so seeing this one means others are somewhere close by. You *never* see one by itself. And they are very territorial."

"Is it going to eat us?" Jenni asked, worried.

"No, they are herbivores." The gatekeeper sighed, feeling slightly better. "It'll spit us out and leave our carcasses for the vultures to clean, then use our bones to line their nests."

Aw crud.

"We're lucky though, they are normally bigger than this."

Aw crud.

The hummingbird screeched loudly, moving its one large blue eye in a scanning motion and ruffling the green feather-shaped scales on its arms.

Not fair. Mine!

Wait. What?

"Aim for the eye," Rick hollered.

It screeched again, shaking its head and stomping its brown webbed foot. *Mean. So mean. Not fair. Mine!*

"Ready. Aim—"

"No," Jenni yelled, jumping to her feet and waving her arms, accidentally hitting herself in the head with a knitting needle. "WAIT. Don't shoot."

"Hold your fire," Rick hollered while everyone turned to her in shock and confusion. Ignoring them and her new headache, she dropped the needles and raced to the front of the wagon, bounding down the stairs two at a time. Misjudging the height of the final step off the ground, she landed badly, falling ungracefully into the dirt.

Scrambling upright and disregarding the dirt and weeds now covering her body, she ran through the outriders toward the large beast.

"Someone get that lunatic."

"Lady, get back."

"She's going to get us all killed!"

"She's in my line of fire."

Jenni raced onward, only stopping a few short yards before the animal. "What…is…unfair?" she asked through heaving, panting breaths.

The beast gasped and leveled its one eye at her. *You talk,* it exclaimed in shocked disbelief.

Suddenly, Elliott appeared in front of her with mini swords in each of his hands. He stood slightly to the side, not blocking her view of the lizardbird, but ready should the animal lunge.

"Yes…" she answered through heaving breaths. She needed to exercise more. "I can… Please…don't hurt us."

It lifted its overgrown nose shaped like a beak high into the air and waved its feathered scaled wings. *Hungry. Mine. You steal.*

The tone. The timbre of the cadence. The petulance. Oh dear. It sounded very, very familiar to her.

"Where are your parents?" she asked sympathetically, her breath finally even enough to talk semi-normally. "Are you lost?"

The creature stood indignantly, puffed its chest out, stomped its feet and clucked at her.

Not lost. Big boy now. Don't need them.

"So you ran away," she said.

It shrugged. Its own version of the gesture, but still an adolescent shrug.

Don't need them.

"Yes, you do," she answered sternly. "They are your family. Families stick together."

Mean, it screeched at her, stepping forward and pushing its face closer than Elliott apparently liked, causing him to step between them. She leaned around him and shoved on his arm, punching him lightly and shooting a glare at him before turning back to the overgrown, hormonal, teenage cycloptic lizardbird.

"How are they mean?"

The animal ducked its head in close. Elliot growled in warning.

"Back off or bugger off," she hissed at her bodyguard through clenched teeth. "He's talking. Don't screw this up for us."

If she hadn't known him for twenty-five years, she wouldn't have the ability to translate the look in his eyes as his mouth pinched shut while he kept his vigilant stare forward. But she knew inside he swore proficiently and profusely, telling her he didn't care if that thing could talk or not, he'd damn well do whatever needed to keep her safe if he thought her in danger.

Fine. Time to get them both to back up.

"Sit down," she ordered in her most authoritative "high school teacher" voice and pointed at the ground. The lizardbird looked at her in shock for a second, but plunked down to the ground, its feet splayed out in front. She ignored the shocked gasps from the company of travelers behind her. She disregarded Rick's voice as he shouted instructions. "What is your name?"

****

Anger and adrenaline coursed through Elliott's veins, warring with pride and admiration at her bravery as he listened to the animal make two clicks and a caw in answer to Jenni's question of its name. Of all the stupid, foolhardy, obnoxious things she'd done in her life, racing in front of a massive reptilian bird ranked as one of the worst. And she very well may have saved several lives in outing herself as "special" to the company of people they traveled with.

He didn't give a damn if she didn't like him growling at this thing. He might not be able to talk to it like she could, but some things were universal and with his own form of communication, he let Garbonzo here know exactly what would happen if it decided to get squirrely.

She imitated the sound and continued. "How are they mean?"

She listened to each shriek, click and caw of its answer, asking questions occasionally until finally she surprised Elliott with, "At least they love you enough to pay attention." Wait. What? "It's not that they don't want you to have any fun," she argued, "but what if the branch broke?"

They dealt with a recalcitrant child? He rolled his eyes, sighing. No wonder she managed this thing so well. Still, he kept his guard high. Adolescents were notoriously unpredictable, and in this case, possibly dangerous. But he felt slightly better about the whole situation.

The animal obviously did not want to relent, and Jenni continued her argument. "Your poor mother is probably worried out of her mind. And with your grandfather sick, she already has a lot to worry about."

Lizardbird hung its head low.

She made the sound for its name, and it looked up at her. "Maybe you should go home and tell them you're sorry, and you miss them."

It made some more noise in answer.

"I promise, we're passing through. We are not

hunters." She turned to give Rick and his men pointed looks. The guardian nodded at her. "We are not looking for your family's nesting ground, and we will not trespass long. We only need safe passage. In fact, you can escort us through; just to make sure we won't poach your territory."

It spoke again and Elliott saw Jenni's gaze dart in his direction for a second, her eyes apologetic and concerned.

"Um…" she hemmed. "Yes."

"What did you agree to?" he asked through gritted teeth.

Instead of answering him, she turned to face the wagons and outriders. "He will take us through his territory, but we have to keep up. Everyone needs to hold on tight, it's going to be a fast ride. He says if you don't keep up, he'll call the family." Under her breath, she addressed him. "Hurry and mount up, or you'll be left behind."

Without further warning, she darted past Elliott and onto the bird's outstretched wing. Using it as a ladder, she settled onto the bird's back and with lightning speed, it jumped to its feet and ran.

Swearing profusely, he sheathed the machetes in the back scabbards and sprinted for his horse through the crowd now scrambling. One leap and he mounted his horse, galloping at full speed. The bird thing ran as if on fire, disappearing with his wife on its back.

If Elliott ever got hold of Jenni again, he'd strangle her.

****

Jenni held on for dear life, watching the landscape fly by in a blur, trying to remain calm. This thing ran faster than the zebra cats, and it reminded her of riding a motorcycle on the highway without a helmet, only with a higher view. Her stomach in her throat, she clutched at the scaly feathers with white knuckles, trying to breathe with only marginal success. Afraid of knocking them off balance, she didn't even turn to see if the company kept up.

At long last, the cycloptic bird slowed, then came to a stop at the edge of a ravine.

This is clear of the boundary, he declared. *Travel away and don't come back.*

"Thank you for your help," she said as she slid off his back onto shaky legs. "Remember go home and talk to your parents."

It nodded at her, then turned to watch as the wagons emerged over the horizon, headed toward them at their fastest possible speed, Elliott and Rick in the lead at full gallop, a few riders slightly behind them. Finally, she saw the look on her husband's face and cringed. Big trouble. She never saw him in this state of fury before.

When it seemed the creature felt secure the interlopers were free of its territory, it nodded at Jenni, then ran away without another word as the two men came within shouting distance.

"We're clear," she called out, hoping to waylay the inevitable.

Their horses thundered toward her, and they pulled up a short distance away, Elliott jumping off in one smooth fluid movement and walking forward with careful deliberation. "Ms. Carter," he said through teeth clenched tightly together, glaring fiercely at her, "are you injured?"

"No," she assured him. "I am fine."

"Don't you *ever* pull a stunt like that again," he growled at her, voice low. She looked worriedly to the other riders, but Rick distracted them with orders.

"I had no choice," she hissed back. "He'd have killed people, Elliott."

"You take me with you," he said gruffly. "That's the deal, Jenni. You do stupid stuff, *you take me with you*. Period. No negotiation."

"You're not the boss of me," she growled in anger.

"No, sweetheart," he answered with vehemence, "I'm the other half of 'us.' "

Without another word, without giving her a chance to reply, he turned and stormed away to the wagons finally approaching, checking amongst the other riders and passengers for any injuries resulting from their speedy exodus. He didn't even look in her direction for the rest of the evening, engrossing himself in the setup of camp.

Rick somehow convinced everyone Jenni participated in a scientific study of Hummingbirds, in which she spent a vast amount of time learning their indigenous language and habits. How he managed to get that one to fly, she never knew, but she took the win without complaint, and the witch trial died before it began.

Later in the evening, sitting near a bonfire and roasting marshmallows, Milliscent quietly parked a canvas chair next to her and plopped down. They sat together in silence for a few minutes.

"So today," the young woman finally said.

"Yup."

"Will I be able to do that?"

"I don't have the foggiest idea."

"It's pretty awesome," the teen said in obvious glowing approval.

"Thanks."

"Elliott growled at me to tell you to eat more than just marshmallows tonight." She held out a granola bar, and Jenni's lips lifted upward slightly as she pulled it from her fingers.

"I'm not hungry." Despite her lack of appetite, she ripped open the package and nibbled at the edge, knowing granola was better than puffed sugar for her knotted stomach.

"He's pretty mad right now. I don't know why he's worried about what you're eating."

Jenni looked over at the young woman staring into the fire, now rotating her own marshmallow over the flames. She shrugged before answering. "Because he loves me."

Her young friend didn't seem to know how to respond, so they lapsed into silence.

Their days became routine after "the incident." The company traveled at a sedate pace all day, stopping occasionally for pit stops, camp in the evenings and after setup and dinner, Jennifer and her employees hosted entertainment. Bonfires. Dancing. Cards. Stories. Dodging Trevor. Bed.

Jenni found it maddening not talking to Elliott to clear the air, enduring his silent treatment. But two days later, she entered the tent she shared with Milliscent to find a folded paper on her pillow along with a freshly-picked yellow wildflower. Her heart jumped into her throat. Carefully, she reached forward and lifted the parchment. Sitting on the edge of her cot, she slowly unfolded it, trying to hold back sudden and inexplicable tears.

Through her watery eyes, she read, "You are such a dorkface sometimes" and instant laugher burst from her, the tears actually escaping now.

Milliscent grabbed the note from her fingers and read it, confusion clouding her face. "Seriously? This is what he writes? And you are laughing?"

Jenni breathed a few times to regain control before answering. "Yes. It's perfect."

"If you say so," the young woman said doubtfully before dropping the note on the pillow and heading out of the tent.

Anxious to see her husband again, Jenni followed close behind. Scanning the crowd of revelers, she finally found him leaning against a tree a short distance from the crowd. He looked up and they locked gazes. His lips lifted tentatively, his eyes questioning. She smiled and nodded. He smiled and nodded in return.

Everything clicked back into place, the world righting itself once again.

****

A long slow whistle made Elliott look over his shoulder to find Paul behind him. The young man saw his questioning look. "What on earth did you write in her note?" he asked. "The smile on the gate's face could light up this entire camp."

Elliott turned back to the campers, purposely moving Jenni out of his direct vision, hoping to keep any blatant longing from his face. Not completely surprised by the youth's question; he'd asked quite a few throughout the weeks.

"I apologized for yelling and I forgave her for

182

giving me a heart attack. I asked her to be careful in the future because she's my everything and I'd be completely lost without her. I told her she is beautiful and I miss her. And I reminded her of some good times we've had."

Kind of personal. He'd never normally share that kind of information with anyone, but if Paul seriously considered trying to have an actual relationship, he needed to know a man sometimes had to bite the bullet.

Long-term girls liked mushy crap.

"You said all that in six words?" the kid said in apparent disbelief.

Elliott coughed, trying unsuccessfully not to smile. "We've developed our own shorthand over the years."

"So what did you actually say to her?"

His gaze darted to Paul for a second and then back to the partiers again. "Never you mind."

"Well, I'm not the only one who noticed her smile tonight."

Sure enough, several men vied for Jenni's attention. He watched in amusement as she entertained them all with good humor, playing with her necklace the entire time. Her gaze flicked over to his for a split second when she lifted the empty ring and playfully tapped it against her lips, causing him to chuckle. He knew those other men thought she flirted with them, when in actuality, she kissed him long distance.

"Doesn't that make you mad?"

"Not in the slightest," he said, tapping the bracer on his wrist with two fingers and smiling wider as she laughed, supposedly at something one of her admirer's said.

"You two are so weird."

Trevor sidled up next to Jenni, standing a little too close, smiling a little too wide and Elliott watched as Jenni's entire aura cringed. "That does, though."

"What's the difference?"

"She doesn't want him there. Go ask her to dance."

"But—"

"Please. Because if you don't, we might have another incident on our hands."

"You're not gonna break my legs, right?"

"I'll buy you a drink."

Paul nodded and Elliot watched as the young man wove through the small crowd until finally getting close enough to grab Jenni's hand and gently tug. He saw the kid's mouth moving, and whatever he said caused a look of relief to flood Jenni's face, and she willingly followed him to the dance floor.

Elliott leaned against the tree, rooting himself to the spot and counted to a thousand, living a horrible deja vu. Not high school anymore. Nor college. He couldn't fall back on old solutions. How many times did he bust the nose of any boy or man who made her unhappy, creeped her out or maligned her honor? He lost count long ago. Even before their truce, everyone knew treat Jenni right, or leave her alone.

Breathing deeply to calm down and shoving his hands in his pockets, he watched from his peripheral vision while she danced with Paul, then Rick. And when she excused herself to return to her tent, he mentally patted himself on the back for his restraint. Maybe he had finally gotten the hang of this adult thing.

Chapter 14

Jenni sat on the edge of the cot feeling drained of all energy. Weird, because she didn't really do anything all day. Maybe the problem developed from days on end of riding in a wagon, making her weak. She needed some exercise. Briefly, she thought of getting up and going for a stroll around the campsite, but tossed the idea away as quickly as it came. She didn't feel like dealing with Trevor hitting on her.

His vibe still creeped her out. She didn't mind talking and socializing with Eric and Matthew and Jayson and James, or any of the rest of the men. Last night, she played a game of cards with the J brothers and had a fabulous time. She roasted marshmallows next to Stephen and enjoyed a long conversation with Matthew a couple of nights ago. She even danced a couple of square dances with Paul and a few others. They were all friendly, and she enjoyed their company.

But Trevor made her skin crawl. The look in his eyes when they talked. Weeks ago, next to the lake, Elliott offered to handle the situation, but she didn't want him to bring attention to himself. Besides, as a big girl she could handle her own problems, and didn't need her husband to make everything go away.

The tent flap smacking against the canvas wall heralded Milliscent storming into their shared living quarters. If she could slam the door, Jenni had no doubt it would've cracked loudly indeed. Tears threatened under the young woman's heavy eye liner, and she blinked to keep them inside while she paced in the tent, seething.

"What happened?" Jenni asked.

"I hate him," her roommate hissed. "I absolutely hate him. I'm not going to do it. They can't make me, no matter what. I'd rather die."

"What? What is going on? Who's making you do what?"

"Uncle Rick," Milliscent spat. "I just had to sit through another stupid lecture about my stupid soul mate and my stupid mission in life."

"Oh."

"I won't do it. They can't make me get married."

"Forget the married part." Jenni stood and pulled the shaking young woman into her arms. "We talked about this, remember? No one can make you do anything you don't want to do."

The teen burst into tears, and held onto Jenni as her sobs progressively worsened. The poor girl was terrified. And Rick, of all people, should understand how his niece felt and not push so hard. When Milliscent finally calmed down enough for a nap, Jenni decided to take that stroll, hoping to clear her mind and help her figure out how to approach Rick about his problem.

Barely paying attention to where her feet led her, she wandered away from the campsite, watching the deep blue sky of the late evening fade ever so slightly. A purple bird overhead caught her eye and she watched its gymnastic show with awe. If Elliott were here, he'd write a poem about it so she could always

186

remember this moment. Maybe she should try.

The purple bird flew overhead against the blue of the sky

It dipped and flipped and...

Yup, official. Call her a lousy poet. She could, however, tell you it flew in concentric circles. But enough of that. Milliscent needed help. How to approach Rick?

"Hello, Jenni. This is a nice spot."

She looked up find herself dead-ended in a semi-circle of tall boulders, Trevor blocking her exit on the path.

"It seems pretty," she agreed as congenially as possible with alarms blaring in her mind and her heart's sudden racing. She tried to laugh, but it came out a little strangled. "Guess I'll head back now."

"Don't be shy, sugar."

"I'm not shy, Trevor. I just want to go back to the company."

He stepped closer, forcing her to back up. "You've been playing hard to get for weeks, and now you've caught me."

"I'm not interested."

He stepped closer, in her space now, and leaned in slightly. "You will be." One of his arms braced above her head on the boulder, the other trailed a finger over her cheek. "This will feel good."

"Get off me now, or you will regret it."

"No one can hear us out here, Darlin'. You picked a nice, secluded spot."

Slimy ooze crawled down her spine and she found herself momentarily frozen with fright, horror, shock and disgust. But then his hand dropped from her face, his knuckles grazing her breast, a part of her body no one other than Elliott ever touched, and rage drowned all her senses.

Her right hand slipped into her belt and pulled free the dagger Elliott insisted she carry. She shoved it into Trevor's groin area, maintaining enough control to stop when she heard the rip of the blade slicing through his pants and felt the pressure of his body against the sharp tip.

He felt it, too. His eyes bulged in shock and all color drained from his face.

She spoke each word carefully, distinctly, enunciating to erase all doubt. "Get. Your. Nasty. Hand. Off. Me." The offending appendage fell away. "Now hear me clearly, you chunk of horse crap, No means no.' 'I'm not interested' means don't talk to me, don't look at me, and don't breathe in my direction. Ever. Under any circumstances. Now I am going to walk away and you will leave me alone for the rest of this godforsaken trip and if I so much as see you smile at any woman in this company, I will report you to Jennifer."

Which meant castration. These people didn't play around. And he knew it.

His mouth opened and closed a few times, a small strangling noise escaping when she twisted the knife slightly, and she took that as acknowledgement of the conditions of his release.

Sliding between the rocks and his body, she held the dagger out in front of her as she backed toward the exit. When she passed the boulders, she turned and ran.

Elliott. I need Elliott. She didn't care about rules or if they were caught or consequences, she needed her rock, her best friend. She needed him to wrap his arms around her and calm her nerves as only he could. Tears streamed down her cheeks as she ran, and with the waning light, she didn't see an outcropping of weeds in the path until she tripped over them, stumbling to her knees. The forgotten knife dropped from her fingers, skittering in the dirt.

The jolt brought her back to reality, and the truth of her situation rolled over her in waves. She left camp, alone, left Elliott behind. Again. She dodged Trevor for weeks instead of simply handling the situation in the first place like she swore to her husband. This whole thing could have been avoided. Shame poured over her.

She pictured Elliott's face, how he'd react as she told him. His concern. His disappointment. His anger at her for being so foolish. His fury at Trevor.

Oh no, Elliott was going to kill him.

She couldn't tell him. She had to keep it a secret. Jenni pushed herself up, choking on a sob as she snatched the dagger out of the dirt and pushed it back into its sheath and ran again. She couldn't tell her husband what happened, he'd commit murder, and she couldn't let him do that to himself. Running as hard as possible and avoiding the neutral areas, she headed straight for the women's section, grateful for the first time for its sanctuary. With tears still streaming down her face, she went straight to the bathing tent.

Maybe, if she scrubbed hard enough, she could wash off the feeling of Trevor's hand on her.

****

Elliott leaned closer to get a better look at the foot on the log in front of him, trying his best to act professional and not let disgust show on his face. "Yup.

189

That's infected." Greenish gook slowly oozed from a break in the skin. "You should have come to me earlier," he said, pulling a bar of anti-bacterial soap, a tube of anti-bacterial ointment and a packet of pills from his medic box.

The woman shrugged, looking away. "Didn't think it would get this bad. I've been washing it every morning. Am I gonna be all right?"

"Yes, you'll be fine," he assured her, grateful when he saw the fear in her eyes ebbing away. "I'll show you how to take care of this, and you'll need to take these pills every day for two weeks. When we get to the next township, you need to follow up with a doctor."

He finished showing his patient how to care for her injury and escorted her to the door. As he held the flap open, he saw Jenni run through the encampment and dash into the women's bathing tent. Unable to see the look on her face, an uneasy vibe crawled into his midsection. He couldn't do anything about it now, but Milliscent could provide him with answers at dinner.

Barely sitting back down in his medic tent, Rick stormed in, flopping onto a chair across the folding table Elliot used for his equipment. With a grunt, the guardian pulled out a long, thin cheroot and lit it before sitting back and taking a long puff.

Elliott choked and waved his hand in the air. "Dude, you're gonna kill me."

"Don't you have any vices?" Rick asked in irritation, stubbing it out and rubbing a hand over his lightning bolt beard.

"You're not here to talk about my bad habits. What pissed in your oatmeal?"

"That girl is going to be the death of me."

"Jennifer tell you to kick rocks again?" he asked with a smile.

"Not her, you idiot. Milliscent. She just doesn't get it. How many times have you treated her these last couple weeks for her…you know," he said vaguely, waving his arm in the air to encompass everything. "I didn't even know you could lessen the symptoms like that—"

"It used to help Je—my gate on the rough days."

"Yeah, well, I simply mentioned when she got to where she's going and mar…made things official, things will be fixed permanently. You'd think I told her to take a swan dive into a vat of acid, with her reaction."

"Well, maybe if you—"

Loud scuffling preceded the tent flap slamming open and Trevor stormed in with a red face, chest heaving, and the crotch of his pants sliced open. "Rick, that bitch assaulted me."

Red hot anger and adrenaline spiked through every millimeter of Elliot as he jumped up, muscles poised to complete one task, but Rick appeared in front of him, arms out. Loud roaring in his ears drowned out the man's fuzzy voice calling to him. He paused, breathing deeply, trying to gain some small amount of control. He heard the bastard's voice, but he focused on Rick, trying desperately to bring his mind back to human levels of thinking.

Mumble, mumble, mumble "… Jenni, she needs you…" mumble, mumble, mumble.

The one thing in the universe that could have pulled him back from the brink of killing Trevor right now. Grabbing his medic bag, Elliott ran from the tent.

He ignored the protests of the sentries at the dividing line between the neutral zone and the women's section, merely holding up his bag to show his free ticket to no-man's-land.

With single purpose of mind, he headed straight for the bathing tent. Sheila, a female soldier, stepped in front of the entrance as he approached. "Woah there, Doc, where do you think you are going?"

"Ms. Carter sent for me."

Sheila's face clouded, suddenly suspicious. "She came in here crying, and she's been in there for a long time. Did someone—?"

"I don't know, but I need to…" He anxiously waved his hand in the direction of the door.

"Yeah," she answered darkly, stepping aside. "Go in."

Elliott stepped through the door, closely followed by the sentry. He saw Jenni's head at the end of a large metal tub, fluffy white bubbles covering the water and hiding her entire body. A few wisps clung to her wet hair.

"Jenni, honey," Sheila spoke, "Doc says you sent for him, is that true?"

His heart nearly broke when Jenni wrapped her arms around her already concealed breasts and turned her face to them, revealing red and puffy eyes. She wouldn't look at him. "He can come in," she answered, not confirming his lie, but not sending him away, either.

"Do you want me to stay with you?" the woman asked gently.

Jenni shook her head and gulped in a deep breath of air. "No. Thank you though. I'd rather…" Her voice trailed off.

"All right, but if you need me all you have to do is call out. I'm right there at the door."

"Thank you."

Elliott carefully approached the tub, inwardly calling out for her to look up at him. She didn't. Slowly, he knelt beside her. Reaching up, with the greatest of care, he placed his thumb and forefinger on her chin, pulling her face toward his. Her gaze rested on his chin, his nose, his ear, until finally, finally her red eyes met his.

"I love you," he whispered.

She launched herself sideways at him with an agonizing cry and, unprepared for the assault, he nearly fell over. Water splashed over him as her arms locked around his neck and she buried her face in his neck.

Sheila ran into the room, only to freeze at the sight of Jenni holding the camp medic in a death-grip hug while completely naked. He held up a hand and sent the soldier an imploring look as he rubbed Jenni's back with his other hand. Pinching her lips, she backed out of the room once again.

"I'm such a big baby." His wife sobbed against his neck.

"No, sweetheart, you are not a baby. You are the bravest person I know."

Jenni choked and gasped for second. "I am too a big baby," she refuted. "He didn't even…" Her voice trailed off.

Sharp, instant, relief flooded through Elliott's system until he felt like he might collapse. "He didn't touch you?" he asked with fervent hope.

"He didn't rape me," she said, and he caught the clarification with a mixture of sadness, anger and relief.

"He barely touched me before I pulled your knife on him."

The sight of Trevor's cut pants filled Elliott's mind, and he didn't even try to stop the smile from covering his face. "I saw the damage you did," he said with pride. "That was pretty badass."

He heard her broken giggle as he stood with her still wrapped around him. He only lifted them high enough for her to pull her legs out of the metal tub, then settled her on his lap.

"Do you want to tell me what happened?" he whispered.

Worried she might be cold, he reached over for a large towel on a table nearby and wrapped it around her like a blanket. She took several long, calming breaths and snuggled closer to his body.

"I went for a walk to clear my head," she started. "So wrapped up in my thoughts, I didn't pay attention to the path. Trevor followed me and trapped me in some boulders. He wouldn't let me go, and I just stood there like an idiot—"

Elliott hissed through his teeth. "You're not an idiot, you were scared. You haven't been trained like the rest of us."

Why didn't she join in the sparring sessions all those years? Okay, so she's not as physically coordinated as everyone else in the families, but they couldn't teach her *anything*? Did they really think he'd be there every second of every day?

He failed her. He had one job in this universe. Born with one function in life, to take care of her, he failed.

"You saved me, you know," she interrupted his self-flagellation. His arms wrapped tighter around her, but he couldn't find words. "I stood there frozen in shock but then he…" She gulped again, took a deep breath and continued, "He put his hand on my breast and it grossed me out and made me angry. So I pulled out the knife you gave me and shoved it in the place I knew he cared most about." She giggled on a hiccup and the sound made Elliot smile, despite the feeling of failure still coursing through him. "And *I* scared *him*."

"You absolutely terrified him."

"Even though you weren't there, Elliott, your knife saved me, the one you gave me. Your belief that I'm strong enough to use it gave me the strength I needed. You always take care of me."

He kissed her hair with reverence. Barely escaping a rape attempt and she comforted him. "You are the most incredible person ever."

"I still feel his hands on me," she said with disgust. "No matter how hard I scrub, I can't get the feel of him off me."

"How can I help you, sweetheart?"

"Touch me. Please."

A lump formed in his chest. "Are you sure?"

Jenni nodded and looked up into his eyes. "I need you to replace him. You're the only one I've ever wanted to touch me. Please, take him away."

He started with her face. Her beautiful face. His fingertips trace her eyes, her nose, her lips, her jaw, her ear. Gently pulling the towel aside, he slowly trailed his fingers over her neck and shoulder, feeling her collarbone before caressing the swell of her breast. She gasped and his eyes darted to hers with fear. But the love shining through her reassured him and he continued his ministrations. He didn't try to arouse her, wanting only to give comfort, another memory to hold on to.

She leaned into his hand, and he cupped her fully, running a thumb over her sensitive spot and feeling satisfaction over the happy relief in her eyes. Unable to stop himself, he leaned over and placed one kiss next to his favorite freckle before slowly pulling the towel back up over her shoulder.

"I love you, Elliott. Thank you."

"You're welcome." He considered the limits of their time—Sheila might walk through the door at any moment.

"Please don't kill Trevor if you haven't yet."

"Tell me why I shouldn't."

"Because you'd hate yourself, and I don't want you to live with the guilt."

She had no idea he wouldn't feel guilty killing Trevor at all, but Jenni deserved a husband better than that.

"Rick will handle any punishments," he promised, though the thought galled him.

"How did you find out?"

Climbing out of his lap, she dried the last of the water on her body. Elliott stood and stretched his legs in an attempt to get blood flowing into them once again, ignoring the chill of his soggy clothes.

"The dumbass came into the medic tent looking for Rick to blame you."

Jenni froze, towel against her head.

"Don't worry," he assured. "No one's gonna believe him."

"But it's only my word against his," she said in a slightly panicky voice. "And he's the one with the cut crotch."

Elliot snickered, trying to muffle it when her expression changed to outrage. "It's not funny."

"What he did isn't, no, but that crotch thing, yes it is. Trust me, Jenni. You will not be blamed."

She hurriedly threw on her clothes, and he waited until she finished before standing in front of her, holding onto her upper arms and looking into her eyes, searching.

"Are you all right?"

She opened her mouth, then closed it. Paused a second and said, "I'm better. I still feel a little shaky, but I think I'll recover after a while."

He nodded, swallowing a fresh wave of rage and fervently wishing he hadn't promised to let Rick handle the situation. "Come on, then," he said, heading for the door.

"Elliott?" she called and he turned to face her. "I'm sorry I left you behind again."

"No, Jenni," he assured her fervently. "Going for a walk is worlds away different than jumping on the back of a massive cycloptic lizard. You are not at fault, honey. In any way, shape or form. I don't expect us to be joined at the hip. We'd kill each other."

She smiled and chuckled ruefully, some of the darkness in her eyes lightening. "Isn't that the truth."

As she passed him, she tiptoed and kissed his jaw before walking away, and he knew then she'd be all right. Eventually.

Chapter 15

To Jenni's surprise, she never saw Trevor again. She expected some sort of trial where they presented their own version of events, and he'd hurl insults at her and accuse her of trying to seduce him. But it never happened. Escorted to the administrator's tent, she relayed to Jennifer everything she remembered about the events as they transpired. When the company owner wanted exact details, she even demonstrated where and how his hand touched her.

As simple as that.

Jennifer nodded, her mouth set in a concerned line. "I'm sorry this happened to you, Ms. Carter. The company strives to screen all individuals, and our patrons' safety is our utmost concern."

"It's nobody's fault, I shouldn't have wandered so far from the camp."

"No," the woman corrected. "Don't go there. You are allowed to explore, it's the whole purpose of traveling this way. To meet people, to make friends and to experience the world we are always blocked away from. We travel this way to stretch out of the confines of the city. Unfortunately, it's the Trevors of the world which made the division necessary and the safe havens for women so crucial."

"Not all men are like him."

"No, honey, they aren't. I've been told you seemed

to trust the medic fairly easily." Jennifer eyed her shrewdly, one side of her mouth tilted upwards.

Ouch.

"Poor guy. I broke down crying, and he probably didn't know what else to do. I wonder if he has to double as a shrink a lot. It's hard not to trust doctors, you know?" *Will that deflect any suspicions?*

"It helps he's pretty easy on the eyes, too." Jennifer smiled kindly at her. "If you need to hook him for the night to get your head back on straight and help you get over this incident, I'll look the other way this once about employees fraternizing with customers. Only if he wants to, you know, I won't obligate him."

Jenni choked slightly, wishing she could see the look on Elliott's face when he heard. "Um, thank you," she finally said, blushing slightly to her mortification. "I'm not sure if I feel particularly amorous though."

"Entirely understandable. But don't take the option off the table completely; a good shag really helps to clear the mind sometimes."

She couldn't really refute that, so simply nodded.

"Trevor will be dealt with," Jennifer told her. "You will never have to see him again."

"What's going to happen to him?"

"Well, he won't be castrated since you stopped him in time, but one of my outriders is escorting him directly to the city and warning the local lawman. He'll be banned from any neutral sections for several years, in any city. He won't be allowed to travel by caravan ever again, so he's stuck with the light rails."

"Can I ask…" Jenni trailed off, wondering if she should continue or if she'd shoot herself in the foot.

"What is it?"

"Why are you taking my word for everything that happened?"

"Several witnesses came forward about how he's been harassing you. How you've told him multiple times you weren't interested, and he still pursued you." She paused for a second, pursing her lips tightly. "I'm sorry you felt as though you couldn't report him to us."

"At the time, I thought I overreacted to everything. And I thought him simply annoying and I could handle it."

"We're here for your safety, Jenni. If you have any further issues, please, tell one of my workers or me. We're here for you."

"Yes, ma'am."

"And remember, if you need Mr. Hamilton's assistance for a while…" She paused for a split second and a smile grew on her lips. "Well, let's just say I'm pretty sure he'll be interested." At Jenni's questioning gaze, she explained. "I'm observant. He's into you. But he's too much of a professional to cross that line without my okay. I'll let him know if you approach him, he has a green light."

"Yes, ma'am." Jenni swallowed. *Oh boy*.

So glad she'd miss *that* conversation.

****

"Excuse me?" Elliott asked in shock, his eyes blinking rapidly a few times as he tried to control his reaction. Heat crawled up his neck. "Did you order me to have sex with Ms. Carter?"

If he heard correctly, his boss just pimped him out to a client. Granted, his wife, but this lady didn't know about their matrimonial status. It was the principle of the matter.

"No," Jennifer said hurriedly, cringing. "Not in the slightest. You don't have to do anything you don't want to do. I merely mean your employment will not be negatively impacted if you do choose to enter into a liaison with Ms. Carter."

"And you say this at the same time you make the observation Ms. Carter seems to really trust me and this company needs to do everything in its power to help her through this crisis."

"Okay, so it all came out wrong," his employer huffed, shoulders sagging slightly. "That's not what I meant at all. I merely meant she seems to like you, since you helped her yesterday. You are totally into her." He scoffed in disagreement, but she shot him a look that said she recognized his bluff. "If Ms. Carter approaches you and you want to hook up for a time, you won't lose your job. That's all I meant. But it probably won't be an issue anyway, but I wanted to cover all the bases in case she changed her mind."

"What do you mean?"

"She said she didn't feel very amorous right now, so you probably won't get your shot. But like I said, in case she changes her mind, I thought I'd let you know I told her she could approach you if she wished. I told her you had to be completely on board. You won't lose your job if you turn her down. Just…do it nicely."

Wow. What if it had been one of the other women?

"Thank you for the green light."

Nothing like getting permission from your boss to have sex with your wife. This had to count as the most awkward conversation ever.

Apparently, Jennifer felt as uncomfortable as he, because she escaped as quickly as possible. Coward.

He followed her retreat through the crowd of passengers until Milliscent caught his eye, leaning against the women's bus with a frown on her face and an idea formed in his mind. He put fingers to lips and gave off a short, sharp whistle. The young woman's gaze darted to him with an eyebrow raised and he motioned for her to come over, then put his hands in a praying position to silently say "please." She smirked and sauntered over to him.

"Hey," he said in greeting, smiling sheepishly as she came within voice range. "Sorry, I didn't know how else to get your attention."

"What's up?"

"I need your help."

She quirked an eyebrow so high it disappeared under her green-tipped bangs, put a hand on her hip and blew a bubble out of a piece of gum he didn't realize she'd been chewing. "Seriously?"

"I need you get Jenni to a campsite tonight, and I need you to keep watch." She already did it once for them, forever ago it seemed now, surely she won't mind.

Her face, however, screwed up in disgust. "What, you a perv?"

"No," he denied with forced patience. "I'm not a perv. I need to make sure no one stumbles on us out there."

"From I've been told, you've been given permission to get your freak on so even if anyone did stumble on you—"

"Jenni doesn't need a lover right now," he said through a clenched jaw, hanging on to his patience with white knuckles. "She needs her best friend. And if anyone stumbles on us out there to find us *not* in a compromising position, we're in trouble."

The teenager stared at him for a moment, her face a mask of confusion. "So what are you going to do out there?"

"Can I borrow a deck of cards?"

Milliscent's jaw dropped open. "You're kidding me."

"No. I'm not."

She shook her head. "Yeah. I have cards you can borrow. But I can't believe you two won't get…you know." She waved her hand in the air vaguely.

"If it happens, I promise you I'll take it into the privacy tent the company provides for these interludes, okay? And then you won't need to keep watch because we'll be doing what everyone expects anyway."

"This is so weird."

"So can you get her there around dusk?"

"Yeah, no problem."

He pulled her into a quick, grateful hug. "Thank you." He threw one last smile in her direction to show his appreciation, and then let his mind start working on the details of tonight as he wandered away to execute his plans. Everything had to be perfect.

****

Elliott paced anxiously in the small clearing he prepared. Everything sat ready for their night together. Frankly, he had fun setting the scene, the process reminded him of his old scout days… ignoring the girl factor. Short table lashed together with two-by-fours—check. Cushions to sit on—check. Lantern for after sunset—check. Picnic basket filled with food chosen specifically to bring back fond memories—check.

Privacy tent, as promised to Milliscent—check. Teenage lookout sitting high in the branches of tree far enough away for semi privacy—check.

Their young friend didn't have a terribly tough job ahead of her; he chose this particular spot for its strategic qualities. Nestled against a cliff face and surrounded by thick forest and undergrowth, no one could sneak up on them—intruders had to approach from a single trail. The one remaining woefully empty.

Where the hell was she?

He circled the clearing again. Maybe he should go find her. Maybe…

Slow footsteps on gravel interrupted his thoughts, and Jenni approached on the path. The tension in his muscles disappeared, his entire body relaxing, and he pulled in a long breath of air, releasing it slowly. Sadness swirled through him as he saw his wife held her knife out in front of her, grasped tightly in her fist. Her wide eyes darted amongst the trees, and it looked like she wanted to see everything at one time. His confident, brash, energetic wife was scared out of her mind.

That bastard took away her sense of security, and Elliott wished again he hadn't promised to stay out of any punishment. Swallowing to keep the fury from his voice, he took another breath. He could do this. Keep it light. Help Jenni forget.

"It's about damned time," he called across the distance and watched her eyes search, then find him. "What have you been doing, watching the daisies grow?"

The shock on Jenni's face made him smile and Milliscent giggled high in the tree, but he ignored the teen. Their young observer, with binoculars in hand, would witness a lot of things tonight he and Jenni never shared with anyone. He sighed to himself and mentally shrugged.

"What are you doing?" Jenni asked in disbelief as she dropped her arms to her sides and abandoned her watchful, fearful approach, striding confidently closer.

He gestured to the table. "You owe me a rematch, sweetcakes. It's time to pay the piper."

"Rummy." She stopped where the trail met their campsite, eyeing him with amusement.

"Yes."

"Dearest love, you know we can't."

"Oh, no dearest love, yes we can. And it's time you realized I took it easy on you last time." He folded his arms across his chest to ramp up the challenge. While committing ego suicide, one must do the job thoroughly.

"You can't win a game of rummy against me and you know it." Yes, he did. "So unless you brought Scrabble with you, this will only end in your defeat and yet another embarrassment." For half a second, his heart longed for his ivory tiles and spinning board. "But that's beside the point." She sheathed her weapon and put her hands on her hips, walking closer and stopping a few feet in front of him. *Atta girl, there's the old fighting spirit.* "What if someone comes by?"

"We've been given permission," he informed her, winking for effect.

"To, and I quote, 'shag,' " Jenni clarified. "Not to play cards and—did you bring dinner?" Her eyes, suddenly wide, darted to the basket. He just won.

Laughing, feeling carefree for the first time in

forever, Elliott pulled Jenni close, his left hand holding her right hand, his other arm snaking around her back, and began dancing. Jenni fell into perfect step, and he sighed in contentment.

"If someone comes by," *step, step, twirl,* "we'll start making out." *Step, step, shimmy step.* "I have a lookout posted." He wiggled his eyebrows at her and she giggled as he spun them once and continued in his random pattern.

"How much time do we have?" Jenni asked, looking increasingly happy about the turn of events.

"Well," Elliott spun them again, "you know what a stud I can be. I think I can keep you busy for the rest of the night. What do you think?"

"I think you, sir, must be a stallion."

"Yes, ma'am." He pulled her even closer, their bodies flush, faces mere inches apart as he continued to guide them in the music-less dance. He stared into his wife's eyes, letting her see his hunger and desire. "I can play rummy *all night long.*"

Jenni's eyes half closed, as though in ecstasy, throwing her head back without breaking their step. "Ooooo," she sighed in mock breathlessness, sending his blood to places it didn't need to travel tonight. This platonic night. "Promises, promises," she said in a low, sultry voice. Elliott, for all his bravado, could barely breathe. "But you'll be crying by sunrise, when I kick your butt."

"Lucky game." His voice cracked, but oh well.

Step, step, shimmy step.

"For six years?"

"Yes."

She laughed, he laughed, and he lifted her right

hand in the air above their heads, spinning her before landing her at the table.

"Time to eat." Time to lighten the mood. He desperately needed the sexual tension to diminish a notch.

He sat cross-legged on the other side of the table and picked up the borrowed deck of cards, shuffling while Jenni dug into the basket. Watching her from the corner of his eye, pleasure filled him when her head shot up for a second, jaw dropped slightly and her eyes softened. Pulling out a metal canteen of water and two peanut butter and jelly sandwiches, she placed them on their table, one in front of each of them, eyeing him with a wide smile.

She picked up hers and took a large bite. "You are such a romantic," she said around her food.

Elliott blushed slightly as he began dealing the cards, and he hoped Milliscent was looking elsewhere right then. "I don't know what you're talking about. Don't go spreading rumors about me."

"Uh-huh."

"They only had crunchy, so it's not exactly the same."

"Close enough."

Elliott lifted an eyebrow in her direction while he continued to deal cards between them. Time to change the subject. The last thing he needed was some sixteen-year-old girl to know what a sap he was, and why peanut butter meant something. Besides, he and Jenni hadn't simply talked since they arrived to this stinkin' reality, and he wanted to hear every adventure he missed.

"So tell me all about Starflower. Did she keep you

busy? Show you all the sights? Did she take you to see the Sheekespire festival? I mean, how weird is that?" He still couldn't reconcile the famous playwright as a woman. "I thought her version of *Romeo and Juliet* rather well done."

"You know I can't stand Shakespeare's version, why would I go see it in another universe?" Jenni picked up her cards and sorted them. "You're just trying to distract me."

He studied his cards, moving them here and there. "It's going to work, too." He shot a cocky smile, the one that annoyed her, in her direction, pointing to the draw pile indicating she needed to start the game. "But you totally missed out; you would have liked this one."

She harrumphed. "Starflower took me shopping a lot. Bought these boots." Jenni stuck her legs out to the side and wiggled her feet, a goofy smile on her face.

Elliott obligingly leaned over to the side of the table to investigate the boots fully. "Niiiice," he said, drawing out the vowel for punctuation. "Lots of buckles and straps. Isn't that heel higher than you usually like?"

"A little bit, but it's wider around the base, so I can keep my balance better. They'll go really great with my skinny jeans."

He made a sound of appreciation. "Yeah, they will. They'll also look really hot with your red dress." The visual jumped into his head and he allowed half his mind to enjoy the view while leaving the other half to their conversation.

"You think so?"

"Oh yeah."

"I don't even know where that is anymore."

Oops. The picture popped out of existence like a

burst balloon. "It's hanging up in the closet of our bedroom at home." Twilight cast shadows over his cards, so he lit the lantern and retrieved his cards again.

"It's been with you the whole time?" Jenni asked, laughing. "I thought maybe Ilsy stole it when she came to visit." Yeah, a renown clothes thief amongst the women of the families, he could see why she'd blame his sister. "Turns out you're the guilty party. Is there something we need to discuss? Cause I found my bra hanging on the bathroom mirror, too."

He shrugged. "Are we going to play tonight, or not?"

Jenni picked up a card, shuffled it among the cards in her hand and discarded, then stared at him. He knew she wanted an answer to the dress thing, but he was too busy trying to make a decent play with the crap cards in his hand. Maybe if he picked up that five…grumbling to himself, he picked up from the draw pile and cringed at the queen. Totally useless.

His wife still stared at him expectantly. "Okay," he finally answered her unspoken question, still irritated over the state of his hand. And then he sheepishly remembered the answer he needed to provide. "So I didn't want you wearing that dress anywhere without me around. Get mad. You look totally hot in it, and—"

Jenni laughed so hard Elliott gave up and let his explanation peter out with a shrug.

"I meant the bra, Mister," she lowered her voice in a mock imitation of his tone, "our Bathroom Isn't a Damn Laundry Room!"

"Oh shut up." It would have sounded better if he wasn't laughing. "You hang a bra in our bathroom, it's homeless laundry. I hang my wife's bra on a mirror in my bachelor pad, and it's a legitimate interior design choice."

"Uh huh."

"I missed you. It helped me pretend you weren't so far away." He realized Milliscent could hear all of this and inwardly cringed. There went his mancard. Damn it all. Maybe he should have stationed Pete up there too—the kid could use a lesson or two. Luckily, Jenni turned the conversation in a general direction.

Adam, Trevor, and Shelton helped her pack the car to move, sending the message they'd be around in a month to check out the cabin. He'd have to thank their brothers someday. The month timeframe passed long ago, but maybe Jenni's mom told everyone that the two middle children fell through the rabbit hole. Pushed, actually.

How many siblings in the families knew about this whole "gate" thing, and were they the only ones kept in the dark all these years?

Shirley's pregnant. Again.

The Clemptons next door adopted a new dog, a real sweetheart. Sheepdog.

He let her know he found a perfect space in the backyard of the cabin for a sunflower garden, despite how much they stink. She disagreed with his opinion on the smell, and they childishly went back and forth a few times with, "no they don't," "yes they do," for nostalgia's sake until she ended the argument with the standard "whatever."

Jenni told him about Amanda's knitting tutelage, and despite the fact his luck with the cards changed and his hand was coming together brilliantly, he lost himself in her enthusiasm. Her eyes sparkled, her smile wide. Happiness poured outward, and he soaked it in. She planned to make a blanket for Cricket, and his heart ached for the baby they waited for so long. While she detailed booties and hats, he pictured her rocking their infant.

"But this first project is for you, it's a scarf."

Wait.

What?

His face froze, and while he tried to re-arrange his features to emulate enthusiasm, he gave himself a mental high-five for stopping the chagrin and horror from manifesting. His lips lifted upward, and her joy made the effort worthwhile. "That's great," he said. "I can't wait to wear it." If it made her smile like that, he'd wear that ugly thing every single day. Proudly.

He drew a card. Yes! Score. One more to go and he'd win for the first time. Legs cramping, he stretched them under the table, his calf resting against Jenni's thigh. Absently, he twisted his foot back and forth, bumping her hip with the toe of his boot.

"What happened at the training center?"

Elliott froze, his heart pummeling in his chest. She knew. She somehow learned what a monster he'd become. Bile rose from his stomach as shame slithered through his veins. He shifted on his cushion again, studying his cards intently, trying to find the words to explain. He cleared his throat.

"Rick," he choked out. "He, uh. He wanted to prove a point to me and his boys." His gaze darted up to his wife's for a second, but he didn't want to see her horror, or worse, pity, and turned back to his cards. He shuffled them around in his fingers.

Jenny remained quiet for a few seconds before

finally asking, "What point can that possibly be?"

He clamped his jaw tightly. "That we all had a whole lot to learn."

"What did he do to you?"

He flung his cards down on the table and rubbed his hands over his face, then his fingers through his hair, pulling the long strands back. His gaze landed on his wife as the remembered fear twisted his gut once more. "He made me think you were in trouble, and then tried to stop me from getting to you."

Jenni recoiled.

"Yeah. It was bad."

"I saw the newscast." She reached under the table and rubbed his leg.

Elliott took a deep breath, letting her touch work it's calming magic. He peeked back up at Jenni, but she seemed neither disgusted nor horrified, only worried. In an attempt to distract himself, he picked up his cards again, searching, drawing and discarding. Still not the card he needed.

"He changed his tactics after that."

"I'll bet he did. Creep. Did he teach you anything new?"

A slow smile grew on his face, the mood easing. "A few things."

"Do you have superpowers now?"

"Not really." Damn it. "Basically, I'm 'better'. I can see better, move faster, that sort of thing. My hearing is off the chart now, that's awesome. My night vision is improving. I get a super-boost when danger is high, but like chugging caffeine, the drop afterward is ugly."

"Yeah, I remember." After a pause, she continued.

"I'm sorry you didn't get laser vision."

He nodded absently, staring at the cards in his hand. "That would've been cool, yes."

"You also didn't get super card-playing skills either." Elliott's head shot up in time to see Jenni throw her wad of cards on the table. "Rummy."

"No!"

"Yes."

"No! I only needed one more card," he lamented, holding up a finger. "*One!*"

But Jenni ignored his rant, too busy dancing a victory jig next to the table chanting "I'm the win-*ner*! I'm the win-*ner*!" Legs and arms flapping around obnoxiously.

Elliott growled, pouncing from the table and scooped Jenni into his arms, spinning her around once while she shrieked, red faced and laughing. "You cheated," he said and tickled her relentlessly.

She shrieked again. "No! No, I didn't you big baby." Struggling to free herself, she twisted and kicked her legs, but he had her pinned against him. He wasn't too proud to admit her curves felt incredibly pleasant.

"Admit you cheated and I'll let you go," he demanded around her continuous cries.

She didn't. Wouldn't. He accepted this fact, but since he never expected to win anyway, he stopped his torture.

Already in his arms, Jenni didn't falter in the slightest when he started humming an old swing song the jazz band at their high school used to play and twisted her around. Instantly falling into step, she doo-wapped the harmony. He pulled her in close, pushed her out, sidestepped and twisted, arms over each other, around, back. They missed each other's hands a couple of times and turned the wrong way once or twice, but they only laughed harder.

Near the end of the song, the music growing in crescendo, a crazy idea popped into Elliott's head. Could they do it? Would she catch on quick enough? Trying to remember the move correctly, he grabbed hold of Jenni's waist, picking her up and bringing her in close. As though reading his mind, her legs wrapped around him, then he pushed her out and swung her to one side, then the other. Now for the finale—the Big Spin. He pushed her high in the air. She flipped on cue. He twisted. Their arms reached for each other…they missed the catch. Their bodies collided, and Elliott and Jenni fell in a tangled mess. Laughing uncontrollably, they lay unmoving for far too long and he heard Milliscent shifting on the branch.

He waved a hand to let the teen know they were fine.

"Ms. Dunham would be absolutely horrified," his wife finally said through her giggles as she stirred, beginning the process to extricate herself from the knot of their arms and legs.

"Probably, but we haven't tried that move in eight years." Elliott freed an arm. "I think we did pretty good."

"I hated that old dragon lady for making us partners." They disentangled their legs.

"You? I actually tried to pay Groucho to swap with me."

"Because you hated me or because he'd been paired with Victoria?"

The less said on that matter, the better. "A win-win

situation all round. But Dragonlady wouldn't let us."

Deciding not to make the effort to actually stand, they crawled over to the table and drank deeply from the canteen. While Jenni took her turn, Elliott removed two wooden legs from the short table, leaving it slanted to the side. Pushing the mats against his new support, he leaned back, dragging Jenni between his legs until he held her in his arms. He turned off the lamp, plunging them into darkness. She laid back, her head against his chest and sighed in contentment, staring up at the stars.

"Tell me a story, Elliott."

"Do you want to hear about Benjamin, the little green snake, or Billy, the lonely sea monster?"

He couldn't see her smile, but he heard it in her voice. "Benjamin."

He chuckled slightly, congratulating himself on already knowing her choice. She pointed at the snake that first day on the trail for a reason, and he'd worked on that tale ever since. "Once, there was a little green snake named Benjamin…"

Elliott lowered his voice so Milliscent couldn't hear his poem. Jenni relaxed against him more and more until her breathing evened. He continued for a few more minutes, until he knew she'd fallen asleep, then stopped his story. Gently, so as not to wake her, he reached up and pulled some hair from her face, then gently kissed her temple.

"Thank you for helping us tonight, Milly," he said in a voice barely loud enough to carry to the teen in the tree. "We both needed this."

"You didn't fool around."

"No, we didn't fool around. We made love."

Elliott wrapped his arms a little tighter around

Jenni's sleeping form. His lower half started to lose feeling, so he lifted his right knee, pulling his foot in closer to his butt to adjust his back, prop them up, and to circulate some blood in the problem area. He smiled to himself, watching the stars and ruminating on his growing abilities.

His night vision continued to improve each passing week. Without the lantern, he could still see the foliage surrounding them on three sides clearly, and Milliscent sitting high in the branches of the tree where she kept watch all evening.

He listened to the sounds of bats hunting, owls hooting. Crickets chirping. A four legged animal quietly slinked past the campsite. A small creature scurried through the underbrush. Closing his eyes, he breathed in deeply, letting the scent of pine and cedar fill his lungs. He could stay here forever.

Well.

Almost.

His lower half lost feeling again. Stretching his right leg out, pulling up the left, he scooted slightly to adjust, trying to move Jenni as little as possible. Elliott needn't have worried; his wife snored slightly and cuddled in closer, mouth hanging slightly open. He chuckled to himself.

Soft footsteps on the trail caught his attention, and he lifted his eyes to Milliscent. Their friend eyed the path through binoculars, then dropped them to her chest, apparently unconcerned.

"Don't worry, it's just me," Rick's hushed voice floated to him, and he relaxed.

Listening to the man's approach, he waited until the guardian came into view. Their eyes met and they nodded to each other.

"Where is she?"

Elliott pointed to the lookout post, ignoring the young woman's indignant huff.

"Traitor," Milliscent called out, unaware that she didn't need to yell, he could hear her perfectly well from this distance. He smiled again, loving his improved hearing.

The older man cut through the camp and walked to Milliscent's perch, stopping at the base. He stretched his neck to look up at his niece while she eyed him from above.

"Can I come up?" he asked softly.

"That depends."

"I just want to talk."

"I'm not in the mood for another lecture."

The older man sighed. "No lectures. I promise."

Milliscent sighed dramatically, rolled her eyes and scooted over a little. "Fine."

Rick jumped, grasping the lowest branch and pulled himself up, swinging his legs and propelling himself higher. Limb by limb, he climbed upward until he finally settled on a bough near the young woman. The two sat in silence for several moments, and Elliott watched as Milliscent fiddled with the straps on her binoculars while her uncle scratched his head, then his beard, then wrung his fingers.

"I'm sorry," the older man finally blurted, and Milliscent's face swung around, her eyes wide, her mouth hanging slightly open.

"What was that?"

"Jenni cornered me this morning and laid into me. I'm sorry. I'm not trying to run your life, I wanted to give you hope."

The teen grunted. "You have a funny way to go about it."

"It's easy to forget you're a child of this world now."

They fell into silence for a couple of seconds. "I've never been around married people," Milliscent finally said. "Not that I really remember, anyway. All my memories of Mom and Dad are vague. All I know is what I've been taught at school." Her voice dropped low, and Elliott figured she thought he could no longer hear. "These two, they don't match any of that."

Rick shook his head, smiling. "No. They don't."

Another pause. "If I tell you something, do you promise to just sit and listen?"

"Yes. I promise."

"I wanted to hate Elliott. I mean, he married Jenni, which meant he wanted a slave, right? He had to be a selfish jackass. And I couldn't understand why any woman would subject herself to a man like that, so I figured Jenni was weak."

Rick chuckled, and Milliscent smiled ruefully.

"She's not weak."

"No," Milliscent agreed, shaking her head. "She's not. She's smart. And despite what I thought, Elliott turned out to be a good guy." She swallowed and took a deep breath. "It's hard to dislike someone who wakes up at three in the morning to make sure you're not in too much pain from your freaky glowy powers trying to activate, and never once complains about giving magic foot massages." She paused, chewing on her bottom lip. "Figuring out all those pressure points, to know exactly what combination to push in what order to minimize the pain on whatever limb happens to be activating at the moment, must have taken a lot of years of trial and error, you know?" Rick nodded without answering. "That's dedication."

"Yes, it is."

"He's my friend now."

"Glad to hear it. You can trust him."

"I watched them tonight; they did a lot of talking."

"They had a lot to catch up on."

"Very little of it made any sense. They talked about people and places and things I had no context for. It's like they have their own secret language."

"Yeah, that happens a lot with long-term relationships."

"You think that'll happen to Jeremy and me?"

Rick cleared his throat. "It's a possibility."

"Jenni waxed long and poetic over her new knitting hobby." Milliscent shrugged and shook her head. "I wonder how on earth Elliott managed to pretend enthusiasm for the excruciating details of the color scheme for baby slippers."

Elliott chuckled to himself as the vision of Jenni rocking their baby entered his mind again. Why wouldn't baby slippers interest him? Especially, if they are made for his child by the woman he loves?

The teen continued with her ramblings. "She went on and on about plans for a baby blanket for some poor kid named Cricket."

Not kid, Elliott corrected mentally. *Unborn baby.* They still couldn't agree on an actual name yet—the nickname represented a compromise of epic proportions.

"But what really got me," the teen continued, "was

when Jenni excitedly proclaimed her current monstrosity of a scarf for Elliot, he didn't even flinch." If only she knew. Milly snickered. "Though his smile did become slightly strained."

The young woman's eyes stared into the distance. "Right that moment, it dawned on me. Elliott actually planned on wearing The Thing. I saw it in his face, the set of his jaw, the look of panic in his eyes. He planned on wearing the globby, misshapen ugly mess and pretend to love it. And I wondered, why? And then Jenni's voice from days ago came back to me. 'Because he loves me.' "

Rick wisely sat quiet, letting the teen work through her thoughts and emotions without interruption.

Milliscent rubbed her chest absently, staring in front of her. "Earlier today, he said to me, 'She doesn't need a lover right now, she needs her best friend'." She paused. "I could use a best friend." Another long moment of silence. "I wonder what Jeremy is like. Do you think he'll be an all right guy?"

"I think you are an amazing young woman, and I think you wouldn't have chosen him, otherwise."

After a long pause, Milliscent said, "Jenni said he could fill this black hole in my heart." She rubbed her chest again. "Maybe it won't be *so* bad."

"Maybe it won't."

"I mean, Jenni isn't a slave or a servant."

"No."

"These two, they serve each other. They look out for each other. They help each other. They fight and they make up and they laugh and cry together." She paused. "It goes against everything I've been taught since going to boarding school. But…it goes with everything I remember of Mom and Dad."

"Sounds like you have some things to think about."

"Honesty. The key to their relationship is honesty." Milliscent seemed to speak to herself now. "I can do that." A look of resolve settled on her features. "I'll be honest. I'll tell Jeremy I don't believe in love at first sight. I'll tell him I don't want to get married for a long, long time, if at all. I only want friendship."

"I think that's a great idea."

"If he agrees, then maybe this whole 'destiny' thing won't be so terrifying."

"If he doesn't, he's an idiot."

Milliscent smiled warmly at her uncle.

"You've got a lot to think about. How about you head back, and I'll finish up watch tonight?"

"No. If it's all right with you, I'll stay here."

"Suit yourself. Love you, kiddo."

"Love you too, Uncle Rick."

The older man deftly climbed down the tree. As he passed Elliott and Jenni he whispered, "Thank you."

Elliott nodded. Nighttime settled around them, and he felt fatigue creeping in.

He must have fallen asleep—he woke to Jenni adjusting against his body. Pink rays of morning light ebbed over the horizon. Beautiful, but it marked the end of their interlude. Now came the hard part.

He poked Jenni in the side. "Hey," he coaxed. "It's time to go."

Jenni grumbled slightly but, thank heavens, stretched and stood sluggishly without her usual arguments.

"Mornin'."

Elliott tried to stand, but the entire bottom half of

his body fell asleep and thousands of pins and needles attacked his limbs after hours of stagnation.

Jenni held out a hand. "Here."

Their hands connected, and a sonic concussion slammed through his body.

Ah, damn.

Chapter 16

"Son of a—"

"Elliott, watch out," Jenni screamed, pointing with her free hand over his right shoulder to the massive *thing* swinging a giant metal staff at her husband's head, momentarily distracted from the nausea gripping her stomach.

"Run," he yelled as he rolled to the side, wrenching his hand from hers.

Stupid man, did he not get the concept they couldn't gate out of this mess without physical contact? She still felt the low hum of power running through her body, and if he just—

"Run," he hollered again as the eight foot bulbous grayish-clear insect turned what might be a head in her direction and swung the staff toward her with speed defying its gelatinous form.

She spun, hoping the movement wouldn't make her vomit, as Elliott vaulted himself toward her attacker, pummeling into it and grabbing it around its middle. The massive stick swept less than an inch past her face as she fell backward. Landing with a jolting *thud*, all of the air knocked from her lungs and she gasped, stunned for a second before crab walking away from the wrestling insect and her husband.

Fighting dizziness, she desperately searched for a rock or a stick to aid in the fight; vaguely registering they had landed in the middle of some battle between humans and these creatures.

Fabulous.

If it's not a cliff, it's a stinking war.

Surrounded by mayhem, the humans shouted to each other, calling battle cries and working in pairs to cut down the giant bugs screeching at ear splitting decibels. Each pair of warriors grasped long silver sticks with sharp bulbs at the end, and their main focus lay in ramming it into the gut of the massive mutant tick-like things, causing blue lightning to shoot out the end and melting the insides of their victims.

"Dammit woman, run!" Elliott hollered at her again as he fought to ward off the pincers in his face. He pulled a huge knife from somewhere off his person and stabbed the thing in the back, but it merely screeched without even flinching as it continued to attack. He stabbed again and again as they rolled on the rocky ground, but the monster remained unaffected, oozing grayish-clear liquid through the new holes.

Finding a big sharp rock, Jenni grabbed it off the ground beside her, jumping to her feet. Ignoring the roiling earth around her, she chucked it with all her strength at the monster trying to kill her husband. The two combatants rolled and, despite the fact her projectile actually flew with perfect aim for once, it managed to hit both of them in a ricochet effect, opening another oozing gash in the creature which dripped onto Elliott's neck—directly onto the angry red scratch where her rock bounced off him. As the thick, slimy gray pus landed on his skin, smoke drifted upward with a low hissing noise barely discernable through her husband's scream of pain and the monster's screech of anger.

Terrifying war cries pierced the air and two children ran past her, jumping on the massive creature. The boy and girl, no more than eleven or twelve years old and dressed like peasant villagers escaped from a renaissance fair, each wielded one of those weird lightning sticks and worked in tandem. Hitting, poking, yelling, slicing, they angered the insect until it crawled off Elliott and bounded for the girl. As it jumped toward her, the boy lunged and twisted his weapon, causing the blue lightning to erupt the insect's gut into a storm within its clear cavity.

Screeching, it fell to the ground, motionless.

"Get to the inner circle," the boy shouted as he and his partner rushed off to fight another one.

Breathing deeply in an attempt to gain control of the nausea, Jenni watched in horrified fascination as the duo engaged another monster, dodging, cart-wheeling like acrobats, lunging, spinning and jabbing until it too fell. They were only children. Appalled, she looked closer at the battle around her and realized all of the teams paired as male/female, and ranged in age from the children to middle-aged. All of this she observed in a matter of moments, while Elliott scrambled to his feet and rushed toward her. Grabbing her arm, he tried pulling her away from the carnage.

She planted her feet, resisting. "Elliott, we have to help them."

"Jenni," he leveled his sweaty, dirty, face at her, his neck red and raw, his eyes relentlessly determined. "We don't know how. We are a liability to them; we will only get in their way." Angry turmoil rolled through her, and as Elliott's eyes held her hostage, he must have seen her inner conflict. His shoulders slunk a little, his voice softened slightly. "Honey, Milliscent will die if we don't find a way back. And we can't find a way back if one of us is dead."

"I hate this," she grumbled as she finally allowed him to pull her away from the mayhem. "I feel like we're abandoning them. Did you see those children?"

"Yes, I saw them. Impressive training."

"You're okay with that?" She couldn't believe the admiration in his voice.

"I'm okay with any society teaching their people how to survive," he said as they hurried to a large boulder near a grove of trees. "You can bet Cricket will know how to take down a wildebeest by the time she's eight."

"So you're going to turn into your father?"

"My respect for him grows by leaps and bounds with each passing day."

"What if I want him to be a scholar?" she asked indignantly, stumbling slightly as dizziness got the better of her for a second, nausea still clawing at her midsection.

"She'll be a ninja scholar." Elliott shrugged, pulling her closer to prop her against his body as they rushed to safety. "I don't see the problem."

They reached a large outcropping of boulders and ducked behind them. To her surprise, Elliott grabbed her by the shoulders and pushed her against the rocks, his eyes boring into her. Before she could get angry, he kissed her, cutting off her response.

And then he ruined it.

"We have to talk, Jenni." His hands fell away, and he ran them through his hair. "When I tell you to run, you need to run, damn it."

"I'm not running away when—"

"I don't think you're weak, okay?" He threw his arms up in exasperation. "I'm not sending you off as some macho super-ego thing." He huffed, frustrated. "Frankly, you are untrained and when I tell you to run, it's a strategic decision." His mouth pinched for a second, but he took a breath and continued with the brutal truth, pointing to his neck. "You could get us both killed when you don't listen to me. So until I have a chance to teach you," she rolled her eyes in disbelief, "and I *will*, you need to listen to me. I promise, I promise, I *promise* you I will not tell you to run unless it's the most strategically sound decision." He raised his eyebrows, and she couldn't look away. "Okay?" She nodded, irritated and feeling like dead weight. "Let me do what I do best, and I'll let you do what you do best."

She snorted. "Right, what I do best."

"Yes, like keeping us alive. Remember the cats? I could have ignored you when you yelled at me to stop, and we would have died at that oasis." He pointed at her. "I trust you. I need you to trust me." He pointed at himself.

"Oh." When he said it like that.

"We're a team, Jenni. We're 'us,' remember?" He paused for a second and he must have misinterpreted her grimace of pain for something other than the infernal nausea when he continued. "You are my number one priority, every single time. But to keep you alive and get you home, I have to keep myself alive so you *can* go home. I promise I will not throw myself on a sword for that purpose alone."

"That's a lot of promising in a short amount of

time."

"You know I'm good for them."

Yes. Yes, he was. "I'm not the type to stand on the side screaming helplessly while her man gets his butt kicked."

"Please don't. But play to your strengths, honey. And let's be honest. Combat isn't one of them right now."

She glared at him. "I wanted to gate us out of there, but you let go of me."

"Yeah, well, I thought you might prefer to gate me intact, without my head missing."

"At the moment, I'm not so sure."

He rolled his eyes. "Speaking of gating us out of here…" He grabbed her wrist and held up her glowing hand. "Does this mean you're juiced up?"

"I believe so. We can only try."

"How do you want to try this? Should we—"

Her stomach finally turned inside out, doubling her over and bringing her to her knees as she wretched and gagged on acid. Every muscle in her body convulsed and tears pooled in her eyes as wave after wave of nausea assaulted her. Elliot's large callused hand braced her forehead while his other arm snaked around her waist for him to rub her belly gently, easing the knotted mess slightly.

She heard his voice whispering, but the words folded in on each other. The world spun and her husband's iron grip kept her from nose-diving into the rocky ground beneath her.

"Here we go, Jenni, you're doing it."

Blinking to clear her eyes of moisture, she realized the world actually turned blurry. "Yay me," she gasped, then heaved again. She spit. "Doing what I do best."

Elliott had the gall to chuckle, and she collapsed sideways into him since she didn't have the fortitude to reach up and hit him. He simply caught her and pulled her into his lap, wrapping his arms around her in a vise grip.

"Careful," she warned breathing deeply, wondering if the spinning sensation came from her head or the gating process which seemed to work on ultra-slow motion at this moment. "I'm oozing like that tick right now."

"S'all good," he said, rubbing her back. "You owe me one."

She closed her eyes, unable to stand watching the blur of white and shapes trapping them in the eye of a vortex and slowly picking up speed. "Tell me when it's over."

"You're driving this bus, honey; you should probably keep your eyes open."

Groaning, she lifted her lids and swallowed convulsively. "Okay." Breathe. Breathe. Breathe. "Tell me what you see."

"I see swirling white mist, like we're stuck in a cloud whirlpool."

"No doors?"

"Nope."

"No brown streaks that might be our kitchen table stretched out in a bizzaro shape?"

"Nope."

"No dancing purple penguins?"

"Really?"

"No, but that would be cool."

He laughed. "Tell me about the doors. Are they

stationary or swirling?"

"Neither, they're kind of jumping around and fading in and out. Getting to one will be like playing a twisted game of whack-a-mole."

"Okay, no problem. I'm good at whack-a-mole."

"No, you're not. Eddie beat you every time."

"But he's the only one who could. Adam, Seth, Trevor, Gary…I trounced them all."

"Well, it doesn't matter because they are too high in the air. Ground level is scarier."

"Why?"

"Because I think I might be able to get us back to our kitchen."

"Ouch. That hurts."

"Yes. It does. What if this is our last chance? These pictures, they keep fading and jumping too, but if I calculate it right, I might be able to jump us home."

"Your call, Jenni."

"Don't lay this all on me."

"I know what you're going to pick, and I'm okay with it. Home is where you are, darlin'. I can make a cabin anywhere."

Tears swamped her, choking her again, and she recoiled in horror at her over-the-top reaction. "I hate my mom," she wailed, disgusted by the petulance in her voice and wondering where the emotional outburst came from and feeling stupid.

Really, they had no choice.

She must find a way back to Milliscent. "How did you know I wouldn't pick home?"

"For the same reason your mom knew if she sent us here, we'd help."

Jenni sighed heavily. "We are such pushovers."

"Yup."

"All right." They stared at the cloudy twirling mass for a second while she rallied her strength and resolve. "Okay."

Climbing out of Elliott's lap, she lost her footing and landed on her hands and knees, but pushed up. Using his shoulders to steady herself, she climbed to a standing position. Rubbing her hands together and breathing deeply to master the nausea still lurking in the background, she eyed the swirling mass around them in speculation.

"Why aren't you carsick?" she grumbled as she counted flashing intervals and watched Elliott pick himself off the ground from the corner of her eye.

He placed a hand on the small of her back. "I don't know, love. Don't jump without me."

The rhythm began to emerge, and she scooted one foot slightly in front of the other, bending her knees to loosen her body in readiness. Arms bent at the elbows, she pumped them back and forth a few times.

"Jump when I say jump."

"Wait!"

"What?"

Elliott reached down and unbuckled his belt, stripping it from his pants.

"Later, Elliott, I'm getting in the zone." And she still felt like puking. Total mood killer.

He chuckled, wrapping his belt through hers and then through two of the belt loops on the side of his pants before re-buckling the leather. "Since I don't have rope."

"Ah. Got it."

She pulled them closer to the wall of clouds in

front of them and re-poised herself for the jump. Her husband followed her example.

"You know we look like dorks like this, right?" she asked, staring intently at the vortex a few scant feet away.

"Maybe, but we're dorks who stay together."

"One. Two. Three. Four. One. Two. Three. Four. One and two and three and four-five, what? Dangit!" She breathed heavily through her lips a few times, cracked her neck by bending her head to touch an ear to each shoulder, all while staring intently. "It's mathematical."

"Oh thank heavens," Elliott breathed out, relief palpable in his voice.

"I always told you about real world applications for all the stuff you were forced to learn."

"Yes, dear. Because gating to other realities is so commonplace."

"Okay, I have it. On the count of three, jump right *there*." She pointed to a random spot in the all-consuming white mist, her finger disappearing into the void momentarily before she pulled it back, and Elliott stared at that spot intently, as though trying to burn that exact placement into his psyche.

"Got it."

"One…two…three…"

****

They bumped into each other a split second before entering the mist, but the stomach-lurching freefall and the blue sky overhead consumed Elliott's entire attention until his back crashed into multiple sharp objects, and he bounced outward and sideways. Brown and green now mixed with the blue, and he felt each stab, thump and smack as a tree broke his fall. Down he went, scrambling to grab a branch, twig, leaf, anything at all, but his fingers could not find purchase. His body flipped and turned, showing him the ground many yards below and he braced for imminent connection, but a sharp jolting halt and pain around his waist signaled the end of his descent. Contorting his head to look up over his shoulder, he found one of the sexiest sights he ever saw in his life.

Jenni hung upside down, legs wrapped around a tree branch, body and arms stretched outward, holding on for dear life to the waistband of his pants. His belt, still looped through hers, hung against the side of her body, obviously ripped free from his pants at some point during the fall. Her shirt slouched around her armpits, giving him a generous view of her stomach and the bottoms of her breasts as her bra rode up (or would that be down?) as well. Ill-timed and inappropriate, a few choice lyrical phrases zipped through his mind, but her grunt of physical strain interrupted his mental flow.

"My hero," he called out to her. He had to give credit where credit was due.

"Shut up and help me, you weigh a ton," she gasped, her red face now twisted in fervent agony. The tomato effect ruined the sexy factor a little bit, but one had to make allowances for gravity.

"You are so hot."

She grunted. "Still not helping."

He reached over to a nearby branch, but missed it by a few inches. "You need to swing me."

She obliged and few seconds later, he grasped a branch and swung his body and legs around to straddle it. Settling himself, he looked up to see Jenni sitting on a nearby branch, adjusting her bra.

"Darn."

"Feeling feisty today, I see."

"I'm learning all kinds of new things about myself. But seriously, you have this extra shiny glow thing going on."

She snorted. "That's left over from the nausea."

"Still bad?"

"Not at all. Actually, I'm starving."

Jaguar-like snarling interrupted their conversation and they looked down to find two giant black and white striped, saber-toothed cats on the ground beneath them.

"Nithlam? Shesta?" Jenni asked in shock.

The two animals snarled in response.

"Well," Elliot said, trying to be pragmatic about the situation. "I guess we can stock up on cat spit now."

****

Jenni giggled.

She couldn't help it, the look on Nithlam's face—a strange combination of shock, disbelief, horror and disgust—all combined with cat eyes and prehistoric teeth made his expression hilarious. Especially since the animal levied his expression at her husband…who stared back unabashed less than three feet away from those fangs.

"What?" Elliott asked in innocence. "I'm not asking you for anything vital," he said in defense. "Just spit a few times." He held the small container outward, toward the zebra cat.

Elliott and Jenni sat cross legged in a cave, surrounded by Shesta, Nithlam and their cubs. Light filtered in from the entrance a few yards away. She felt a low hum of power in her veins, but so far they'd been unsuccessful in opening another vortex mist-tornado to gate. She pondered for a second over the odd fact that the weird cloudy stuff only happened this last time, and not any of the previous jumps, and wondered why.

The two cats, shocked by the gatekeeper's re-appearance a mere day after dropping them at the hunter's cabin, another puzzling time zone difference, begrudgingly brought them home to meet the family. And here they sat. Two little girl cubs snuggled against Elliott's side, one even laying her head in his lap as he absently scratched behind her ear with one hand. The youth purred contentedly. An older male cub sat alert behind them, reminding Jenni of a noble Egyptian statue.

Jenni translated Elliott's words, and Nithlam's mouth scrunched to the side as his eyes narrowed to slits. *Poachers hunt us for our healing abilities, and sell our body parts for money. I never thought I'd see the day when a gatekeeper turned heartless like that.*

"No, no, no," she said. "Elliott is a healer. He's not trying to make a buck; he only wants to help people. Honestly, I think he wants a stockpile for me, 'cause I keep getting into all kinds of trouble."

She held up her scratched arms to prove her point. "He'll never ever sell the stuff, or make money when he helps people with it." She elbowed her husband in the rib cage and gave him a deliberate look. "Right, Elliott?"

He nodded. "Promise."

"He gives his word. And we're not *taking* it from you, we're asking. Nicely." She pulled her lips back in the biggest, toothiest, cheesiest smile she could stretch across her face without traipsing into "creepy serial killer" territory. Shesta snorted and Nithlam rolled his eyes, shaking his head. He even chuckled slightly, though it came out as a bit of snarl. Elliott cleared his throat and swirled the bottle around, gaze darting around the small group.

The animal then trailed his tongue up and down one of his large teeth, apparently stimulating a saliva gland, as he drooled into the small container in Elliott's hand. Jenni cringed, once again holding back nausea, knowing the clear slimy liquid would eventually be spread on some part of her body at some point. Her husband, on the other hand, smiled with enthusiasm.

"Awesome, man. Thank you very much."

Nithlam repeated the procedure several times until the vial was full. Elliott capped it and tucked it into the pocket of his jeans, jostling the girl cub lying in his lap while he maneuvered to gain access. She didn't move. If anything, she batted her eyelashes.

Jenni smiled to herself, thinking of several nieces during holidays doing the exact same thing. *He captures hearts everywhere he goes.*

"Okay," her husband said, once again scratching behind the cat's ear and focusing on Nithlam and Shesta. "Now that's out of the way. Can we ask a few questions?"

She translated back and forth during their conversation.

"What would you like to know?"

"Not that we're complaining, but why are you helping us?"

"We owe a debt to one of your forefathers. It can never be repaid, but we will do all we can. If you ever find yourself in need, you can gate here and find sanctuary."

"Which forefathers? And how do you know who we're related to?"

Shesta smiled and Elliott scooted back slightly, earning a grunt of displeasure from the young cub in his lap. "You look remarkably like him, young warrior. We cannot say his human name, but we call him Thunder."

Jenni started laughing and explained to him. "Uncle Malachi," they said together.

"We call his gate Summer Breeze. We have not seen them in many seasons."

Jenni sighed, regret and sadness coursing through her. She swallowed a lump in her throat to answer. "Aunt Rita passed away about seven years ago now. Uncle Malachi can't jump anymore without her, I guess."

"We are sorry for his loss. She was a generous and kind being. We will truly miss her."

"If we ever make it home—"

"When we make it home," Elliott grumbled under his breath.

"*When* we make it home, would you like us to give him a message?"

The animals hesitated, looked at each other as if in silent communication then turned back. "Tell him the north wind is yellow and purple tonight. And let him know Delean," Shesta nodded at her son still stoically standing at attention behind the group, "awaits a rematch."

"We will definitely do that. We have so many questions. A guardian named Rick mentioned something about a group called The Underground. Do you know anything about them, or what their mission is

237

or—"

A massive burst of power stole her breath, cutting off her sentence as her entire body turned into a giant lightbulb. Her head flew back, her chest out, her muscles rigid. Elliott reached for her, but she flinched away. "Don't touch me," she gasped harshly, pushing back and standing.

"Jenni, we need—"

"Cekubra, she's still touching you."

Her entire body ached with overwhelming need. Unbearable pressure pushed outward, and fear she might explode slithered through her as she watched Nithlam grab his daughter's scruff in his massive mouth, pulling her to safety.

Elliott jumped to his feet and reached with both hands, calmly placing a palm on each of her arms. White mist instantly enveloped them. No whirlpool, no doors, no flashing pictures, not even solid ground beneath their feet. Jenni now hung suspended by an intangible tether in a cloudy void, surrounded on all sides by a thousand whispering voices mixing together in a cacophony of unintelligible blather. Their urgency clawed at her, pushed her, pulled her, begging for attention.

Two hands shook her upper arms, snapping her focus to Elliott standing before her in the void, mouthing the words "what's happening" with exaggerated enunciation.

She shook her head, terrified. The invisible tether tightened and pulled, yanking them backward and causing her stomach to revolt yet again. Adrenaline pumped through her veins and black spots formed at the edges of her vision. Then, as they flew through the incorporeal nightmare rollercoaster, her body started to stretch. The ridiculous memory of Saturday morning cartoon men with stretchy powers flew through her mind as she watched her legs, arms, and torso elongate to unnatural proportions.

Hyperventilation assaulted her. Unrelenting, the whispering voices crowded her brain, urgent, angry, desperate. Warm lips pressed against hers, shocking her enough to force her lungs to open fully. Warm assurance poured into her. The lips moved to her ear and Elliott's voice sliced through the babble.

"I've got you. Let's enjoy the ride."

Enjoy this madness? Yeah. Right.

She exploded, her vision blacking out as her pieces scattered like shrapnel across the universe. Her lungs coughed on dust over here. One arm, way over there, throbbed. One knee pulsed. A foot, over in another area completely, twitched. The ringing in her ears either drowned out the voices or they finally decided to leave her alone. Tiny elves played bongo drums on her brain.

Her stomach, ironically enough, felt perfectly fine.

Groaning, she blinked a few times to find a world beginning to focus above her.

"Jenni?" a familiar voice called to her with joy and disbelief. "Elliott?"

Lifting her head, Jenni made the visual realization all her appendages were, in fact, attached properly. "Ouch."

Her head flopped backward onto leaves.

"Yeah," her husband's voice agreed from a few feet away, sounding a bit strained. "Let's avoid that kind of entry in the future."

"Did you hear those voices?" she asked, still

blinking, but unable to get the gumption to move anything else. At least the high pitched squeal receded.

"Jenni, what's wrong?" Milliscent knelt beside her. Black mascara ran in ghoulish lines down her face. Her red puffy eyes blinked rapidly, probably in an attempt to hold back tears.

"Just give me a minute, that last reentry was a doozy."

"You came back," the young woman cried and buried her face in Jenni's neck.

"Of course, we came back." She managed to lift an arm high enough to pat her friend on the back.

Air stirred next to her, and she pushed her head over to see Elliott on his back, his elbows propping himself up. "We're going to move heaven and two earths and several realities to make sure you get to Porthinch safely, Milly." He smiled tiredly at the girl before resting his eyes on Jenni. "I heard the voices, too." He sounded grim.

"Did you understand them?" Jenni decided to experiment and push herself to her elbows, mirroring her husband's posture. Surprisingly, she held firm.

"Sort of. I think I heard my dad arguing with your mom. Adam and John tried to tell us something, but I couldn't make out what. Some of the voices, I didn't recognize."

"Who's Adam and John?" Milliscent interrupted. "Brothers," Jenni answered. "Adam is his, John is mine." She turned her attention back to Elliott. "You did better than me. I only heard incoherent blabber. I thought I lost my mind."

"You can't," he assured her lovingly. "It's already gone. I drove you crazy years ago."

"True, true."

She watched him turn over to his hands and knees, then gingerly stand up. He stretched a couple of times, then hopped up and down on the balls of his feet as if to test out his strength.

"Huh. It's not as bad as it seems. Come on." He held a hand in her direction.

"No," Milliscent hollered, throwing herself between them, landing across Jenni's body in an inelegant tackle. "No touching,"

They sighed and looked at each other over the teenage body, shrugging simultaneously.

"She's right," Elliott said.

"I just spent the worst ten minutes of my life thinking I would die a horribly long, drawn out and painful death. If you guys touch each other again, you better touch me, too."

"How long were we gone?"

"Ten minutes," Milliscent answered as she climbed off Jenni and helped her to her feet. "I gotta ask, what happened to you guys? You look like hell." She covered her mouth and nose with her hand, cringing. "You smell like it, too."

Jenni looked at Elliott, trying to see him through Milliscent's eyes. Hair, matted and greasy, stood in a thousand directions, one clump defying gravity in the back of his head and another standing straight up. An angry raw burn on his neck. He looked like a man who finished rolling in the dirt while fighting for his life and then used a tree to break his fall after popping into the sky. His poor clothes, ripped, dirty, and splattered with blood and gray tick goo, were a total loss.

She could only guess she didn't look any better.

"Giant mutant insects," Jenni answered, slowly heading down the path toward camp.

"Medieval battles," Elliott added, following her.

"Rock throwing."

"Lightning sticks."

"Running in heels."

"Acid pus."

"Flying."

"Attack trees."

"Cuddly cats."

"Sadistic parents."

The young girl's eyes grew wider and wider along with her mouth. "All in ten minutes?"

Elliott shook his head. "Time is apparently relative. It felt like we were gone for about three or four hours, total. I should get a watch."

Jenni snorted.

Voices ahead alerted them to the fact they neared the camp and her husband tapped the bracer on his left wrist a couple of times with two fingers, nodding at Jenni before strolling away to the men's section.

"Come on," the teen pulled on her arm. "You have to bathe."

"I need to eat."

"Bathe first."

"Listen kid, I have been up for *hours* and I am *starving*." Her stomach growled loudly and she pointed at the noise, feeling vindicated.

"Fine." Milliscent rolled her eyes. "Go take a bath, and I'll go get you something to eat. What do you want?"

"Rhubarb puffs. Three of them."

The girl's eyebrows shot up. "Three? Seriously?"

"I'm hungry."

"Fine," she relented on a long suffering sigh. "I'll see if I can snag three of them."

Jenni headed to the washing tent with determination, but quickly realized how badly she looked as women stopped to stare at her with shock and horror. More embarrassing, several of the passersby raised their eyebrows, sharing a knowing smile, surely surmising for themselves how she and Elliott spent their hours together. Beet red, she hurried to the shower, eyes straight ahead. No leisurely bath for her, they'd already been torn down for the daily move.

Blessedly, Milliscent returned with three of the promised pastries and, towel wrapped around her chest, Jenni fell on them with unabashed enthusiasm without waiting to dress. The first bite, her eyes rolled back into her head as the flavors and sweetness exploded in her mouth. "Oh," she said around her food, "this is soooo good."

Finishing off the first, she finally slowed down enough to put on the clean clothes her friend supplied, taking time to steal bites of the second puff between arm holes, leg holes, zippers and buttons and ties.

Finally dressed, she plopped onto the bench and leisurcly finished the third.

"You ate all three."

"Yup."

Her friend merely nodded, smiling. "Impressive."

The rest of the day continued in a blessedly anti-climactic fashion. Camp broken down, riding on the bus. Napping for several hours at Milliscent's feet, using a satchel as a pillow. Knitting with Amanda.

****

Jenni awoke two mornings later feeling like a wet dishrag. Stomach churning and roiling, she rushed outside to heave into the bushes next to the tent. As her muscles contracted again and again, she grumbled at the cosmos for her ravenous appetite the previous evening, wherein she ate two full helpings of chicken and dumplings. Bent over at the waist, hands resting on her knees, she breathed heavily in an attempt to bring normalcy back to her system. A wet cloth appeared before her, and she grabbed it thankfully, wiping her mouth.

"Sorry, I know this grosses you out," she told her teenage friend.

"Yeah, it does."

She glanced up to see the twitching smile on the young woman's face before it turned serious. "This is a bad morning for you to catch a stomach bug, though."

"Today?" Jenni gasped as her stomach turned over once again.

"The signal came in last night, but now…"

"No. I'm in." She swallowed a few times with deep breaths. "Let's get this over with. Tell me when and point which direction you want me to run, and I'll make it."

"I don't know."

"I'll make it," Jenni insisted.

She didn't know where she'd get the energy, but she'd pull it from somewhere.

"Rick needs to know—"

"No," she barked, and Milliscent flinched. She didn't want that man to see her weakness. "You can't tell him. Or Elliott either." Her stomach lurched, and she weakly pushed the hair out of her eyes. "Promise me."

"If you can't keep up, you'll get us all killed," the young women hissed at her, gaze darting around, probably in an effort to make sure their argument wasn't overheard.

"If I've learned anything from being around you people, it's that timing is everything. It's too late to change anything now."

"Elliott will get mad when he finds out I didn't tell him."

"I thought…" She took a deep breath as another wave of nausea rolled over her, and she leaned against the tree next to her. "You were a hardcore feminist, and here you are…" Another deep breath. "Threatening to tell on me to my husband. Shame on you."

Loud, heavy gunfire shattered the morning peace, interrupting their dispute and rendering the entire argument moot.

"Um." Milliscent gulped heavily, her face draining of all natural color. "This isn't the plan."

Chapter 17

Elliott burst through the foliage dressed to kill.
Literally.

Once again looking like a stuntman in a barbarian warrior movie with his swords sticking up in back, multiple weapons around his waist, bracers on his wrists, knives strapped to his thighs and ankles and guns in a shoulder holster, he ran toward the two women with grim determination. "You packed?" he asked gruffly, scanning the surrounding area meticulously, pulling one gun out of its holster and holding it at a "ready" position.

Men shouted nearby. Women screamed. Guns fired continuously. Something crashed.

"Yeah, I did it last night," Milliscent answered.

"Grab 'em, we gotta go."

The teen disappeared into the tent with haste, and he glanced up at Jenni still leaning against the tree and then did a double-take. He breathed in, eyes narrowed, and she could tell he wanted to ask her something, but he must have changed his mind. He merely snapped his mouth shut and pinched his lips together, shaking his head.

"Where's Uncle Rick?" Milliscent asked, emerging from the tent with two framed backpacks and a pair of boots, handing the footwear to Jenni.

"He's not coming."

"*What?*"

"He has to stay behind," he explained, holstering his gun. After Jenni slid the boots onto her feet and tucked in the laces without taking the time to tie them, he helped her shoulder her backpack, meticulously careful to refrain from skin to skin contact. He fussed for several seconds over fitting and clipping the straps around her waist so the weight of the bag rested on her hips instead of her back. "Some group called The Outlanders attacked—"

"They're slavers."

"He's staying to fight, but if we have to leave right now or risk getting caught."

"Elliott, we can't leave them helpless." Jenni finally found her voice. "They'll need a doctor."

"Jenni my love, we cannot stay."

"This isn't you, Elliott. You're not like this."

"I have to make a choice," he shouted in anger, then dropped his volume, once again searching the surrounding woods. He continued in a loud whisper, "I can either save you and Milliscent or I can stay here. I choose you." He pointed at her. "You choose Milliscent. We've already gone through this."

Yes, they had. She clamped her mouth shut and hated the truth with every fiber of her being. What if something happened to Amanda, though? Or Jennifer? What if that young kid, Pete, got injured fighting and needed assistance?

Her husband didn't watch her turmoil, already turned to the younger gate. "Rick says you know how to get us to the rendezvous."

Milliscent nodded.

Elliott swept his hand in front of him. "You take

the lead. Jenni, you stay right on her tail, I've got your back. You still have the dagger?"

She nodded, swallowing the guilt and regret and bile in the back of her throat. Her stomach lurched again, and she didn't know if the persistent stomach bug caused it, or culpability in abandoning her friends when they needed her. Maybe both.

Elliott looked at Milliscent. "Don't go too fast." His gaze darted to Jenni for a split second before landing back on the young woman. "We don't want to be loud and…" His eyes darted to her again. "We don't want to stumble on any surprises, but we can't dally."

Rapid gunfire punctuated his statement of urgency.

"I'm fine," Jenni protested between clenched teeth as she followed the youth already starting down an invisible path.

"You're as gray as a corpse," Milliscent said over her shoulder. "You aren't hiding jack squat from anyone."

"My reasons are still valid," her husband whispered behind her. "Which means shut up and move."

She growled inwardly, angry she couldn't argue with him further. The adrenaline gave her weak limbs mobility and for a short stretch, she kept a brisk pace. Her stomach, however, revolted and she stopped to vomit into some ferns. Instead of holding her head like yesterday, Elliott stood alert beside her. Feeling his rising consternation, she took several steps, threw up, then continued moving.

"Here," Elliott whispered, stopping her for a second. He pulled a familiar small rod off his belt and tapped the end. The sides shot out to form the sleek staff he acquired from the hunting cabin long ago and held it out to her.

With her new support and down to dry-heaving every three or four paces, she didn't even bother to stop any more, but continued to move through the gagging process. Occasionally, when she lost her balance, Elliott's hand on her pack stopped her from toppling over.

The sounds of chaos slowly faded behind them, and she wondered if they made a clean escape when movement from the corner of her eye caught her attention. A man emerged from behind a tree, shotgun leveled at them. He wore brown pants, a plaid shirt and grubby cowboy boots. A cowboy hat covered his hair, but the scruff on his jaw hinted to a reddish brown tint. Hazel eyes glared at them coldly.

"Well, well, well. What do we have here?" he asked slowly. He glanced at Elliott with a smirk on his lips. "Think you're a warrior, huh?"

A weird *thwoop* sounded next to her a fraction of a second before the gunman gagged horrifically, reached for his throat with one hand, and then dropped to the ground motionless. Stunned, Jenni stared dumbly for a second at the prone body while Elliott returned his dart gun to the right wrist bracer.

"Did you kill him?" she asked, worried. Milliscent tugged on her arm, but she couldn't seem to look away.

"Probably not." He gestured for her to follow the teen. "But I've never hit anyone in the throat with that paralytic agent before, so I can't say for sure."

Probably not? Elliott may have just killed someone, and he stood there emotionless, waiting for her to keep moving. He must be in shock. The guilt would eat him alive when they escaped from this situation. Her feet stumbled forward, and the trio continued on their journey.

Oddly, she didn't feel like hurling anymore, but her energy sank to non-existent. Trudging forward, she took small victories in every single step, amazed her body remained upright and each foot continued to pick itself up and shuffle onward. Step, stick, step. Step, stick, step. She held no illusion the other two could have doubled or tripled their speed, but other than the occasional long-suffering sigh from the young woman guiding them, no one complained.

Her spirits sank and tears welled in her eyes. Rick said she couldn't make this trip safely, that she could get them all killed. She should have listened back then. She held them back. Milliscent and Elliot, they could be captured, turned into slaves, all because she couldn't suck it up enough to move a little faster. But she felt so *tired*.

Keep moving. Keep moving. Step, stick, step. The lopsided boulder up there, make it to that. Good girl! The tree looking like Groucho Marx, that's not too far away. Go there before you beg for them to rest a second.

"Stop." Elliott's voice commanded. Both women turned to look at him in question. "There's been no sign of anyone for a while now, and we need to stop and drink water or we'll start to fall out." He held up his canteen, looking pointedly at Jenni. "Drink."

Jenni wanted to argue with him. She wanted to shove the canteen back at him for the principal of the matter—arrogant, overbearing, dictatorial, chauvinistic pig. But she was thirsty. And tired. And she simply didn't have the fire right now.

"Thank you." It came out meeker than she intended and shame for her weakness washed over her as she reached out and grabbed the offered item and tipped it to her mouth. She saw the look of shock and then worry transform Elliott's face over the bottom of the canister, but he didn't say anything.

After several guzzles, she handed the container to Milliscent. Stumbling to the nearest tree, she leaned heavily and sighed in relief. Gravity won, and she felt her body begin a slow descent against the bark, her hand simultaneously sliding down her walking stick.

"Don't sit down," her husband said, grabbing her pack to keep her from going all the way down. "You won't be able to get back up, sweetheart. I'm sorry."

All of his earlier brusqueness gone, his voice broke on the last two words, and she suddenly realized with perfect clarity his bluster had been a defense mechanism. Knowing how sucky she felt, the difficulty of every single step, he tried to keep her just irritated enough to continue moving on adrenaline. He wanted to carry her, but couldn't. He wanted to carry the pack for her, but couldn't. He didn't want to force her on this trek, but had to. This left him powerless.

She only nodded. "Thank you. It's all right. I'm all right."

"We're getting closer," Milliscent said from a few feet away. "I'd say another half hour at most."

Jenni nodded, breathed in deeply and pushed away from the tree. "Let's do this."

****

Elliott kept one eye on his wife trudging along in front of him while he continuously scanned the area for danger. Heart and stomach in his throat, he mentally shook his fist at the universe…and his mother-in-law for good measure. He used to like the woman. Now, he'd have to do a bang up job of pretending at the next Christmas party.

And those damn erratic whispering voices weren't helping either. How could a guy keep his concentration with five people muttering unintelligibly in his head? Through static, no less, like an old radio turned down low with really bad reception that kept cutting out. Adam was the worst. He loved his brother, was closer to him than any other of the multitude of siblings in the two families. But if he didn't back off soon, Elliott was going to kick his ass the next time they saw each other. How many times would that idiot force him to listen to the same medley of old Queen songs? Granted, it could've been worse. With Adam's sense of humor, he could sing "I'm a Little Teapot" on loop, so maybe he shouldn't complain.

Maybe he went crazy. Or schizophrenic. Maybe he finally snapped. Maybe this entire experience, the entirety of the last six weeks since Jenni arrived at the cabin, had been one long hallucination. That would explain a lot.

My name is Elliott, and I'm going insane.

I'm following my wife through a scraggily terrain.

I'm a lame husband because I'm doing nothing to take away her pain.

Bad meter.

Something moved in the bushes several yards away. Jumping forward, he grabbed each woman by the pack and pulled them down with him to the ground. They turned to him with angry eyes, but he placed his fingers to his lips and gestured with his chin. They understood and their mouths snapped shut in eerie unison. He'd laugh if he had it in him. Jenni closed her eyes and laid her head in the mulch, but Milliscent joined him, peering through the underbrush.

The outer world stood in complete silence.

His inner world softly sang "We Are the Champions" and it took concerted effort not to hum along. Two men stepped into view.

"Uncle Kevin," Milliscent hollered and darted away before Elliott could grab her arm to stop her. The young woman ran across the distance and threw herself into the arms of a thirty-something blond man who twirled her around, laughing with her.

"What?" Jenni asked, raising her head and blinking. "Time to go?" Pulling herself to her arms and knees, she crawled forward.

Pride in her fortitude and determination seeped through his cracking heart. "No, Jenni. You can stop now."

"Oh thank heavens," she mumbled and flopped back down again.

The second man, tall and wide with dark blond hair and a beard, left the teen and her uncle and approached Elliott and Jenni cautiously, arms held out to his sides, palms open to show the absence of weaponry. "I understand you need sanctuary," he said slowly, meeting Elliott's eyes with directness. "My name is Joseph. I am here to help."

"I'm Elliot, and this is Jenni. She's sick. She needs help."

"I don't need help," his wife grumbled on the ground beside him, sounding a little drunk. "I got this."

Frustration and irritation, but mostly relief, flooded through him all at the same time, and he snickered. "Jenni, just shut up. We get it; you're a magical warrior princess."

"I wonder if Shesta will be my animal companion?" She didn't even open her eyes, the only muscle moving in her entire body being her mouth.

"Nithlam might take exception to that." Elliott glanced up for a second at the man hovering nearby and saw the look of confusion and indecision on his face. He apparently had no idea what to do with such a strange pair.

"Their son looked old enough to leave home."

"I'm your animal companion, Jenni, don't go making me jealous."

She snorted and finally lifted her eyelids. "Seriously, though. I'm all right. I feel better, only weak." Crawling to her hands and knees once more, she grabbed the forgotten staff off the ground near her head and used it to prop herself up to her knees. "See? Magical warrior princess. Hear me roar."

"Let's hear it then," he teased as he stood up and tugged on her backpack to help her the rest of the way. Her guttural, heartfelt roar took him by surprise and he laughed. "Impressive, impressive. Now take off your pack."

"No."

He stepped in close and a strange, faint, rhythmic *thump, thump, thumping* sensation prickled at the back of his consciousness, underneath Adam belting out "Somebody to Love." His brother had a decent voice, but only a couple static filled words at a time came through, frequently cut off. Like being stuck in a malfunctioning fast-food drive through with the volume turned down to the lowest setting. Ignoring his descent into madness, he lowered his voice and addressed Jenni.

"You'll walk faster without it. If you and I were alone out here, I'd let you kill yourself hauling it around. You know I would. But there are three other people besides us. Do the math."

She growled, but unsnapped the clip at her waist and let the bag fall to the ground as she glared at him. "Fine."

"Fine." He grabbed her bag, lifting it to his side.

"Will you two quit flirtin'?" Milliscent broke into their argument. "I want to introduce you to my mother's brother. Kevin, this is Elliott and Jenni."

All three of them exchanged nods and nice-to-meet-yous.

"I'll take that," Joseph said, holding a hand toward Jenni's pack. "I know you want your hands free." Elliott reluctantly handed it over.

"You're in safe territory now," Kevin assured them with a smile. "You don't have to pretend anymore."

"Pretend about what?" Jenni asked, letting her gaze slide pointedly to Joseph and then back to Milliscent's uncle.

He cleared his throat and nodded. "Ah, yes. I mean you can be open about your relationship now. No more hiding."

"Oh. Right," they answered in unison and waited for direction.

All five people stared at each other awkwardly for a second, Joseph's eyes narrowing slightly, Kevin shifting from one foot to the other.

"Is something wrong?" Elliott asked.

"Usually at this point," Joseph answered, "people tend to embrace, or kiss…laugh. Show some kind of relief or happiness."

"Oh. Yeah. Well, I'd kiss her and all, but she's got cooties today, so, you know."

"And his hugs," Jenni said, shaking her head with disappointment, "they are sooooo lame." She rolled her eyes for emphasis, leaning heavily on the staff.

The look of shock, horror, and bewilderment on the face of the men sent Jenni into a fit of giggles and when she snorted, Elliott couldn't hold back a snicker. The longer she laughed, the worse his own humor tickled him until he couldn't hold back any longer. Milliscent rolled her eyes at them, smiling widely.

"We're private," Elliott assured Joseph. "The next time I kiss my wife will not be an acceptable public display of affection." Better than saying he couldn't touch her because they might zap into another reality, leaving a teenager behind to die. It probably wouldn't go over well, to admit that.

"Ah, yes. Well, let's get going. The sanctuary is this way." The poor man turned with speed and headed down a narrow path winding haphazardly through the woods.

Soon, Elliott assured himself, watching Jenni begin the trek again with renewed determination and following close behind her. *Soon this will all be over.*

Now if he could get Adam to shut the hell up because listening to his brother singing in his brain about wanting to ride his bicycle in a falsetto voice was just wrong. And what was with the thumping?

Chapter 18

The five travelers continued through the woods, following an invisible path known only to Kevin and Joseph. Jenni knew Elliott followed closely behind her, she heard him singing softly, something about a bicycle for some bizarre reason. Thick underbrush hid the path beneath their feet, and she frequently couldn't see where each footfall landed. Her exhaustion, untied boots, and poor visibility over the uneven terrain made for a hazardous trek. Inevitably, her foot caught on a vine, then twisted on a rock, and she felt herself catapult forward.

Joseph turned around at her surprised yelp, and she landed inelegantly on his side. His right arm instinctively caught her, his left still holding her pack. She extricated herself as quickly as possible, embarrassed over her clumsiness.

"Sorry about that," she mumbled.

"Don't worry about it. Your husband is right, you need help."

"I'm fine."

"Milliscent," Elliott called out, and the teen turned around. "Jenni's staff isn't cutting it anymore. Will you help her?"

"Sure, no problem."

Jenni glared at her husband for his high-handedness, but he ignored her, kneeling at her feet.

"Here, this should help."

He tied her boots, treating her like some kindergartener. How embarrassing. When he finally rose, he smiled his fake smile. Something was wrong. Maybe the man he darted earlier weighed on his mind.

The small group continued on the path, and after fifteen minutes, they broke through the woods into a settlement of small cabins. Haphazardly scattered throughout the trees, there seemed no rhyme or reason to their placement. The community existed in an odd state of modern-meets-frontier. Some wore jeans and t-shirts, while others wore clothes straight out of a prairie show.

"Milliscent," a woman's voice shouted.

"Mom!" The young woman bolted away.

With her support ripped away, Jenni felt herself dropping and aimed her fall into Joseph's body in an attempt to not meet the ground again. She landed with a hard *thud* and she heard his gasp of surprise. Propping her up against his side, he shuffled toward the embracing women like a trooper. She thought maybe his gaze darted in Elliott's direction a few times, but he didn't comment or drop her.

Elliott's jaw looked like he welded it together, but he didn't say anything, keeping a fake pleasant smile on his lips—one that might even fool the strangers around them.

"Jenni, Elliott," Milliscent pulled back from her parent, turning to them with a massive smile, "I'd like you to meet my mother, Zerephine."

They stared at the woman in confusion for a moment. There had to be some mistake. Zerephine could not be any older than early twenties, definitely not old enough to have a sixteen-year-old child unless she started in her tweens. Her long blonde hair hung past her thin waist in rolling waves. Jenni wanted to hate her on sight; she looked like an immortal elf. But the twinkle in her blue eyes and warm smile made it impossible.

Darn it.

"Thank you so much for everything you are doing for my family," Milly's mother said with a shaky voice. "I've been so worried. You are truly angels of mercy."

Elliott reached out and shook the woman's hand, then gestured back to Jenni. "My wife, she's not well. Is there some place she can lay down and rest?"

Instantly, Zerephine's face clouded with concern. "Yes, I'm so sorry. Here, come into my cabin."

Another wave of exhaustion hit and the rest of the journey passed in a fog. They entered a cabin. Milliscent helped her change clothes. Someone brought a drink, and then the blessed comfort of a real bed and a warm quilt embracing her. Jenni sighed in relief as darkness settled.

****

Cup in hand, Jenni stood on the deck in the fading sunset, watching Elliott chopping wood as though a demon taskmaster stood behind his shoulder. This time, he kept his t-shirt on, and sweat stains circled under his armpits and through the charcoal-colored fabric covering his chest and back. A bandana tied around his forehead kept his blondish-brown hair and sweat from falling into his eyes, though he paused for a second to wipe his cheek on his shoulder before continuing. Any of the serene contentment she saw on his face that long ago morning completely absent, his eyes held wild, desperate anger. He let out a sharp "hya!" every couple times the ax slammed into the block.

Grasping the large cup more securely in her hands, she descended the stairs and slowly approached her husband, stopping a few feet away from his work. He finished off his current chunk and glanced up at her, brow raised. She held the drink in his direction, looked him square in the eyes and commanded sternly, "Drink."

One side of his mouth quirked up. "Yes, ma'am."

Sticking the ax into the chopping block, he peeled off his gloves and tossed them beside the ax before grabbing the drink and gulping long and hard. He stopped for a second to breathe heavily a couple times, then finished off the offering with a satisfied "ahhh." Smacking his lips, he held the cup out to her. "Thank you."

She didn't take it back, pulling her arms behind her back and smiling at him with her "I want to play" smile. The one she used to send his mind to the bedroom. "You're welcome. I sauntered over here swinging my hips the way you really like."

She hadn't, honestly, but he raised an eyebrow again, his half smile firmly in place.

"Did you now?"

"Yes. And you were so captivated by my seducing powers you couldn't keep your eyes off me."

"Of course not."

"Now I stand about three inches in front of you, my fingers climbing up your chest which is very firm right now, I must say."

"I love it when your fingers wander."

"I know. And I really love your firm chest. So I

step in closer, and I'm on my tip-toes now, our lips so close. I lick mine."

"That's always sexy."

"And I push fractionally closer until our lips connect."

"So we're kissing right now? In front of Milliscent and her mom and everyone else in this commune?"

"Sanctuary," she corrected. "But, who cares about them, we're lost in our own world. Because I started to do that thing you like." She flicked one eyebrow up for a split second, her smile wide.

"Which one?" he asked, slightly breathless, meeting her eyes intently. "I like a lot of things you do."

"The one with my teeth nibbling your bottom lip."

He sucked in a breath. "Oh yeah. That's a good one."

"And you are so lost in this moment, the energy we have flowing between us, you don't feel me reach into your bracer and pull out the penny."

"Aw, man!"

She held up her hand in his direction, wiggling her fingers. "Come on, come on. You so know it would work."

He huffed indignantly, but pulled out the penny and dropped it into her outstretched palm, making sure to keep his fingers high enough not to touch her. "Brat."

She smiled cheekily at him for a second, flipping it through her fingers, then flicked it into his cup. It pinged as it hit the bottom, then made a clunk on the bounce. "Spill. All of it."

He blew air out heavily through puffy cheeks and glared at her from the corner of his eyes. Undaunted, she plopped her rear end onto the chopping block next to the ax and settled in.

He retrieved the penny and placed the cup on the block with her, on the other side of the ax. "I'm going crazy, Jenni."

What?

He shook his head, and began pacing in front of her. "You know those voices we heard during the last jump?" She nodded. "They never went away. They haunt me. I've got Adam in my freaking head *all the time* now." He pointed to his bandana. "And on top of that, today I had to watch while some other man carried you—"

"He didn't carry me," she said. "He simply let me lean on him."

"That's *my* job. You know, I could have caught you? Twice, I had the power to reach out and stop you from falling, and I let you drop anyway. Into *him*."

"You had no choice. And it's not like I flirted with the guy."

"I know, I don't blame you. I'm not even mad at Joseph, I'm grateful he helped you. But then Milliscent's mom, she helped you change clothes and drink water and tucked you into bed after examining you."

"And it's your job."

"Yes. I'm crawling out of my skin because I *need* to do these things for you, and I'm standing here helpless while other people do it because I can't touch you. We might accidentally gate to Upper Sandusky on Nova Prime, stranding Milliscent here without her key. How do I know she didn't miss something?"

"I'm okay, Elliott."

"I know. It's just…hard. It's always you and me."

Jenni snorted. "And John and Adam and Ilsy and about sixteen or seventeen other siblings. Not to mention cousins, uncles, aunts—"

"You know what I mean."

Yeah. She did. "I'm sorry."

"Don't be, honey. It's my pride I have to get over. This," he waved at the chopping block, "helps to get some of it out. And it mutes Adam a little bit. If I hear 'Bohemian Rhapsody' one more time, I might snap altogether. It's like Chinese water torture, it never ends. Who knows what I might do then?"

Which brought up the original direction she thought this conversation would go. She paused, collecting her thoughts and picking the words carefully. The sun almost completely set, and the stars appeared one by one in the sky. "How are you doing with…that other thing?"

His eyebrows scrunched in confusion. "What other thing?"

Her heart twisted in her chest. Should she drop it? No. He needed to talk about this, too. "That man you darted."

"What about him?"

Um. Really? "You said you weren't sure if you killed him or not."

"Yeah. So?"

"So you may have killed a man, Elliott. I know you. You hate hurting people. You've kept up your training, yeah. But you aren't a murderer. You, the black sheep of both clans, refused to join any of the armed services or police force because you didn't want to get into a situation where you might have to kill someone. You don't hurt people." A memory flashed through her mind. "Anymore." Apparently, in high school he took several shots, remembering her prom date.

He snorted, shocking her. "You, Jenni."

"What?"

"They say I'm your key? Well, I guess you're the key to my dark side because you are right. I will never, ever hurt another human being. Unless they threaten *you*."

She gulped.

"The bastard had a shotgun pointed at you. I don't give a damn if he's dead. And that makes me a monster, yes. I get that. I should be conflicted, tortured. But I'm not. I try to balance out the cosmos by healing everyone else, but the fact remains I will never, ever, hesitate to do whatever it takes to protect you." He paused for second, both in his tirade and his pacing. "It is messed up though I don't feel bad about it, isn't it?"

She didn't know what to say, so she remained quiet. Darkness settled over the night, the moon peeking over the distant horizon. "I don't want you guilt ridden," she finally told him. "I feel…" She struggled, finding the right words. "Overwhelmingly loved. And cherished. Because I know what a selfless, good heart you have."

He snorted.

"You do. You're not a monster."

She saw his face in the starlight, shadows falling here and there. The look he gave her said he disagreed. "Jenni, I have a dark side. I need you to accept my darkness; I can't hide it from you. Everyone else in the world sees what I show them, but I need you to accept this corner of my heart, know it's there. And I need you to love me anyway."

She stood from her seat on his chopping block, walking toward him. She stopped as close as she dared, barely an inch between their bodies. He looked down at her, and she strained her neck looking up at him. "I don't love you in spite of your dark spot, Elliott."

Everything about him drooped slightly—his mouth, his eyes, his shoulders.

"I love you with it. All of you. And I won't pretend it doesn't exist, okay?"

He nodded, swallowing a few times.

"And I say again. You are not a monster."

He took a few deep breaths, staring into her eyes, causing heat to intermix with the gating power slithering through her veins. "I'm throwing my arms around you and hugging you so tightly you can barely breathe," he whispered.

Her breath followed his command and instantly evaporated. She tried to pull in a draught of air, but her lungs merely laughed at her attempt.

"And I am nuzzling you right *here*." His finger hovered over her neck by mere millimeters.

"With your teeth?"

"Uh-huh."

She exhaled, almost feeling it. Something landed in her bra, and she looked down to find the penny nestled between her breasts. "Good aim."

"I have a bird's-eye view. Your turn."

She sighed, stepped back, and walked to the deck. He followed her, and they sat on the top step, side by side, keeping enough distance so as not to touch. The now familiar low current of power continued slithering through her body. Her left heel tapped on the step beneath her feet while he played with his fingers, lacing and unlacing them.

"You wasted a turn, you already know. I'm thinking about you and how much I love you and I'm worried about you."

"There's more," he insisted.

"What makes you say that?"

"My 'Jenni senses' are tingling." He smiled at her, causing the butterflies in her stomach to overload, but she humphed.

"I'm thinking about how we might be home by tomorrow afternoon, but I'm trying not to hope too much, so I'm not overwhelmed with despair when we land in the middle of a freaking swamp with a giant man-eating snot-o-ramus wanting to eat us for dinner."

Elliott chuckled. "Yeah, me too."

"We have one spot of good news, though."

"I could really, really use some good news right about now."

"I talked with Zerephine over dinner, which you missed by the way. We saved you a bowl on the table. She says the gating power won't work if either one of us is asleep, or if I'm aroused."

Elliott froze, shadows cast by the rising moon making his face hard to read. "Seriously?"

Jenni nodded, though she couldn't be sure he could see her. "Yup. So we can't accidentally gate if we're…you know." She waved her hand between the two of them.

"Not if I'm doing my job right, at any rate."

"Like that's ever been a problem for you."

"Aw, you always say the nicest things."

"I wonder why I'm the only one who has to be in a state of arousal to shut down the power? Why not you?"

"Because we'd never get anywhere."

"Oh brother."

"You think I'm joking, but honey, the gating thing is *hot*." She laughed, and he smiled at her. "I'm glad we can't gate while we're sleeping. With our luck, we'd wake up in quicksand."

"Right?" she chuckled. "Zerephine said it's some kind of defense mechanism." She paused for a second, her mind circling back to earlier parts of this conversation. "How's the whole Adam thing going?" she asked. "Is he still serenading you?"

"Thank you for reminding me. For a few moments, I'd managed to relegate him to white noise status and ignore him."

"Maybe you're not going crazy. I heard the voices too, remember?"

"Heard. Past tense. You don't hear them anymore."

"I can understand animals and foreign languages. We're weird, Elliott. We embrace 'weird' in this family." She used her fingers to air quote. "Maybe Adam is actually trying to communicate with you. Have you tried talking to him?"

Elliott stared at her for a second, his expression frozen. "Um. No. I didn't want to feed the crazy."

"Seriously? You know how he is; he won't leave you alone until you answer him. You're lucky he hasn't been singing princess songs the whole time, you know that's all Kayla lets him listen to anymore. The poor guy is probably desperate for adult conversation."

Her husband eyed her with irritation. "You want me to try to talk to the voice in my head?"

"Yes."

"Fine. Hello, Adam." He waited, staring at her. "Oh nice. We've switched to 'Under Pressure'."

Jenni couldn't help but laugh again. "At least he has good taste."

"Until you get a visual in your head of your big brother with big hair and short shorts riding around on a bicycle, and then tell me where the therapy comes in."

She couldn't stop laughing for several minutes, and he simply sat next to her, shaking his head until she calmed down. "That is awesome. I'm going to get Frank to draw that, and we can give it to him for his birthday."

Elliott finally laughed as well. "Perfect."

She wiped tears from her eyes. "Seriously though. You have to really try this time. Close your eyes and try talking to him in your head."

"All right, all right, all right. I feel stupid, though."

She didn't bother answering, merely watched as he closed his eyes. She waited. And waited.

****

Elliott closed his eyes and looked at the darkness of his inner eyelids. He breathed in deeply and tried to ignore the warmth radiating off Jenni next to him. Tried to ignore the odd, rhythmic beat that returned a while ago. It disappeared earlier in the day but returned, stronger now. Not quite a thump, not one he could hear exactly. But he felt it at the edge of his consciousness. Maybe more of a dual *wub, wub* sound. Setting the oddity aside, he concentrated on the voices.

Well…only one voice now. The other's seemed to take a rest, finally, but Adam's voice hung in there, sounding a little hoarse.

"Adam," he thought. His brother continued singing.

He felt dumb. Here he sat, talking to himself. But Jenni wanted him to try, so he ignored the "idiot" sign written across his forehead and tried again.

Adam!

Still, no change. Fine, he'd try one more time, but that's it.

Aaaadaaaaaaamm! He mind shouted it as loud as he could, harkening back to their youth when they screamed across the yard.

The singing stopped.

Ell—at—ou?

Adam? he asked internally, incredulously. *Can you actually hear me?*

Ell it's about da—ime, bro. Took—ou long enou—

Holy cow, I've really gone insane.

His brother laughed. *Tha—wa—lo—time ago, b—dy.*

Ha, ha. You wanna tell me what the hell is going on?

We'll talk mo—wh—n y—et—ome. B—d recepti—

No joke.

We—com—o the da—k si—brother.

You've been waiting for this, haven't you?

For—ong lo—time. Gi—enn—ug fr—m us.

Say hi to Sarah and Kayla. Can't wait to see everyone again.

—ill do, bro. Be ca—efu—ou—there.

Always.

Elliott opened his eyes to realize tears streamed from them, down his face. Jenni stared at him expectantly. "Well?"

"Yeah. Adam spoke to me."

She air pumped a fist twice. "I knew it. You are telepathic. Why didn't Rick mention this earlier?"

"I don't have a clue, but it would have been nice. Somebody needs to write a freakin' manual or something."

"So what did he say? Are they going to rescue us? How is everyone? What is going on?"

"Whoa, whoa," he said, laughing and sniffling, wiping away the stream of tears. "Bad reception, we barely understood each other. He said we'll talk more when we get home, so he obviously thinks we'll make it back. But other than connecting and sending love from his wife and the squirt, we're still in the dark."

"Crap." She paused and they both stared at the stars overhead for a few seconds. "Still. It's nice to know we can communicate. That we have a lifeline to sanity."

"Yes. Yes, it is."

They watched the sky together for another few moments, but Jenni eventually sighed. "I know I took a long nap today, but I'm still exhausted."

"Go to bed. The sooner you fall asleep, the sooner I can join you."

She smiled widely. "It'll be the first night we sleep in the same bed in over three months."

"One hundred and fourteen days."

"But who's counting, right?"

He smiled at her, and she smiled back before she stood and turned into the house. "Goodnight."

The door clicked shut, and he continued to stare at the night sky, trying to identify any familiar constellations. The rhythmic *wubthump* disappeared.

Adam's voice disappeared. For the first time in two days, Elliott finally had his head to himself. Sighing in relief, he pulled off the bandana and rubbed his fingers through his hair to loosen the sweat-dried clumps. Lying back, he settled against the deck and let the night enfold him. Honeysuckle and pine floated on a soft, warm breeze. Crickets chirped in the trees. A frog croaked in the distance. An owl hooted. The moon, three quarters full, hung sleepily in the night sky.

He let himself simply exist for a while, enjoying the fact Jenni lay a few feet away, just behind that wall. They were safe for the moment, and they were together. The nebula above looked like a blob of cotton candy. The field of stars resembled a giant pepperoni pizza.

They needed to eat at Marco's Pizza when they finally made it home.

He needed to eat dinner.

Sighing, he finally stood and entered the darkened cabin. Already given the grand tour, he decided not to turn on the generator he'd been shown earlier and located a lantern on the countertop. Deftly lighting the wick, he found a plate of stew on the table waiting for him. Elliott wolfed it down without even caring about the temperature, and rinsed off the dish in the sink. Taking the lantern with him, he quietly stepped into the shower room to find a fluffy towel and a pair of pajamas Milliscent's mother loaned him. He didn't know where they came from, but they'd fit all right.

Surprised to find the water scalding hot without the generator running, he spent only a moment wondering how they managed that small engineering miracle before deciding he didn't really care. Without hurrying, Elliott allowed the water to pummel and loosen his muscles, draining away the sweat, dirt and grime. Barely able to keep his eyes open, he quickly dried off, pulled on the nightwear and blew out the lamp before silently making his way to the bedroom allotted to them.

Gingerly, he opened the door and squeezed inside, closing it behind him.

Wubthub-wubthub-wubthub…the rhythm competed with Jenni's slow, even breathing. She lay sleeping on the bed. What was that noise? Louder now, he felt it in his chest and heard it. He crept across the room and the beating grew louder. And then it dawned on him. The sound—a heartbeat.

Could she be sick again? He felt the blood drain from his face, and he had to swallow rising panic. Heart in his throat, he gently sat down on the edge of the bed and reached over to place his hand gently on her forehead. No sweating or erratic breathing. He moved his fingers to her wrist, carefully counting his wife's pulse. No, not that. Her heart rate seemed fine- slow and regular.

This beat faster. Much faster.

He closed his eyes and listened intently.

The flutter, it sounded so famil—Holy Hanna!

His eyes shot open in shock, his jaw dropping open, his own heart racing, causing the blood to pound in his ears.

Jenni's pregnant.

Chapter 19

Overwhelming, all consuming, crushing joy poured over Elliott and exploded from the inside. He choked on it, gasping for breath and clutching his heart with shaking hands. Tears streamed unchecked down his cheeks. Closing his eyes, he counted carefully. *Wub-thub-wub-thub-wub-thub.* The hunter's cabin happened a little over six weeks ago, quickly calculating, he sighed in relief. They were right on point, her heart healthy.

Swallowing, he lowered to his stomach on the bed and slowly, reverently, reached out, gently placing his hand on Jenni's lower abdomen. "Hey there, Cricket," he whispered, caressing softly. "Daddy's here." He smiled at the sound of that. Daddy. He had to swallow again. "We've waited a long, long time for you."

Six years, to be precise—at least for him. Not that Jenni knew. She only threw out her birth control two years ago.

He looked over at his wife, sleeping peacefully on her side. Her breathing slow and regular. Her hands tucked under her pillow, her mouth slightly open. So full of emotion for this courageous, strong, determined woman, it poured from him uncontrollably. Surely, she had to feel the actual waves as it flowed from his body and filled the room. His best friend. His co-conspirator. His lover. The mother of his child.

He wanted to wake her up and tell her. He wanted to see her joy. He wanted to share this moment with her. He wanted… it didn't matter what he wanted. She needed sleep. Cricket needed her to sleep. Tomorrow would be long and possibly dangerous. Who knows where they will gate to? Despite Zerephine's assurances, there were no guarantees they'd land in Porthinch on the first try. If Jenni woke up with morning sickness again, it might make their travels even more difficult, and she needed a reserve of energy.

And he knew how his wife would react when she found out—it would be automatic, instinctive, unstoppable. She'd throw her arms around his neck and hug him mercilessly. To ask her to do anything less, to stop any physical contact in the moment she finally realized her greatest wish of the last two years, would be cruel. Heartless. He must wait a little longer.

Thinking about what lay ahead tomorrow, fear settled in the pit of his stomach—festering, clawing, ripping. Would gating harm Cricket? They could transport their child into a battle zone. His breath shorted out, his mind careening at all the horrible scenarios that could possibly happen. Panic bubbled, threatening to burst into full blown terror.

Stop!

Think.

Closing his eyes, he centered his mind on the rhythmic beating and regulated his breathing to match, slow and steady. Breathing in on ten thumps, breathing out on ten. The panic melted around the edges, and he could rationalize coherently. He and Jenni already jumped multiple times since this pregnancy started, and Cricket's heartbeat sounded…and felt…robust and healthy. Gating itself must not be detrimental to the unborn.

Thank heaven.

He held onto that hope, continuing his deep breathing, focusing his mind. Tomorrow would come no matter what he did. They would gate. They might end up in scary situations. But this is the new norm, and he could not spend his life in a state of terror. Jenni needed him to think clearly. To strategize. To be one step ahead of whatever pitfall might open up beneath their feet. To protect Cricket.

He swallowed, feeling calmer. He was made for this. All these years, his true purpose for living finally came to fruition. His father prepared him, and he was good at his job. He and Jenni, they could do this together, no matter what might happen.

Opening his eyes, he leaned in closer to Jenni's reposed form.

"Hey, sweetheart," he whispered to his baby. Tonight, they were safe. This moment of introduction would never come again and he wanted to make the most of it while he could. Carefully, he leaned over and kissed under Jenni's bellybutton. "I know you're just starting out on this whole adventure, and things might be a little rough. But Mommy, she's having a hard time." He caressed where his lips touched. "If you can, try to take it easy on her, okay? She and I, we love you. More than you will ever know." He chuckled. "I made you a crib already…"

He continued talking, telling his child about the nursery, about the booties and blanket Mommy currently worked on. About the tree swing and sandbox he planned to build in their yard. He talked and talked and talked until his words slurred, his eyelids dropped and his hand fell away. At last, he joined his little family in quiet slumber, wrapped in the warm comfort of his baby's heartbeat.

****

Elliott woke in a good mood, the bastard. Like, a really good mood. A fantastic mood. The kind where he hummed under his breath and smiled constantly, which would be fine if it wasn't six-thirty in the friggin morning. Jenni growled and rolled over, pulling the blankets over her head.

"Come on, sleepy head. Time to get up."

Seriously? *Six years of marriage, and he thinks that's going to work?* Did he completely forget The Semester—an entire five months of getting cussed out every morning when he pulled her butt out of bed to make it on time to that stupid early morning class with the stupid professor who only offered the one stupid timeslot?

"You haven't gotten laid in over month, you have no right to be this cheerful," she grumbled at him, fortifying the seal of her cocoon by tucking the ends of the quilt under her body. She knew his tactics.

He only laughed.

Laughed.

At six freaking thirty.

Bastard.

"Go away." *Stupid man. Stupid barbarian who gets up at 5am every stupid day just to work out and train.*

"How do you feel this morning?" he asked solicitously, angering her further.

"I don't know, I'm not awake yet. Give me thirty more minutes."

"All right, honeybunch. Thirty minutes."

She felt pressure against her cheek, where he probably kissed her through the quilt, and then a short hard smack against her butt. And then blessed silence. Oh, thank heavens, he left the room. She didn't stop to ponder why he gave up so easily, simply took the reprieve with gratitude and fell back asleep a few short seconds later.

It was a gift.

As promised, her internal alarm clock activated thirty minutes later and she found herself semi-awake. And starving. The low hum of a generator nearly soothed her back to slumber, but she resisted. Extracting herself from the warm cocoon, she stumbled bleary eyed and disheveled out to the open living room/kitchen area to find Milliscent and Zerephine, sitting at a table eating stacks of pancakes. They looked rested and disgustingly well put together. Elliott stood over the stove holding a spatula and wearing a pink frilly apron. He looked up with a bright smile.

Oh come on. This was so over the top, even for him.

"Hey there, beautiful," he said with a gleaming smile.

She rolled her eyes, knowing full well she looked like the keeper of the crypt right now. Normally, he'd be the first person to point that out to her, but his fabulous mood blinded him, apparently. She grunted at him in greeting and shuffled closer to the kitchen, doing an amazing imitation of a zombie. She looked down to see if any skin was peeling off her arms, just to make sure. Because she felt like one at the moment.

"How's your stomach?" her husband asked,

pointing to the counter where several plates sat waiting for her. "If you're nauseous, I have crackers and water. It'll help calm your stomach to put something in it right away." He pointed to the boring plate to show her the option. "If not, there's pancakes, watermelon, or oatmeal and toast. Or, I can whip up some cream of wheat for you, I know you like it on cold mornings. I'll add blueberries," he said.

"Oatmeal and toast," she answered, trying to get her brain functioning enough to hear past his good cheer and pick something.

"No problem." He waved toward the table while he picked up a bag of bread and headed to the toaster with intent.

"With blueberries."

"You got it."

"And pancakes."

"They are ready on the plate there."

"Where's the watermelon?" No judging.

"On the table." He smiled at her over his shoulder, pushing down the lever on the toaster and bringing the other items she asked for to the table, then returning to his cooking.

"I take back everything I said earlier," Milliscent whispered as she slid into the seat next to the teen. Jenni raised her eyebrow as she reached for the jug of orange juice and poured herself a glass. "You are definitely not his slave," the girl explained. "I think he's yours."

She smiled and chuckled. "He's a little extreme this morning. I think he's excited to get you where you need to be and go home."

The teen's face fell. "I'm sorry for all the trouble

I've put you guys through."

Jenni patted her arm. "We're glad we could help, Milly. Don't, for one second, think we'd ever choose differently."

Then she dug into the food with fervor.

"I thought you'd want to know," their host told them, "Kevin got through to Rick last night. The overland company deflected the slavers with only three people missing—their medic and two passengers. No other major injuries or losses."

Relief swept through her and she sighed in gratitude. "Thank you. I was worried."

"Unfortunately, we're short on time now. Kevin also communicated with Jeremy's father and it seems their region is destabilizing. They won't be able to hold their position much longer. I wanted to give you a day or so of practice, but it looks like we'll have to hurry things along."

Jenni swallowed her watermelon with trepidation. "It's always something, isn't it?"

"After breakfast, we can go over basic techniques in the living room, and give you guys a chance to practice initiating and stopping a jump. When you think you're ready, we'll all pack and take the plunge."

"Why can't Jeremy's parents gate him somewhere else that's safe?" Jenni asked.

"They aren't gaters, they are guardians."

"Wait, so a guardian can give birth to a key or a gate?" Elliott asked from the kitchen.

Zerephine looked at them with compassion. "You really have not been told anything have you?"

"No," Jenni answered grumpily, cutting a triangle of pancakes dripping with syrup and popping it into her mouth. "Everyone likes to tell us as little as possible."

"The race is gatekeeper," Milliscent's mom explained. "As a gatekeeper, you are a gate, a key or a guardian. Two gatekeepers will produce any one of the three as offspring, however, there will always be far more guardians than gaters—gates and keys."

"So all of those men working with Rick?" Jenni asked.

"No," Elliott refuted. "No way. None of them have the strength or skillset to be a natural guardian. My eight-year-old sister is harder to beat than they are."

"He's right," their host confirmed. "It's completely different. They are simply a group of men helping Rick try to change things, but they are not gatekeepers. He felt the title appropriate for his band of renegades." She paused with a small, sad frown. "Since Aaron's disappearance, it's only me, Kevin and Rick now. Being stuck here, he's trying to make the best of things, help where he can. It's the guardian way. They can't help it, it's in their nature."

"Protect and serve," Elliott said, quoting the families' motto as he placed a bowl in front of Jenni.

"Exactly."

No wonder all their siblings were law enforcement, firefighters, or in the armed services. How did Uncle Malachi become a rancher?

"You two are an anomaly," Zerephine said, sitting back in her chair.

Jenni paused with a spoonful of blueberry oatmeal halfway to her mouth. "How's that?"

"It's incredibly rare for a gating team to have both sets of parents as gaters themselves. Everyone expected you two to be supernaturally powerful."

"You mean, for gatekeeper standards," Elliott snarked as he pulled out a chair at the table to join them. He ditched the apron at some point.

Their host smiled. "Yes, the whole thing is unfair, but everyone had very high hopes. The high council was very disappointed when you didn't show any signs of transmorphing."

"Bully for them," Jenni grumbled and chewed the berries indignantly.

"I need to warn you two, you need to stay under their radar. If they find out you've transitioned, you will be—"

The door burst open, and Kevin rushed in. "We're out of time, we have to go now."

Oh good grief, what now?

Elliott didn't suffer from her moment of dithering; he had already jumped to his feet and traveled halfway across the living area. "What's going on?" He stopped at his pile of weapons in the corner and started suiting up.

Jenni, finally coming to her senses, ran to the bedroom to grab the framed backpack she never unpacked. Why were they always jumping in her pajamas? Carrying her bag in one hand and boots in the other, she raced back out to the living area. Plopping down on the sofa, she jammed her feet into the boots vaguely hearing Kevin explain something about earthquakes or a volcano or tsunami…some kind of disaster.

"My power doesn't turn on and off like that. I can't jump on command," she interrupted, tying her laces. She felt the thrum of energy building, but would it be enough?

"You're on cycle right now," Zerephine told her. "So you can do this. You only need some guidance."

"On cycle? I haven't noticed any kind of pattern with this whole thing."

"It's erratic the first little while, but most people settle into a rhythm. Hopefully, you will too, eventually."

Everyone stood in the living area now. Milliscent wore her framed pack and held a large duffel bag in her hands. Zerephine gestured to Elliott. "Come over here and stand in front of your gate." He did as instructed. "Now, Jenni, close your eyes." She lowered her lids and breathed deeply. "You feel that current of electricity?" She nodded. "Good. Concentrate on it. Breathe it in. Visualize it running through your veins. It is a flame. Gently blow on it, stoke it so it grows."

Jenni tried to clear her mind, focusing on the power. She pictured the course of its movement, starting in her heart and traveling outward, through her chest, arms legs, feet hands. She mentally pushed, trying to make it faster, stronger, hotter. Prickles on her skin made her gasp as the intensity grew. Need filled her, consumed her and she heard a whimper escape her lips.

"You're doing great. Now open your eyes."

Elliott stood in front of her, his mouth quirked up in a lopsided smile. "Hello, Glow Girl."

Sure enough, Jenni lit up like a light bulb. She smiled back. "Hello there, handsome. Want some of this?"

"Absolutely."

Kevin coughed.

"What's next?" Elliott asked, not looking away.

"For everyone the trigger is different, but let's try the standard approach first. The more you play with the combination, the smoother you'll get at jumping and more elegant your style." Elegant? They wanted fancy? "Both of you, bring your hands up to face each other, but don't touch."

They followed her instructions, holding their hands as mirror images two inches apart. Light formed between their palms, stretching out from both to meet in the middle, little tiny threads of electricity zapping back and forth. Adrenaline pumped through Jenni's veins and she heard Elliott chuckle.

"It's quite the rush, isn't it?" he whispered.

"We're out of time, we have to go *now*," Kevin interrupted, his head quirked to one side, his eyes glassy and distant. "They had to relocate; we're aiming for the Sherderon Overpass now."

"Did you relay that to Edgar?" Zerephine asked.

"Doing so now."

"Sorry guys, no time to practice. We're going to touch you now, but do not connect until my cue."

"Got it." Every cell in Jenni's body cried out to join hands, to reach across the tiny distance and fuse with her key to ignite this explosion desperate for release, but she held back, gritting her teeth.

"You've got this," Elliott whispered to her as she felt a hand descend on each shoulder. She couldn't look to see anyone's position, her gaze glued to her key, her lifeline, the very breath keeping her grounded. His green eyes stared back at her intently. "You can do this, Jenni. You are woman, hear you roar."

She growled, trying to imitate Shesta, and he chuckled. Sweat beaded on her forehead, her arms and legs shaking, the electricity zapping louder, hotter, burning her.

"Hang in there, baby, hang in here. Let's do this together. Breathe in through your nose, two, three, breathe out your lips, two, three." He breathed in time with her as he counted.

"Now!" Zerephine called and their hands clashed together.

Concussive shockwave, lightning, whirlpool, white mist, standing in the eye of the storm. Loss of air. Hair tossed wildly in the wind. Thousands of voices whispering, calling, cajoling, in her head. Jenni almost felt used to this.

"I've never seen it happen this way before," Zerephine called beside her in shock, still holding onto Jenni's shoulder and staring at the flashing pictures and doors with wide eyes.

"Welcome to our world," Elliott responded ruefully.

Chapter 20

Hey, Adam? Elliott asked inside his head, keeping vigilant watch over his wife as she and Zerephine discussed whatever invisible pictures they saw in the swirling mist and the best options for entrance. Cricket's heartbeat not only remained stable through this whole process, but he felt her heartbeat stronger, more energized and filled with vitality.

Yeah, brother?

He sighed in relief. *What do you know about Porthinch?*

You're not going there? His brother sounded horrified.

We have no choice; a couple of teens will die if we don't.

It's a raging mess right now. They're in the middle of civil war between the three sentient species and yesterday the high council banned all traffic into that realm and locked the doors. Everyone should have already been evacuated. I don't even know how you'll get in there.

Edgar and Martha are supposed to get us in somehow. At least three guardians are still there, I don't know if there're any more.

Doesn't surprise me, his brother grumbled. *The council doesn't give much time to get everyone out when they make these choices, they look better politically to show decisive action.*

Tell me about the Sherderon Overpass.

Forget about the overpass, you need to know about the Tellblock. The only way to take them down is cut off their tail horns.

Tail horns?

And the Jimlick, their spit will burn you.

Great, another thing with acidic bodily fluids. Like the giant tick wasn't enough.

When and how did you get to Alaria? That place has been lost for decades.

Thankfully, a short trip. What does a Jimlick look like?

Bipedal. Green with yellow eyes and big teeth. Do you have any backup, or is it just you? Sarah and I would be there in a heartbeat, but I don't know any gates who can get past the locks.

I have some guy named Kevin with me. Don't know his last name, but he knows Edgar.

I don't know him, so I don't know for sure if he's any good, but if he's friends with Edgar he's probably got skills. You know how him and Dad are. I'll stay on standby and talk you through anything you might need to know.

Thanks, man.

"According to Edgar," Kevin said to the group, looking blindly into the air in front of him as his hand rested on Elliott's shoulder, "Martha says to look for a green haze. It was the only way she could disguise the entrance and still mark it for you."

"Green haze, green haze," both women mumbled under their breath as they scanned the blank white wall.

"Do you see anything?" Milliscent whispered to

him.

He shook his head.

"There!" Zerephine pointed victoriously. "See it?"

Jenni squinted in the general area. "Wait. Yes. There it is."

"It's gone."

"Hold on. Wait for it. There it is again." His wife squinted and bobbed up and down fractionally on loose knees. "One two three, one two four, one two three, one two five, one two…got it." He watched his wife breathe in deeply. "I can time it right, but I feel like I have a thousand tentacles holding me. I can't jump with precise timing while carrying everyone."

"You can let go of one of Elliott's hands," Zerephine instructed. "Kevin, come over here and hold my hand. Milliscent, take Elliott's other." The five lined up in a single line, keeping contact.

"You sure this will work?" Jenni asked doubtfully.

"Pretty sure. I hope the power will transfer all the way through to Kevin. He's the only one in danger of being left behind."

The man didn't look too worried, merely resolute.

"Okay," Jenni said, taking a deep breath. "Everyone take three steps closer." Elliott felt the cold swish of the swirling mist on his nose. "On the count of three. One…two…THREE!"

****

All five jumped, aiming for the exact same point, but nobody crashed into each other. Instant freefall, then an invisible cord around her chest yanked hard, pulling them through a strange greenish tunnel of light. Jenni felt like the lead in a V-shaped flock of birds migrating for the winter. The cord pulled, another force pushed, sending them faster and faster. Snapshots of other worlds and realities against the green light sped by until they became long blurry lines. On and on, the never ending rollercoaster cascaded at inhumane speeds—up down, over, around, spinning.

Jenni felt irrational pride in the fact she hadn't lost her mammoth breakfast yet.

The green tint faded away, slowly replaced by white light, then blue and white fluffy clouds. A world emerged, warped, twisted, bulging big and then contorting inward, shrinking. "Jenni," Elliott yelled over the noise of the whispering voices, "when we land, duck and cover and pull out your dagger."

"Milly, Zepha," Kevin shouted, "run north as fast as you can, we're coming in hot!"

Bam! The ground appeared beneath their feet as if they stood there the entire time, and the world snapped into focus. Instantly, Jenni dropped to the ground, releasing the hands she held and covered her head with one while reaching behind her with the other to pull the dagger out of a side pocket. Metal clashed overhead, grunting, squishy sucking, screaming.

"Jenni," Elliott shouted on a grunt while something hissed angrily, "when I say go, you need to stab up and out with everything you have."

She waited. She counted. One. Two. Three. More grunting, hissing, clashing, yelling.

"Go!"

She sprang, heart pumping, using all her lower body strength to propel herself upward and outward, holding nothing back. The blade sliced into something green with yellow eyes and sharp, dripping fangs. It gurgled and stumbled backward, falling off her knife.

"Duck and cover!"

She dropped and crouched, hands covering her head with the knife sticking straight up, trying to swallow bile rising in her throat and hold tears at bay as a whooshing noise sounded directly above her head.

"Go, Jenni," Elliott yelled. "Run to the water."

She sprang up once again and scanned the battle scene for a split second, purposely choosing to ignore the carnage, searching for her destination. There in the distance, a creek. Jamming the dagger into her waistband and bolting away, she ran as fast as she could, the pack weighing her down and slowing her momentum. A green creature appeared in front of her, trying to cut her off, but she dodged to the side while a large knife sailed past her head and landed in its neck. It gurgled on yellow blood as it dropped to the ground. Its arm landed in her path and she stumbled over it, but something grabbed her pack long enough to keep her from falling.

She kept running. Her lungs burned. Her legs ached. Heavy footfalls and two sets of regulated breathing behind her let her know someone followed, but she didn't stop to look. She only moved. Elliott said if she wanted to keep them alive in battle, then she had to follow his instructions exactly. By all that was holy in all the universes, she would continue to run until he told her to stop or the world ended.

The creek grew closer and she saw Milliscent and Zerephine waving at her, pointing to a bridge. In the distance, on the other side of the creek, three people raced toward them—a man, a woman, and a teenage boy, bows and arrows in their hands. The adults looked like accountants caught up in an apocalypse, while the youngest male had bright purple hair and thick black eye liner, matching his black pants and knee-high boots. Celtic symbols covered his face, neck and arms and he wore a white, short-sleeved tunic top.

Milly was going to love him.

In fact, the young woman froze, jaw dropped, eyes bugging out of her head. She stood transfixed as both teams of three converged on their location from opposite directions. Her hands lit up brightly, the glow slowly spreading up her wrists, then her arms and neck, but she seemed oblivious to her condition.

"Run," Elliott and Kevin yelled to the young woman and her mother from behind Jenni.

"Run!" The three archers hollered from across the creek.

"We'll cover you," the woman called as she drew her bow and notched an arrow, letting it fly. Jenni didn't bother looking to see the target or if it fell, she grabbed Milly's arm on her way past and yanked her into action. They sped across the bridge, past the guardians and up the path their backup traveled down.

She heard an explosion, and still she didn't bother turning, she simply ran. Uphill.

They were so buying a treadmill when they got home.

Jenni's lungs burned, chest heaving in and out as it cried out for more oxygen. Her muscles screamed. A small fortress appeared at the top of the hill, a cement bunker thing with short, wide, high windows.

"Get inside," someone hollered, and she followed Zerephine and Milliscent through the wide front opening.

They stood in a large, dark room. Sunlight filtered

through the windows near the roof, but it did little to warm the space or make it welcoming. More bodies ran in, and three people heaved the door closed. The male accountant/archer stepped over to a ledge under one of the windows and looked out, searching the area.

"I figure we have about thirty minutes, tops, until we're overrun." He turned to the small group of people. "Good to see you, Zerephine. We were sorry to hear about Aaron."

"There's been no news?" the woman asked.

The young mother shook her head. "Not really, but Kevin's connections think the Rogues might have taken him. Once Milliscent transmorphs, Kevin and I will search for him."

At the mention of the teen's name, Jenni's attention shifted to the small drama playing out beneath the parent's noses. The boy and girl eyed each other warily from across the room as Jeremy moved random articles of supplies from one pile to another. Milliscent, still glowing in splotches across her body, took a deep breath, squared her shoulders and marched over to the young man.

"I don't believe in love at first sight," she declared defiantly. "And I don't know if I'll ever want to get married."

Jeremy, wide eyed at first, slumped slightly, a smile growing on his face. "Oh *thank you*," he breathed out in apparent relief, holding up one flat palm and pointing to it with the other hand. "Bring it in, sister, that deserves a high five. Right here." Milly smacked his hand, which he immediately tried to turn into a fist-bump she missed. "I was so afraid," he said, grabbing her wrist and shaping her hand like a fist, then bumping against his, "I would get stuck with some starry-eyed, vapid girl who only wanted to stare at each other dreamily all day."

"Ew."

"Right? Not to mention, we're only sixteen."

"I know. And what if we don't even ever *like* each other like that? Who says we have to be together in that way?"

"Exactly." Jeremy nodded, his purple hair bouncing around with the movement of his head. "So we're in this together, right? We're gonna stand firm? When the whole marriage thing raises its ugly head, we're gonna tell them to go to hell."

Milliscent smiled brightly, and the young man blinked a couple of times. "Absolutely. You're not as bad as I thought you would be."

"Likewise."

Jenni snickered to herself and chewed on her lip.

"Should I warn him?" Elliott whispered beside her.

She shook her head. "Naw. Don't ruin the fun. They'll figure it out on their own."

"The glowing thing is awesome," Jeremy told Milliscent, and Elliott coughed. Jenni elbowed him in the ribs.

"So what's the plan?" Kevin asked, interrupting the conversations in the room. "We don't have much time until all hell breaks loose on us. We're sitting ducks and this won't hold forever. How do we get out of here?"

Ah crud.

Accountant-lady cleared her throat. "Jeremy and Milliscent can transmorph—"

"It doesn't work that way," Jenni, Elliott and Zerephine all said simultaneously.

Every guardian stared at them in confusion. "That's the whole point of bringing you here. You said she was activating."

"Yes," Jenni said, "but it's not automatic. I don't know how long Zerephine suffered through her attacks before she finally changed, but I went *years* before the final event."

Zerephine cleared her throat. "Milliscent is far enough along they could transmorph at any minute, if they stay in physical contact with each other. Or it could be hours, maybe days. Yes, it will happen soon, but, like giving birth, there's no exact science. It happens when it happens and can't be forced."

"Well, Elliott and I have to gate everyone out of here anyways, what's two more, right?" Jenni asked with more confidence than she actually felt. "I can't tell you where we'll end up, but it can't be any worse than being stuck in a war zone with no exit strategy, right? Kevin, can you get my dad to tell Mom to push us somewhere? Anywhere?"

"Can't, communication is down, the locks have blocked everything."

"Yeah, I lost Adam the second we touched down as well," Elliott confirmed.

An explosion blasted outside, several yards away from the bunker, shaking the ground. "Fabulous," Jenni grumbled, trying to stay upright.

"Why are they attacking you anyways?" Milliscent asked. "What did you guys do to these people?"

"They aren't attacking us," Jeremy's dad said, once again scanning through the window. He suddenly ducked back as another explosion hit. "Two of the factions are fighting each other, and we are stuck in the middle. Both sides will take down anyone not of their own species."

Another explosion shook the building.

"Jenni," Elliott asked under his breath worry coloring his tone, "do you really think you can do this? Are you juiced enough?" His eyes searched hers, and she couldn't lie.

"I don't have a choice, do I? I can't leave anyone behind."

"We'll stay," Jeremy's mom said instantly, pointing to herself and her husband. "You'll have a better chance the fewer people—"

"No," Jenni insisted. She would not leave anyone. Period. "We all go. I can do this. Get your stuff together while I…while I get my juices flowing."

She ignored the look of shock and doubt on Zerephine's face, the look of disbelief on Kevin's. The look of concern on her husband's face. She could do this. She just needed to push harder. Be more.

"Stand here," she pointed to the floor directly in front of her.

"Yes, ma'am," Elliott responded somberly and obeyed.

His toes spaced only an inch away from hers, his body threatened to accidentally bump against her, and his nearness substantially increased the low hum she felt slithering through her system. She loosened her muscles and stared at his chest in front of her. Concentrating on the dark fabric of his shirt, she zoned out, letting the power in her veins become her entire reality. Jenni visualized the energizing force, its light and brilliance. Reaching into the core of her being, she pushed, growing the light. She felt it, swimming through her, getting bigger, stronger, heavier, but it wasn't enough.

She needed more. She needed more fuel. Where did a gate get fuel?

Elliot. The light between their hands on the last jump.

"I need your energy," she gasped.

"How?"

Holding her hands up and out to her sides, palms flat, her husband mirrored her movement. Tickling threads arched between them. The air crackled, thick with electricity, the pressure inside her body starting to build. His hands began glowing white, the light stretching outward, meeting hers in the small empty space between their palms. Breathing hard, sweat now trickling down her forehead, she baited the power, pushed it, made it grow like the hot core of a volcano.

"More Elliott, give me everything you've got."

She heard him gasp. His hands, like hers, shook, his biceps bulging. She daren't look up to see his face, because she knew they might not survive this. She was killing him, sucking his life force away and he let her, fed her, pushed harder. The pressure mounted inside her stomach, inside her head, inside her chest, legs, arms. The molten lava now coursing through her veins screamed mercilessly for release- the explosion inevitable.

"Everyone, hold on," she screamed.

She felt pressure as people made connection.

"Now!"

Their hands clashed and a thousand suns erupted, shattering reality, blinding her, scattering her particles to the universe.

Chapter 21

Wind and white mist erupted through the blinding explosion of light, whipping Elliott's hair around his head and sucking what little breath remained in his lungs. Jenni collapsed against his body, causing fear to spike through him. Miraculously, to his eternal relief, he held her weight as she drained his life energy, sucking it into her own system to combine it with hers and pushed it outward. How long could they maintain before they both were drained and this gate collapsed?

If it fell before they jumped, would they all die? Would they be trapped forever between realms? He looked down to find Jenni with jaw clenched, gasping for air through her nose, crying inwardly on a low moan. For everything she took from him, she gave ten times more, sending it to fuel this massive white tornado. He tried to hear Cricket's heartbeat, but the wind and shouting voices erased any hope of that assurance.

"Hang in there, honey, you're doing it. You're doing great." His voice sounded strained to his own ears, and he tried not to cringe.

"This has never been done before," Zerephine hollered to be heard over the whirlpool. "No one has ever gated this many people in a single jump."

"Look at me," Jenni gasped, a shudder rippling through her body. "Doing what I do best."

"Where are we going?" Kevin asked, staring at the blank white swirling mass surrounding them.

Jenni choked, her legs giving out and Elliott wrapped his already straining arms around her and her pack to hold her up. "I'm going to lose it soon."

"There," Zerephine said, pointing to some obscure spot in the white mist that, to Elliott, looked only like white cloud. "Thumdalla, it's perfect. I have a cousin there who'll—"

"Jump," Jenni yelled. "Show them where to jump and go."

"We have to go together," Zerephine insisted.

"No, I'll push the energy through, but each of you jump. I can get Elliott and I home, but you guys need to jump first. Grab your bags and get out."

"This has never been done before. No one has ever gated people to two different locations on a single jump."

"There's a first for everything. All we can do is try." Another shudder passed through his wife's body and panic bloomed. Elliott needed to calm down, he needed to stay strong. His legs buckled and he landed on his knees, still holding Jenni close to his chest.

"Jeremy and Milliscent first."

The group, keeping constant physical contact, reassembled into a long chain. Holding hands, their human rope reached the edge of the vortex. They scooted closer until they skimmed the exact spot Zerephine indicated. Jeremy pushed out his hand, then his arm. The entire chain scooted closer as he walked through. Then Milliscent, then Jeremy's mother. One by one, they disappeared until only Zerephine remained. She turned back to Elliott and Jenni with awe and fear.

"Don't ever let the high council know what you have done here today."

"Why—"

But she jumped, leaving their questions unanswered.

The vortex tightened. Jenni gasped. Another shudder ran through her body. Did he have enough strength to jump for them both? "Hold on a little longer, Jenni. We're almost home."

She nodded.

"Where do I go? Point the way, I'll get us there."

He wanted to rip the framed pack off her back to get a better grip around her torso, but he had to conserve all his remaining strength for the jump, so he merely adjusted his hold and staggered to his feet again. They now held each other upright. It would not last long.

"Over there," she croaked, pointing a shaking finger.

Together they lurched, step by agonizing step, closer to the white wall until he felt the cold chill sweep against his skin.

"On the count of three," she whispered. "One…two…three."

They collapsed forward, completely spent, landing with an agonizing *thud* on hardwood floor. Long, loud, cold wind rushed into him on a *whoosh*, pouring the drained life force back into his body, and he felt vitality bury itself deep below his aches and pains and fatigue. The whirlpool vanished behind them. The cacophony of whispering voices died.

Multiple weapons jabbed into his body in various

places, but he couldn't move or shift to adjust the pressure. *Wubthubwubthubwhubthub*. The most beautiful sound in existence graced his ears, and he laughed in grateful relief.

"Ouch."

"Yeah," he agreed, taking small breaths in an attempt to regulate something, somewhere. This inability to move felt strikingly similar to what happened after Nithlam and Shesta chased them all those weeks ago.

"Where are we?"

He opened one eye to find them laying in the entryway separating their living room and dining room at home. "We're home," he gasped. "You did it, Jenni. You brought us home."

He tilted his head in her direction to see her swallow heavily, tears streaming from closed eyes down her cheeks to drip on the floor beneath her face. "What day is it?"

Without moving any limbs, he glanced toward the table and saw his phone lying at the edge where he left it that first morning. "I'll go look."

Elliott. Adam's worried voice called out to him as he experimented with turning over.

He found moderate success, flopping inelegantly. *Hey Adam, we made it. We're back home. The others, did they make it?*

Yes, all of them are safely in Thumdalla, you guys did it.

Relief washed over him, pulling his stomach into his throat and bringing tears to his eyes. "Jenni," he choked, "they made it. Everyone landed safely."

"Oh thank heavens," his wife breathed and more

tears flowed over her cheeks. "Elliott, I don't know if I'll ever be able to gate again. I think I'm broken."

"Honey, we'll figure this out, okay?" he said aloud, then switched back to his mind. *Adam, the family is going to try to descend on us, but you have to keep them away.*

I don't know if I ca—

Seventy-two hours, brother, or I will bring the darkest pits of hell down on everyone. You tell them. Give me and my wife seventy-two frickin' hours without any calls, texts, e-mails, visits, anything. I'm turning off everything electronic and nobody better knock on this door. We have a thousand questions for you guys, but we need to repair first.

All right, I'll keep them away.

Thank you.

Glad to have you back.

Elliott grunted and managed to successfully turn over to pull himself to his hands and knees. Reaching up to his chest, he unclipped one strap after another, listening to his largest weapons crash to the floor. Free of his swords and guns, he slowly crawled his way to the kitchen table, ignoring the weight of his weapon belt still around his waist and the knife sheaths on his legs. Finally achieving his goal, he placed one hand on the tabletop and pulled himself to his knees. Swiping the phone from the surface, he pushed the button experimentally.

Huh.

"Phone's still charged."

Looking at the date, he blinked. *This can't be right.*

"What's it say?" Jenni asked, still lying on her stomach with her eyes closed.

"It says we've been gone for a total of six hours."

How could Adam know what happened if they'd only been gone six hours? Technically, didn't they go backward in time, so then the events that just happened hadn't actually happened yet, right?

So many questions.

Later.

"Come on, Jenni. Let's get you to bed."

She only grunted.

"It's either that or I call an ambulance."

"And tell them what? 'My wife exploded while transporting eight people to another universe'? Yeah. Right. Try it."

He sighed. She had a point. He tried to use the edge of the table as leverage to haul himself to his feet, but his legs didn't want to cooperate and he fell down again. Jenni opened her eyes finally, searching for him.

"Maybe we should lay here for a few minutes?" she suggested.

"We can do this," he encouraged. "You and I, we're good at impossible now."

"Uuuuuugghhhhhnhnnnnnnnnn," she groaned, moving her arms and legs, pulling them under her body and pushing herself to her hands and knees. "I'll negotiate," she said breathlessly. "Meet you at the throw rug in front of the fireplace. Last one there is a rotten egg."

"You're on," he said, grateful to hear her gumption return. And he realized asking either of them to make it up the stairs was unrealistic. There was impossible, and then just plain ludicrous. He pushed himself back to his hands and knees while she unclipped her backpack and slipped it off her shoulders.

Their race to beat each other to the rug involved ten minutes of slow crawling and heckling each other. Turtles would have passed them with superior disdain. Old people would have teased them. Jenni, by warrant of being closer to the rug to begin with, made it first and sprawled victoriously in the center, her maniacal laugh somewhat wheezy and strained. She flopped onto her back, stretching her arms out beside her as though preparing to make a rug-angel.

Elliott finally reached the edge of the purple boundary and pushed himself up to his knees, unbuckling his belt.

"I'm ready if you are," Jenni said with a tired, saucy smile, "but I have to warn you, I'm not at the top of my game right now."

He smiled widely as he pulled the leather from his pants and listened to his backup weapons drop to the floor. He tossed the belt aside and pulled the sheaths off his thighs before sighing in relief. Only one more thing to do before he could collapse. Slowly, he crawled over her until one knee rested against her outer thigh, the other nestled in the junction between her legs. He placed one hand on either side of her head and gradually, bit by bit, lowered his body onto hers, letting only enough weight settle until her eyes showed the relief she always felt by this closeness. Shifting to his elbows, he combed his fingers into her hair until he cupped her head in the palms of his hands.

"My body," he said slowly, "my soul…my heart belong to you."

He recited the words somberly, staring into her brown eyes, so she not only heard the words for a second time, but knew in her heart, in her core, how deeply they were meant, how they spoke the essence of his very soul. She swallowed convulsively, meeting his gaze steadily. He continued, softly, choking on the words, realizing now how much more they meant now, and how truer since he wrote them on that cold lonely night.

"I surrender my existence into your loving care—willingly, gladly. Let your essence surround me, fill me, consume me. For you are my air, my sunshine, my lifeblood. Let the world melt away, let reality dissolve. While I have you, your fire, your tempest, your kiss…" he took a quick breath, "…our child…" he paused again, meeting her gaze intently, then shifted far enough to place a palm on her lower belly. "I am immortal."

He watched the play of emotions in her eyes as she worked through his meaning. The initial blank incomprehension. Her brows scrunching in confusion for a second, her mind turning his words over, analyzing. Her mouth dropping open as she switched to incredible disbelief.

"Wait…" She shifted slightly underneath him. "Are you saying… Am I…"

He nodded, knowing the smile on his face had to be smug and cocky. He couldn't help it. "Yeah, honey. I am saying. You are. Cricket is with us."

"No!"

"Yes."

Reserved hope shone through her eyes. "How do you know?"

"I can hear her heartbeat. She's strong and healthy."

"Really?"

He nodded. "Since last night. I wanted to tell you sooner—"

"He's here!" Jenni cried out in joy, wrapping her arms around Elliott's neck and pulling him down to her in a tight hug. "He's here. He's finally here."

Firmly in her grip, he rolled to the side and adjusted their bodies until they lay in each other's arms. Fabric brushed against his cheek and he realized an afghan from the couch partially fell over the cushion. Pulling it the rest of the way down, he covered their bodies, cocooning them. For good measure, he pulled off a couch pillow and tucked it under their heads. Her chanting turned into sobs and he rubbed her back while she worked through her maelstrom of emotion.

"I'm so happy," she cried on a wail which seemed to belie her sentiment, but he completely understood.

"Me too, sweetheart. Me, too."

She kissed his neck. He kissed the top of her head.

So they weren't completely human. So tomorrow they might get stuck in the quagmires of Ooba Looba fighting killer neon hamsters. So the laws of physics, time, and reality were all inconsequential lies.

Right now, who gave a damn?

He wrapped his arms tighter around his wife, listening as she calmed and her fatigue won. Her breath finally settled into an even rhythm as she drifted into deep sleep, leaving him alone with Cricket's steady heartbeats. Then he, too, joined Jenni in the land of slumber.

A word about the author…

Margie lives with her husband, five boys, and a dog in central Arizona. She's wanted to be an author since the age of nine, when her third grade teacher made the mistake of telling her that her story "Detective Snoop and the Haunted House" was very good, instantly planting delusions of grandeur into her young, impressionable mind. When not dragging her teenagers into various dubious adventures, she loves to read and crochet.

www.ingramcontent.com/pod-product-compliance
Lightning Source LLC
Chambersburg PA
CBHW051518260626

47170CB00003B/670